S0-ACC-806

From the same editor:
The Gay Times Book of Short Stories:
New Century, New Writing

First published 2001 by Gay Times Books, an imprint of Millivres Ltd, part of the Millivres Prowler Group, Worldwide House, 116-134 Bayham Street, London NW1 0BA.

A CIP catalogue record for this book is available from the British Library

ISBN 1-902852-38-9

Distributed in Europe by Central Books, 99 Wallis Rd, London E9 5LN
Tel: 020 8986 4854 Fax: 020 8533 5821
Distributed in North America by Consortium Book Sales and Distribution, 145 Westgate Drive, Suite 90, Saint Paul, MN 55114-1065, USA Tel: 651 221 9035 / Toll-free 800 283 3572
Distributed in Australia by Bulldog Books, P0 Box 700, Beaconsfield, NSW 2014
Printed and bound in the EU by WS Bookwell, Juva, Finland

THE GAY TIMES BOOK OF SHORT STORIES: THE NEXT WAVE

Edited by P-P Hartnett

CONTENTS

DEDICATION

This book is dedicated to Boy George

INTRODUCTION

The appeal for submissions for *The Next Wave* was extensive. Besides sending details to US magazines such as *The Advocate*, *Genre* and *Out*, I also wrote to every major gay publication throughout the world, from *Samtakafrettir* in Iceland's Reykjavik and *Tels Quels* in Belgium, to Latvia's *Elwis* plus Australia's *Capital Q*.

Youth groups such as San Francisco's LYRIC, Philadelphia's RAVE, Charlotte's Time Out Youth and New York City's Gay and Lesbian Youth Services boosted awareness via their specialised programmes. Educational organisations such as the Hetrick-Martin Institute and NYAC lent generous support. Amnesty International became involved, helping to spread the word amongst the few gay rights groups in South Africa. UK editors such as Cary James at *Fluid*, Justin Webb at the *Pink Paper*, Nick Stellmacher at *G-News* and, of course, Colin Richardson at this anthology's parent magazine, *Gay Times*, placed features which helped in promoting the project.

An Internet strategy was adopted. In addition to an appeal on the *Gay Times* website, companies such as gay.com, rainbownetwork.com and queercompany.com placed useful mentions, all of which were much appreciated. So, from the Gay Albania Foundation to Uruguay's Homosexuales Unidos, awareness grew and grew of the world's first collection of short stories by gay, bisexual, transgender and questioning men under the age of twenty-five.

There were four hundred and sixty-three submissions, from all over the UK, Republic of Ireland, USA, Canada, Australia, Israel and – to my surprise – Saudi Arabia. Amongst these came writers from Romania, Singapore and Sri Lanka. A feature in *Joey* provoked a massive response, as did encouraging mentions in *City Life* by Wayne Clews and *NOW* by Gordon Hopps.

I had no idea what kind of material would pour through my letter box. From envelope after envelope came chunks of narrative energy, connecting me to a new generation – ultra-literary at one extreme, post-literate at the other. Writers such as Keith Munro and Lewis Gill certainly surprised me in both content and style. Geezer's female-to-male story 'Bloke' made me laugh out loud, whilst reminding of the torments so many endure.

If anything, I feel that the stories which I have selected for this anthology tap into a vast, diverse, and growing anti-assimilationist queer movement far away from the Budweiser-sponsored Pride parades. The stories collected here make a connection with the hopes, fears, preoccupations and dreams of gay, bisexual, transgendered and questioning youth. Many of the pieces come from a search within themselves, facing issues which shape their lives. Their words certainly affirm their courage in the midst of frequent isolation and harassment, proving that there is still a long way to go in terms of acceptance.

P-P Hartnett
Colne, Lancashire
September 2001

ANTHONY BAULCH

Telling Mother

The only thing Tony ever really minded about San Francisco was the deceptive nature of its weather. Usually the city was blanketed in fog, which he didn't mind because at least with fog he knew what he had in store. But sometimes he would wake up in the morning with the sun streaming through the windows like a promotional ad for California travel. He would be ecstatic – he hadn't seen blue skies since the last time he saw *Baywatch* (it was an accident while flipping through channels). He'd have breakfast, get dressed, and prepare for his day in a marvellous mood, feeling the world was at his feet. As soon as he got outside into the glorious sunshine, however, he'd feel his hair being whipped by wind. The trees would be blowing and his body would be attacked by cold, prompting him to rush back inside to dress warmer. Even when the sun shines in the city by the bay, chances are you're still liable to catch a chill.

That was one of the first things Tony remembered about January 6, 1999. He thought it was going to be a sunny day but upon leaving his door feared he would contract pneumonia.

Thursday, January 7, 1999, had more reason to be memorable to Tony than just the weather. At this time he was a freshman at School of the Arts. He was fourteen, and unsure. He was also gay, and he just so happened to make his first public acknowledgment of his sexuality on this day. Tony was someone who liked to plan things ahead of time, he felt that if he was going to do something he might bother to do it right. But his coming out was near spontaneous, and when he thought about it later he almost wished he had done it in a more formal way, something to give the occasion the dignity it deserved.

Every Thursday Tony had his world literature class. Although he loved the subject he despised the teacher, who, in the second week of school, had given a strenuously long lecture (strenuous for the students, not the teacher). Like most of the other students, Tony had fallen into a state between sleep and consciousness, but twelve minutes before the end of class his ears perked up.

It seemed that the teacher was discussing one of Tony's favourite plays, *The Little Foxes*. In addition to misquoting the play several times, the teacher also misidentified the author, citing Tennessee Williams when in fact Lillian

Hellman had penned the work. After class, when the other students had left, Tony politely approached the teacher and made his error known. This sent the man into a rage. "Well, I see you must have graduated first in your class at Julliard to have such a fine knowledge of theatre history!" he declared, pushing past Tony to the teachers' lounge.

Since that day world literature was not so much educational as treacherous.

On the day of Tony's coming out, though, the gruff literature teacher was nowhere to be seen. The substitute told the students under his charge they had two options. They could either watch the film *Waiting for Guffman* or go outside and talk. Because most of his friends had already seen the film, Tony opted to go outside. While the actual temperature might not have been high, the sun was shining brightly. To waste a free period indoors would be tragic.

Joining Tony were his three female friends, Mara, Tessa and Ruby, all of whom were equally as grateful for the sun and the teacher's absence.

Tessa wanted to be a filmmaker when she grew up, she constantly walked around framing views in her mind and spoke like a storyboard. She would one day win an Oscar, but she assured her friends she would not accept it because she was her only critic.

Tony was confident she would get to the awards an hour early.

Ruby was adorably quiet and everyone's parents liked her. Almost all the teachers (world literature excluded) liked her. None of her classmates could think of a reason to dislike her.

Tony thought Ruby might be planning world domination behind her innocent exterior.

Mara was Tony's best friend, she had been Tony's best friend since the second week of school. It was January now, and that felt like an eternity. Mara was sweet and romantic and mooned over her love for Matt Damon, who she knew was her soul mate since the first time she saw *The Rainmaker*.

Mara and Tony had more in common than they thought.

While the four friends were sitting outside, the conversation turned to a popular subject: boys. The three girls instinctually mooned over the latest topic of discussion, as closeted Tony sat in silence. When he thought about it later he didn't remember who they were talking about exactly but he said quietly, "He's not really my type."

He was shocked to hear the words come out of his mouth. He had never really thought about it but he supposed this meant he was gay. The three girls all turned to look at him, their collective motion creating a slight breeze.

"Who *is* your type?" Tessa asked, ever the investigative journalist. He thought about that for a minute and answered, "Matt Damon, maybe."

Mara let out a little gasp.

Ruby, being relatively astute, leaned her head towards him inquisitively and asked, "So, does that mean you like boys?"

Duh.

There was no turning back now, to do anything but make an honest reply would be cheating. There was no reason to head back into the closet.

"Yes," he answered, firmly and declaratively. "I'm gay."

The three girls stared silently at Tony. Then Mara spoke.

"Well, good for you!" she said, moving to embrace her newly out friend. But then as she was hugging him she whispered, "I still have first call on Matt Damon!" Then the conversation continued as normal, only with Tony being an active member of the discussion about men.

After that, Tony slowly came out to his other friends at school. There were no giant shocks, no screams of horror, and no real congratulations either. This was San Francisco, there was only a faint murmur of, "Oh, that's nice," and then the party would go on to seek his opinion about which he preferred, the blond or brunet Brad Pitt. It was an easy process: as Tony realised how comfortable other people were with his sexuality, he became more comfortable. But at this point he still had no intention of telling his parents.

When he thought back on this later, it seemed downright ridiculous that he had planned to keep it from them. His parents had bushels of queer friends throughout his childhood; his mother was an antiques dealer for crying out loud! Years later he even found out that a woman he was told to address as Aunt Jessica was actually a transitional transsexual.

Tony certainly had a leg up on most queer kids. Plus, it wasn't like there was a lack of signs.

While it would be a bit shocking to some parents if their overtly macho son announced one day that he was queer, Tony's sexuality had always been a matter for speculation among his family. His second week of preschool, the faculty called his mother to break the news to her that instead of playing with the other children at recess, Tony would stand in a far-off corner of the playground announcing to all who would listen, "I am She-Ra, Princess of Power!" His mother just asked if he had injured anyone in the process and upon being told no she responded, "So, what's the point?" And although he *did* play baseball for a season in second grade, it was hardly successful.

It was around the time the Madonna film *A League of Their Own* came out at theatres and Tony was obsessed with Madonna. Playing baseball was just another way he emulated her, as natural as lip-syncing to 'Like a Virgin'. However, he was less than skilled. As soon as he discovered the actual game was far less glamorous than Hollywood had portrayed it, Tony became bored with the outfield and began absent mindedly picking daisies. After practice one day the coach sought to reprimand him by whining that he wasn't trying hard enough and that he "played ball like a girl". Tony took this to be a compliment: "Did you see *A League of Their Own*? Those girls could *kill* you!" His father, outraged at the coach's misconduct and a bit embarrassed by his son's smart mouth, took him home and ended his career in the outfield.

With parents like this, it's amazing he didn't perk up and tell them sooner, like in the third grade or so, but he was still frightened. Although his parents were tolerant of other people being gay, would they be tolerant of their *son*? And yes, he had succeeded in coming out to his friends but that wasn't as big a deal as telling his parents. Tony could always get new friends but getting new family members was another matter. So, like the coward that he was, he kept his secret and waited. And waited. Tony waited almost five months.

Then one day he just couldn't keep it to himself any longer, he felt estranged from his parents by not telling them. He had another life at school, and another part of himself his parents didn't know about. It all hit him on a Saturday afternoon. For almost an hour he sat in his room in tears. He cried endlessly that day, he cried and wrote in his journal:

"I think that death will be the only way I can ever find peace… Someone reassure me that my parents will love me no matter what I am… No one should have to live this way, in pain, in fear. I didn't ask to be different, if I could change it all I would, just so I could stop being afraid."

On and on the entries went that day, sounding like a combination suicide letter and script for *Schindler's List*. Then he broke down, he heard the sound of his father's car leaving the driveway and knew he and his brother would be gone. Tony was alone with his mother.

He suddenly had a plan. He would tell his mother while his father was out, and then if she threw him out of the house he would never have to face the rest of the family in shame. That was it, perfect. In a grand dramatic gesture he threw open the door to his bedroom. But he couldn't move, as a kind of rigor mortis had set in at his feet.

Tony slunk back to his bed and tried to regroup. He told himself he would try again in ten minutes, but as fear set in, ten became twenty, and twenty, thirty, and thirty became another bout of crying.

Finally, when he could cry no longer, he tried again. Although his feet were unusually heavy, he made it up the stairs. His hands were like ice, his face red from crying. He entered his mother's room; she was on the bed, thumbing her way half-heartedly through a *Vanity Fair*.

"Mother," he announced in a mock-judicial tone, "I'd like to see you in my office."

This was a family saying. As a child Tony remembered his mother calling the familiar phrase from all sorts of places around the house. Her 'office' would be the kitchen table, her bed, or even the bathtub. In his case 'office' meant his bedroom. Tony figured a little bit of humour couldn't hurt. His mother got up and followed. When they entered his room they both took a place on the bed.

Tony looked down at his hands nervously, he didn't know how he was supposed to start this discussion. "Mom, I…" he started, in a voice belonging more to a five-year-old than a fifteen-year-old. "I, I, I…" The words wouldn't come out. His mother knew he had something big to say, he hadn't stuttered since he was three. But he knew he had to continue. "Mom, I'm, I…"

The tears began to roll down his cheeks. His mother moved closer and took him in her arms. With her embrace she gave him the strength to finish his sentence.

"Mom, I'm gay." By this time Tony was openly hysterical, and his mother was the only thing that kept him from falling off the bed. There, he had said it, he had told her his biggest secret, now what would happen?

His mother moved away from him and took his face in her hands. She raised his chin so she looked him in the eyes. He was so afraid, he didn't know what she thought.

"Oh, honey," she began, "I know that, I was just wondering when you would figure it out."

A sigh of relief overcame him and, after one last outburst of tears, Tony regained his composure. He looked up at his mother again, this time not out of fear, but out of gratitude.

"How long have you known?" she asked.

Tony thought about it, really thought about it and answered, "Since the sixth grade, but I didn't know what it was."

She considered that for a moment and then asked, "Have you told anyone else?"

Here's where the hard part came. If there was anything Tony's mother hated, it was being the last to know.

"Only my girlfriends at school," he said. "I hope you're not mad but it was easier telling them – I can always get new friends – but I was afraid to tell you. I didn't want you to be upset."

She looked at her son more closely, her brown eyes warm with compassion.

"Tony, you don't ever have to be afraid to tell me anything."

He nodded in agreement, and she continued. "Before you were born your father and I said that we would love you no matter what, that if only we were given the chance to raise children we would make sure that we could be the kind of parents who would let you tell us anything. Nothing you can tell me will ever change that, and nothing you can ever say or be will make me love you any less." She was getting teary.

"You need to know that, no matter what, your father and I will continue to love you. And nothing will ever change that. We're willing to protect you for whatever reason there is." She stopped a moment and looked down, then she took his hand and continued.

"But you're right to be afraid. People in this country will hate you for this, people at that school we sent you to hated you for this. And they will try to hurt you. But you need to know that you should never be afraid of anyone in this house, no one in this family will ever hurt you. Your father and I promise you that. No matter what happens, we will defend you, but that doesn't mean you're safe."

She began to cry a little. Suddenly he knew she needed him to put his arms around her, Tony understood that *she* needed protecting.

"People will try to hurt you. It's not fair to you or me or anyone, but people will hate you just because you're happy with who you are and love other people. It scares me to think of you in the world out there, with so many horrible things waiting. You know it's not easy, it wasn't easy for my friends ten and twenty years ago, and while things have gotten better they won't be easy for you now."

She drew him near. For a moment mother and son just sat there holding each other, each reassuring the other. She continued.

"I knew you would say this to me some day, but I never thought you'd be this young. You're so brave to do this, it makes me love you so much more to know that at fifteen you can no longer live a lie."

They looked at each other again, both moved. It was Tony's turn now.

"I love you, Mom," he said, repeating words he had said countless times but which took on new meaning after all they had said.

"I love you, too." She leaned in to hug her boy, and they collapsed into each other, knowing so much more than they did a half-hour ago. A few minutes later they regained their composure.

"Well, I'm glad we did this," Tony's mother said as she pulled herself off the bed. She took a quick glance at her face in the mirror and let out a joking little laugh. She took out a tissue and wiped the mascara from under her eyes and straightened her face.

"Me too," Tony replied.

Then it seemed as if some thought had been illuminated inside both of their heads. Tony and his mother turned to each, and asked simultaneously:

"When are we going to tell Dad?"

GORDON BEEFERMAN

Scar Tissue

Rafi was getting really tired of men asking him how he got his scar. Since January he had been out with at least seven different guys, and not one of them could get halfway through the first date without asking him where it came from. It was a prominent scar, running across his left cheek from the edge of his lip almost all the way to his ear, an angry raised ridge that rose up in a gentle arc from his mouth before settling into a straight line. If you looked closely enough you could even see where he'd had the stitches.

It was a pretty awful scar, but after all, Rafi was a good-looking guy and men still went for him easily. Occasionally he would meet someone on the street, or in the subway; the guy might give him a funny look when he saw the scar up close, but they'd exchange numbers and meet later in the week. When Rafi could finally afford a computer he also experimented with putting out a personal ad online, including a photo of himself in profile – the right side, without the scar showing. But, inevitably, when he'd meet guys this way, they'd say something like "Wow, your picture didn't show that you had a scar." As if he would purposely show it off so people could ask him about it.

Really, he resented being asked by these guys, on the first date too. And they all did it, one after another. First there was the guy who was a strict vegan, and wouldn't eat at any of Rafi's favourite restaurants; they ended up going to these expensive places where everything tasted like it was made of cardboard. Then there was the one who insisted on showing Rafi his Prince Albert in the middle of a crowded café ("What, c'mon, you squeamish?"). There was the one who, when he found out that Rafi knew a little Italian, begged him over and over again to say something in Italian, because it was *soooo* sexy, until Rafi told him "Fuck off" in Italian, and the guy acted really turned on until he happened to ask Rafi what it meant in English. There was also the one who never went anywhere without his pet rat on his shoulder, even when they went to sit in the park and make out. And then there was the one who started sending Rafi presents in the mail: bubble bath, CDs of romantic piano concertos, and then annoying self-help paperbacks with titles like *1001 Mantras for the Gay Man.* They were all crazy, and they had all asked him about his scar before the first date was over.

And at least two of them had reached over and touched it and given him some line like "Poor baby." These guys made Rafi want to retch. What were these morons thinking, that they had a right to just reach over and touch it? It pissed him off. One after another, he stopped returning their calls. He couldn't stand to be treated like that. Like he was some freak or something.

Until about a month ago, an early Friday afternoon, when he met this quiet, strange guy. He was awfully good-looking, almost unusually so, not because of any distinguishing feature (such as a Prince Albert), but because of the placid, peaceful expression he had on his face – a round pale face, with a faint blue five o'clock shadow on his cheeks and chin, smooth brown hair that draped gently across his forehead, and wet dark eyes that seemed to be just a bit too large for their sockets. He wasn't tall, but he was slender and had a vaguely muscular feeling to him, as if he had played sports as a kid and it showed in his adult body.

There was something strangely relaxing about the guy, something about the way he moved, and the way he looked at things. Even from the moment Rafi spotted him in the bookstore, he instantly forgot all about his paycheques taking forever to clear, and stopped worrying how he could find time to do his laundry before he ran completely out of underwear.

Seeing Rafi staring at him, the man had languidly closed the book he was reading (Rafi couldn't make out the title, but it had a picture on the front of a huge, modern, glass-covered building) and walked towards Rafi, where he was idling sullenly by the magazine rack. They ended up spending the rest of the day together, walking aimlessly around the city and sitting in the park eating sandwiches, until it started to get late; it was turning cold and windy.

They were standing on a corner by the subway. The guy zipped up his coat and looked up at the clock on top of the bank across the street. All at once it was strangely quiet between them, and the sounds of taxis speeding by rushed up between them like water. Rafi suddenly realised he'd been doing most of the talking the whole time, and he started to feel awkward, having said so much. They stood there for a moment, looking in opposite directions. Finally Rafi asked the guy if he wanted to come over to his place, rent a movie and hang out. Still looking up at the clock on the bank, the guy said "No thanks, maybe another time" in a plain, polite voice, and, turning towards Rafi at once, shrugged apologetically, and made a little expression with his mouth. So they exchanged numbers and agreed to see each other sometime that weekend.

*

All Saturday afternoon it was grey, and though it didn't rain, it seemed as though it would start pouring down any moment. Rafi sat at his kitchen table in his sweatshirt, looking out his front window onto the street. People walked by quickly, huddled in their coats, staring down in front of them. Occasionally a couple would walk by holding hands, or a young mother pushing a stroller with a plastic covering, a little kid in tow. Teenage boys crashed by, jostling each other.

Since he'd gotten up that morning, Rafi hadn't stopped thinking about the pretty guy he'd met. He'd been kind of bummed that the guy hadn't wanted to come over the previous night. When he'd arrived home by himself, there was just a short lacklustre message on the machine from an old friend from Jersey who he hadn't seen in a long while, and there wasn't much in the fridge except for some leftover Chinese takeout. So Rafi had turned on the TV and folded himself up on the couch. Sometime after the nightly news and *Star Trek* reruns, he threw off his pants and fell into bed, into a shallow, noisy sleep crowded with nightmares.

When Rafi woke up early in the afternoon, he felt dazed and grimy, like a pasty residue of the TV shows had stuck to the inside of his mouth. As he adjusted to the dull daylight, the first coherent thought that popped into his head was of the pretty, brown-eyed guy he'd met. Rafi had liked him right away, but a part of him had expected the guy to be at least as bad as the others, as far as the scar issue was concerned.

Sitting down at his table, Rafi thought he should be pleased that the guy hadn't asked him even once, didn't even screw up his eyes and lean closer, trying to examine it; still, he gradually became aware of an uneasy feeling that came from just behind his bellybutton and spiralled out to his extremities. Even his own right arm, leaning on the table, felt out of place.

He picked up the little piece of paper with the guy's number from the pile of receipts and change on the rug, where he'd emptied the contents of his pockets the night before. Absent-mindedly he unfolded and re-folded it over and over, examining the number carefully each time, as if memorising it. Abruptly he got up and opened and shut his fridge, and opened and shut it again. At once he went to pick up his phone and dialled with a haste that surprised him.

★

They met up Sunday night and went out to an art-movie house downtown, had ice cream and walked around. Rafi invited the pretty guy over to his house again, but he turned Rafi down, just as before, making that weird little expression with his mouth.

Friday they went to an art opening where the guy introduced Rafi to a bunch of people who examined him curiously as the "steady date." Rafi felt over-scrutinised, as if these people were looking at him under a microscope, and he was squirming around strapped to the glass slide. The guy's friends asked Rafi a lot of questions, even some personal ones, but for some reason none of them said a word about the scar.

Once the reception was over, the pretty-faced guy finally agreed to come over to Rafi's house, and they sat on the rug, facing each other, and held hands. Rafi couldn't help staring at the pretty guy, who seemed so thoughtful and polite. Rafi felt like he had so much to say to him, and really wanted to touch him. But the guy didn't seem in the mood – he just sat there and didn't say much. Rafi tried to enjoy just sitting there with him in the silence. After a while the guy stood up and said he had to go. As he put on his coat, Rafi said he hoped they could meet up later over the weekend.

After the guy left, Rafi stood at his sink in his T-shirt, brushing his teeth – brushing and brushing and brushing them – and examining himself in the mirror, turning around, squinting at himself from all angles and distances, as if to recapture himself from all this strangeness, from the pretty man's placid smile, from all the questions people had asked him at the party. Even doing this, he still felt terribly at odds with himself, as if he were a bookshelf in a library that had been de-alphabetised.

As he leaned forward to spit, he examined his scar, really examined it for the first time in ages, and tried to remember how it felt when brand new, when the stitches had finally come out and people saw him this way for the first time. The new him that even he had been a little afraid of.

Was the pretty guy afraid of him? Maybe that was it. When Rafi was younger he'd always had a little bit of a scowl on his face, a little bit of a don't-fuck-with-me attitude, but really, he didn't think he was intimidating. Could the pretty guy really find him intimidating?

Then the sight of himself in the mirror frightened and confused him, and he quickly shut off the bathroom light. In the darkness, as he tumbled into bed, a vague, tingling sensation slowly rose up in his head like a swarm of flies. Unable to recognise it or to name it, terrified, he shut his eyes and waited helplessly for sleep.

★

All month Rafi felt as if he were waiting for the other shoe to drop. He saw the pretty, brown-eyed guy often, at least twice a week, and still the guy didn't ask him anything about his scar. Of course Rafi hadn't brought up the subject himself, because it wasn't really that important, after all. That was the point. The guy was interested in Rafi, not his scar, and that was why Rafi had kept on seeing him. And Rafi really liked the guy, even though he couldn't completely figure him out.

Rafi always had a nice time with him, just hanging out; he would even get a happy feeling from calling him up and leaving a message on his machine. Rafi felt at ease talking to him – about movies, work, city life, plans for the future, that kind of thing. And the guy really was pretty. Not conventional like the guys in gym ads, but more graceful, slender, well put together, with that peaceful, steady face, and amazing brown eyes.

Rafi would often find himself staring into those big, dark eyes. In certain kinds of light, as in the Middle Eastern café where they would sometimes go, the colour of the guy's eyes seemed to shift, subtly, from one dark shade to another.

Sometimes, when Rafi would have something serious on his mind that he wanted to say, trying to find the right words, the eyes would gradually become so dark that Rafi couldn't see the pupil in them – the eyes became holes, great bottomless pits. At once Rafi would become uncomfortable and look away, perhaps up towards the fluorescent lights, and quickly stir his ice with his straw. Then the guy would laugh, his eyes brown and pretty again. He'd smile at Rafi, and ask him what he was thinking. Rafi would suddenly feel warm and bright once more, and imagine himself reaching under the table to squeeze the guy's hand, as if to reassure himself that everything was OK.

But Rafi couldn't understand the guy's politeness. He seemed so thoughtful; he'd never say that much in the way of response to Rafi's ramblings. The guy's face never seemed to change; it always had that same peaceful, steady look. And Rafi was also puzzled by that little expression the guy made with his mouth. It was a tiny, quick smiling movement, so subtle that if you thought about it too much you almost couldn't believe you had seen it. The guy's lips would turn down at the corners in a kind of pout, while his cheeks would pull back into a kind of smirk. Still, it was a pretty charming little tic, and Rafi assured himself that it was just a private thing that only the two of them shared.

Rafi tried adding it up all different ways, trying to figure this guy out, and how the guy felt about him. At least they had started sleeping together – sort of. It was a Thursday. The guy had invited Rafi over to watch a video, and when the movie was over they discovered it had started snowing furiously. The guy agreed to let him stay over, but said he had to get to work by 8.30 and Rafi would have to agree to get up and be out by eight.

The night had been quiet – almost too quiet. They didn't have sex. The guy didn't seem to have it in mind, and Rafi felt awkward about pressing the issue. They had even slept on opposite sides of the bed. This had really frustrated Rafi, especially after the guy was fast asleep and Rafi was alone in the strange bed, alone with the strange light coming in through the guy's white curtains, alone with the same tingling sensation in his head, and a new feeling this time, a fresh, queasy feeling like there were carbonated bubbles coming up through his stomach and chest.

In the morning, as the guy was taking a shower, Rafi leaned out of bed and pulled one curtain aside. Looking down at the ploughs clearing the street, he was struck by how much snow had fallen during the night, how it had all fallen silently, stealthily.

As he trudged across town in his sneakers, alone, the bubbly sensation started to subside, replaced by a dull, hard feeling. Standing on the corner along with a dozen people in suits, waiting impatiently to cross the avenue, he felt like a nomad, wearing yesterday's clothes, having unmade a bed that was not his own.

★

A few days went by, and he didn't hear from the guy. Rafi was kind of surprised, and a little miffed, so he decided not to call him. Over the weekend he went out bar-hopping with his co-worker, the one with the band, and the next few nights he just stayed home and read old magazines and thought about getting a tattoo. He even called back his old friend from Jersey, but they didn't have that much to say to each other.

Not only did he not feel like talking to the pretty guy at all, Rafi found he didn't much want to talk to anyone else either. At work, going through boxes of CDs with the barcode scanner as usual, he felt like a silent automaton. For the first time he noticed how repetitive the songs on the stereo were, and how stupid. Everything was stuck in his throat. If by accident a word formed on the back of his tongue, he would push it up into his skull behind his right eye and try to forget about it.

Wednesday he started to come down with some kind of flu. All week it had been cold and nasty out, and to make it worse he'd lost his favourite warm hat coming home on the subway. Late that morning he started to feel unusually fatigued, like his muscles and bones had been bruised. Towards mid-afternoon his eyes seemed to become perpetually in danger of closing without warning. He couldn't form a coherent thought; his brain felt as if it were floating in a mist in his head. Arriving home after work, sweating, he threw off his coat and crashed asleep in his bed without even taking off his dripping boots.

By Saturday afternoon he was starting to feel better, but not enough to go out bar-hopping. Around 6.30, he was finally getting his appetite back and was thinking of going out to the corner store to pick up a sandwich, when the phone rang. It was the pretty, brown-eyed guy. He said he was sorry he hadn't called Rafi sooner, but he'd been really busy with work and people visiting from out of town, and he'd really enjoyed their last date together.

Rafi felt his temples throb as the blood rushed, burning, into his head. Sweating now, he squeezed his eyes shut and mumbled something about how he'd been sick all week. He managed to avoid clearing his throat so the guy wouldn't think he was totally contagious.

The guy said it was too bad Rafi had been feeling sick, but did he want to come over tonight? Rafi was a little surprised, but he said sure, he just needed to get a bite to eat first. The guy said why didn't Rafi just grab a sandwich and come over to his house, he'd make tea and they'd watch a movie together. Flustered, Rafi said he'd come over in an hour or so.

They watched some 60s murder mystery movie that took place in Rome. Rafi wasn't sure how close he should sit to the guy, who seemed to be concentrating very hard on the TV screen, but about half an hour into the movie their shoulders touched, then their knees, then their elbows and forearms.

Rafi thought the movie was pretty stupid, but didn't say anything because the pretty guy had picked it out. After a while, the guy finally made some remark about how he couldn't understand why they had named the main killer suspect Ralph, how Ralph was such an unlikely name for a murderer. Rafi took the opportunity to mention that Ralph was actually his own real name, and the guy asked well then where did he get Rafi from? Rafi explained that since seventh grade he'd always hated being called Ralph or Ralphy. A few years back he had read the name Rafi in some music magazine, and thought it was a much better name, so he'd adopted it. Since he'd moved to the city, no one ever called him his old name anymore except his mother and brothers back home. He'd finally got them to stop calling him Ralphy, and if they ever did, he would get really mad about it.

The guy murmured "mm-hm"; he had become distracted by some motorcycle chase happening on the screen. After another fifteen minutes or so, he gently draped his leg over Rafi's knee. Soon afterwards they were holding hands and the guy was cuddling up to Rafi's shoulder.

The movie was rewinding and the guy was coming back from the kitchen with some water. He put down the glasses, sat down very close to Rafi, and looked closely at his face. Rafi suddenly felt very self-conscious about his scar, as if the guy were about to ask him about it. But the guy didn't say a word, and in the silence he reached up and gently stroked Rafi's face, his eyes, his forehead, his chin, even stroked the scar.

Rafi suddenly felt exasperated – why didn't the guy say anything about it? A feeling rose up in him like a knot. It was as if he were a bucket in a well, and the guy was tugging hard on the rope but Rafi was too heavy to lift. Rafi sat there immobilised, a corpse, still staring in the man's pretty eyes, huge dark holes. The only thing Rafi could feel was his own dick stiffening in his pants.

When at last he he was able to move his arm, he ran his hands through the pretty man's hair, but his fingers felt swollen and numb. Soon his hands started to thaw, and he could feel how thick and soft the man's hair was, almost like a child's stuffed animal. The tape rewound, the VCR clicked off, and for a moment there was no sound. Then the guy reached behind Rafi's head and pulled it towards his own.

Rafi was underwater with his eyes closed. Gravity had lost all of its meaning and he felt he might be tumbling and tumbling through the depths unawares, headed for the bottom, never to surface. He clung to the brown-haired man with his mouth, with his hands, not breathing, but speaking, wordlessly. When he could stand it no longer he lunged for the shore, holding the pretty man fast to him, and they were strewn there, gasping, streaked with sand. The man's shoulder tasted like salt; his hair lay damp and tangled like seaweed. Pressed against him, Rafi could hear the rhythms of their two separate breaths, heavy, asynchronous.

They were in the bed. Rafi was helpless, a refugee. It was a land he had visited once before, and in his dreams many times since. He could smell the familiar scent of the pillows – smoke, sweat and shampoo; the curtains, too, were familiar, though rumpled in a slightly different way than he had remembered. New this time were the hands, the hands that smoothed away the uncertainty from his limbs, hands that moulded and re-formed him into a new, unimaginable creature.

Rafi murmured the guy's name, barely recognising the sound of his own voice, or the name he was speaking. In a gentle voice, the guy asked Rafi what was it, what was it that he wanted to do? In the silence that followed, Rafi searched the screen of his brain for *it*, scanning and scanning… He couldn't find it. Lost, empty-handed, he was overcome by a frightening need; a void had opened up in him and desire rushed in to fill it. Rafi murmured a few words in the pretty man's ear, shocking himself at the urgency of his own plea. The guy asked him if he was sure, and Rafi simply replied yes.

Rafi was glad the guy was behind him and couldn't see his face, because his eyes and his cheeks began to twist into terrible expressions, and his mouth hung open, shocked, soundless. He didn't want the guy to know that he had never done this before. The guy buried his nose behind Rafi's right ear and breathed tender assurances into his hair, and Rafi believed them, he believed in them and begged for them. He could feel the weight of his own heart pushing up into his throat, and it seemed that at any moment a bird might fly out, or a bat, or a swarm of flies; and at the same time an immense feeling of lightness spread outward from the centre of his body. He sensed that his whole body had vanished, and he no longer felt anything but the pretty man, could only feel *through* him, only *his* presence, only *his* movements.

And with each movement Rafi felt the pressure in his throat increase dangerously, as if someone were trying to push a brick through it, until finally something snapped, burst. He let out one short, broken moan, and another, the tears started flowing down his face and wouldn't stop, he prayed, he choked, still the waves of lightness pulsed through his body, steady bursts of waves, he grabbed a pillow and buried his face in it, he tried to smother his face; the sounds, still the lightness continued, he was soaked with sweat.

Finally it was over, everything was heavy and dark on him, but his heart still raced like a screaming subway headed right for a head-on collision. But no collision came. Instead, strong arms folded around him, and on the back of his neck he felt a warm moist breath murmuring something soft and unintelligible before dissolving into a faint but regular rise and fall, punctuated by a little hissing sound.

Soon, cool colours, scents, sounds surged over and filled him, in steady, hypnotic waves, but sleep refused to overtake him. He could feel himself drifting over and out of himself; some uncontrollable, unidentifiable ritual was being spun out in his brain. Something was being washed away, and something ancient, something long-buried under the sand was being revealed… He couldn't make it out… No, there it was, slightly worn away by the hands of water and time, but its strange spikes still sharp, its edges still severe. Rafi opened his eyes.

That was it. He wanted to tell the guy about his scar. He wanted to tell him everything.

And how had he gotten it anyway? As hard as he had tried to forget, it was really all too easy to remember. He had often thought he could forget, and at times he had, even for days, weeks at a stretch. Still, it would all come back to him at strange moments, like if he accidentally bumped into an old lady at the grocery store and she gave him an evil look. Then the memory would appear like a dead fish on a silver platter, the cover suddenly removed. Now, again, the events leading up to it suddenly became as clear as if they were happening that very moment.

Back in that dreary summer after he'd dropped out of high school, he and his buddies used to go out to the park late at night, when the faggots would be there, silently walking around in sneakers and baseball caps. He and his buddies would pick one out, usually some smaller, scared-looking guy, and throw him on the ground, maybe kick the shit out of him or something, call him a filthy cocksucker, maybe empty out his wallet if they needed some extra cash. Later, to blow off steam, they'd cruise around in empty mall parking lots, playing bumper cars with stray shopping carts.

One night in the park, they were coming up behind a guy on the path, starting to provoke him a little, when the guy turned around and asked them what the fuck did they want. One of Rafi's buddies laughed and said, well he thought he knew what the guy wanted, that was for sure. It was completely dark and Rafi could barely see anyone's faces, but he could feel the guy's eyes drill into him.

Rafi had stood there paralysed while his buddies moved closer to the guy. The guy shouted something like "Get the fuck away from me you assholes." Rafi's buddies yelled at him to stop just standing there and help them out, so he joined in. Approaching the tangled, struggling mess of dark limbs, he saw something swipe out at him, an arm, a finger. A hot bolt ripped through his face; Rafi screamed out in pain. The faggot had slashed him with a knife and was running away down the path. One of Rafi's buddies chased after him; the other stared at Rafi for a moment, horrified, and said, "Oh fuck, he sliced you?"

Rafi felt his numb face start to burn as the hot tears bubbled out of his eyes. He reached up and felt the wet, sticky blood as he touched his cheek. Shame, rage, fear, terror, mostly terror, all clogged up his throat, and he could say nothing. He could sense his buddy's face blanching with fright. You OK? You gonna be all right?

Then Rafi was standing there alone; both his buddies had fled. For a few minutes he could do nothing, feel nothing, could not move. By the time he made it to the hospital he was a terrible mess, bloody leather jacket and everything. He told the stunned nurses he had gotten into a fight with his friends, that it was OK, he refused to press charges, it was his own fault.

When his face finally healed and the stitches were removed, Rafi started hanging out in the city and soon had his first boyfriend, Andrew, whom he had been with until this past January. Rafi had always been really attached to Andrew, but now that he reflected on it, they had never shown each other that much affection, and had sort of taken each other's presence for granted.

When Andrew abruptly went back in the closet and said he was leaving Rafi for a woman, Rafi shrugged the whole thing off, and said he didn't care that much. Besides, they hadn't even had such a great sex life. But once Andrew was really gone and the weeks went by without a phone call from him or anything, Rafi started to miss him. That's when he realised he was truly single, truly alone for the first time in his life.

Now he was with this amazing, pretty brown-haired guy with the huge, deep eyes, and the gentle, reassuring voice. Rafi would have never expected to be with a guy like this. For one thing, they had totally different tastes, different styles. Plus, physically, the guy wasn't even Rafi's usual type. He was totally the opposite of Andrew. In fact, the pretty guy was exactly the type the younger Rafi would have picked out in a crowd as the faggot. There was something girlish, no, something *boyish* about him, even with his blue five o'clock shadow. In those days Rafi would have never been able to see how deep the guy's eyes were, because he'd have never stared at a guy for that long. But for sure, he was the type Rafi would have singled out, the type that would get him agitated about fags.

So he wanted to tell the guy all about his scar, wanted him to know what had happened. He wanted to unburden himself of it, because he had never really discussed it with anyone – rather, he'd never told anyone the whole story. He had always made the excuse that he'd been in a fight with his buddies, which, since he was perpetually seen with them, everyone thought strange at the time; but after the incident in the park he had avoided them anyway, so he was able to convince everyone they'd had a falling out. Once he moved to the city it was easier not to talk about it, because now he was Rafi. No one he met knew anything about his past and he didn't have to go into it. Even Andrew had never seemed to care about it that much – Rafi had told him the same old version of the story and that had been the end of that. But now Rafi wanted, yes, really needed to tell this guy about the scar. He needed the guy to ask about it, to ask about him, about Rafi, so he could tell him everything. He wanted to tell him everything.

The guy seemed as if he were really sleeping now, judging by the sound of his breathing. But he was holding so tightly to Rafi, Rafi couldn't believe he was completely asleep. Rafi touched the guy's arm and said his name. All he got was a murmur in reply, and another, shorter murmur. Rafi said he wanted to talk to him about something. The guy shifted his arm and said he was too tired, could they talk about it tomorrow?

Rafi felt the bird in his throat sink down into his stomach, and he tried to shift away from the guy. But the guy nibbled gently on the back of his neck and held him even tighter in his arms. Rafi felt an incredible warmth rise up through him, a warmth that dissolved his anxiety, a warmth that completed him, that penetrated to the deepest part of him, making him part of something whole. For only a moment he was alone in his wakefulness; then, squeezing his eyes tightly shut as if to crowd in sleep, he saw the dark matter spinning through the universe, invisible planets hurtling by and disappearing behind him; then the void swallowed him up as well, and, finally at rest, peaceful, he too hurtled through space, himself one of the planets, alone, whole, performing his own dance, the only forces the bare laws of physics, spinning, spinning…

He slept the deepest, heaviest of sleeps; the night was rich with dreams. It might have been that his whole mind, every neuron, every atom in his body stood up to be counted, each joining into a miraculous choir of a billion close tones, the chorus of the uterus of the entire universe, rising up to a celestial volume before dying down into the faintest of sighs.

When Rafi woke up in the morning he was still surrounded by the same familiar arms, warmed by the same gently hissing breath. Only an urgent feeling in his bladder made him tear himself away from that warm, blissful bed. Standing over the toilet, he allowed a shiver of pleasure to course, unmolested, through his body, and catching sight of himself in the mirror, he touched his arm, hardly believing that this transformed, amazing body, the body the pretty man loved, was his own. Still gazing in the mirror, Rafi saw himself smile, and it seemed for an instant that the scar on his cheek was an extension of that smile, and that his whole face was a monument to joy that the whole world should look upon and envy.

As his feet padded back across the floor from the bathroom, speeding that shivering naked body back to the arms that he so deeply desired, he stepped, almost tripped, on something hard. Rafi looked down – he had stepped on the guy's jeans, which had been thrown there so carelessly. But what was that in the pocket, what was it that was so defiantly hard in the back pocket? It was harder, angrier than a wallet, less fluid than a keychain.

Rafi glanced quickly at the guy, who had rolled over to the opposite side of the bed, facing away from him. Crouching over the crumpled jeans, devoid of the miraculous body that gave them life and movement, Rafi reached in and pulled it out. He felt its rough sides, its ivory handle, turning it over and over in his hands. Automatically, coldly, he swung out the blade, and shifted it gently back and forth, trying to catch a glint in the dim light of the room. With great concentration, he glided the sharp edge, cool like a fingernail, along his forearm, shaving off a swath of hair down to the skin. Staring dumbly at the pale, bald patch, he lay the flat side of the blade against his left cheek. The metal was cold against his skin, cold like a hand trying lamely to ease the cruel, hot blow of disappointment.

A rustle of sheets finally pulled Rafi from his stunned reverie.

"Hey, whatcha doing? Come on back to bed."

Flustered, Rafi swiftly put the knife back in the jeans pocket.

He looked for the eyes, the dark centre of the eyes.

For a moment Rafi didn't move. Finally, making that weird, almost sinister expression with his mouth, the guy said, "I always knew you'd like it that way, tough guy."

Pulled back into bed by the pretty, brown-haired man, surrounded by glorious, twining arms, Rafi felt the terror zoom out of him up into the air at a terrific height, where it hovered for a moment before crashing back ecstatically like a wave. Closing his eyes, Rafi felt the pretty man washing over and through him, infiltrating every bit of his being with an intensity great enough, it seemed, to pull his whole body apart. Rafi was putty, a pile of quivering, moist dying flesh, his intestines where his lungs should be, his heart ripped from its cavity, again a bloody mess of veins, standing alone in the dark.

DOMINIC BERRY

Jerk

A boy's wet cheek clung to the piss-smeared, rain-whipped glass of the phone booth. Like a flabby white balloon squashed against a window, the cheek did not move for twenty minutes.

Two mid-teen girls passed by the phone box. They teetered through the puddles on pinprick heels. Raindrop dribbles ran round their tight nipples. Breasts pushed through their long, thick coats, beckoning with every bounce. Both girls paused to assess the pale body, propped against the transparent wall. Piccadilly people revel in the misery of others.

"Sick! C'mon."

Two steps later and their discovery was forgotten. Tonight, they wouldn't need to notice bus stops, phone boxes and below-standard fellas. They didn't need to drink much before they could barely see anything. Their tits were their radar.

They continued up the road, leaving a trail of giggles behind them. But the boy didn't even notice girls.

Staring through the swinging phone-receiver, Josh scrutinised a twisting recollection of the last ten minutes. Tender fists flinched and fumbled further up sweat-laced sleeves.

Tomorrow was Father's Day.

"Shit."

Josh had always hated his father, thinking of him going out at night. He didn't want that man's mind to linger long on the kind of fun his son craved.

More drunks began to sing down the street: men, with fat, chunky voices. Their words slopped out inaudibly, but it was the united force beneath their blood-laced roars that all too coherently yelled to him one simple fact.

They *knew* that they were everything Josh could never be.

Each touch had left its tingling residue under Josh's jeans. Some moments his mind exaggerated, some moments his mind tamed down, although no reiteration of events could justify his silent complicity. But still his mind replayed them.

His arms ached with their severed reflexes. The only reflex reaction Josh recognised was instant obedience. His head would always nod in agreement with any opinion, idea or demand that any man chose to squeeze into his mouth.

Josh had needed no further incentive to obey every command he'd been given. It had been enough just to see the scally's cold-sore-caked lip spit, to hear his bruised eyelids blink beneath his black baseball cap. He might as well have been operating Josh's limbs by remote control.

A dented car shot past the bus stop outside. The broken beat of Sister Bliss spilt from the spluttering radio over the night.

There must be at least a three-sentence conversation in that, Josh thought. John Martyn on a dance track. Dad probably liked John Martin. That would fill part of tomorrow's obligatory ten-minute call.

Josh had to go home.

The streets, for a Saturday night, were surprisingly quiet. Only one Stagecoach bus trundled across Josh's path. Gel-drenched student boys in clinging T-shirts sprawled along the back seat, pigeon arms tangled in matey embrace. Their cluttered facial piercings chinked in rhythm with the limp indie anthems they chanted in teenage anguish. In their identically applied make-up, they somehow retained the look of men you wouldn't mess with. No scally could peel one of them from their camp ensemble and bundle him into a phone box.

Once he'd crossed the road, Josh started running.

"Only an *idiot* would have fought back. Only an *idiot* would have fought back. Only an *idiot* would have fought back."

He hated students. He hated all those blokey-bloke cunts and their oh-so-risky gothic dress-up. All desperately compromising to fit in some clique, but all as desperately alone without their conformist mates to clamber behind. All as desperately inadequate as Josh without someone else's arms to fall into on nights like these.

All as desperately fragile.

Nearly home, he panicked as two pre-teen boys swept around a terrace block's concrete corner, their dirty teeth and zippers glinting in the faint streetlight. Josh felt himself withering under the smaller boy's stench of superiority. They paused to eye him up and down.

Every hair on Josh's body prickled.

The boys rubbed past him.

Their giggles licked his paranoia.

★

"Hey Josh, you in? It's Chris 'ere, callin' t' see if yer fancied a pint or summat tonight, but yer not in, so I'll call later. Right? OK, See ya."

Slumping his body between the settee and his phone, Josh skimmed through the messages. Josh's father had always been uncompromisingly strict regarding when Josh should phone, and what achievements he should, by now, have acquired to report.

But these messages were for his flatmates; endless requests from various students on various irrelevant courses suggesting locations for another over-hyped Saturday night. They'd all be up Piccadilly or down Canal Street by now, wrecked.

Part of Josh longed to join them. He longed to run to Chris and let all his self-doubt bleed into his closest friend's ear. But he had to pull himself together.

For years now, Josh had fought against hating Chris, against such bitter resentment for a guy whose only sin was taking a half-decent Uni degree. Josh shared a crap flat with students, but his similarities with Chris ended there. Josh worked full-time at a working-men's pub in Stockport.

Hands locked behind his head, Josh's face exhaled into his chest. Then he saw his trouser zip was undone.

His trouser zip was still undone.

In the phone box, the last thing he'd thought of was to redo his flies.

Suddenly, he saw the laughter of the two lads that he'd bumped into on the journey home in a new light. What an idiot: walking through Longsight, trying to look all big and tough, and all the time everyone's laughing at you because you've forgotten to zip up. Jerk or what.

Jerk or what. He never even *tried* to stop people pushing him around. He hadn't even tried to resist while being crammed into the phone box.

A Nike branded coat had hung loose around his oppressor's sagging stomach. The giant tick logo: like a teacher's red pen praising the work of a student who's conformed the best to whatever subject's being preached. One massive tick confirming that *this* was right, *this* was what you should aspire to be.

"Right. How much you got?"

A thin syringe needle had sparkled under Josh's chin.

Josh had handed over his wallet almost before being asked. He'd been so submissive, so sickeningly polite, to the extent of apologising for not carrying more money and punctuating the end of every sentence he made with 'mate'. He had cooperated completely, long before any weapon was revealed. He didn't understand why, after claiming Josh's wallet and portable CD player, the man had felt the need to root through his underpants.

"Where's the rest? Eh? Fuck this. You got more than this. Where's the rest?"

Shaking his head speechlessly, Josh had tried to cocoon himself until it was all over, and his whole body *had* been numb until those fingers had brushed, meaninglessly, over the tip of his penis. His body had been a solid lump of wood, his focus never leaving the wavering needle's wet tip, but the hand felt like an axe falling through his fear, splitting his thoughts in two.

Despite his having relinquished hold of all he had of any worth, the serrated edges of oblong nails were slinking to the back of Josh's boxer-shorts. But the terror of injection, the tiny scratch he kept thinking he could feel, the grubby palm that had smoothed the rim of his belt, had pricked his awareness so intensely that every nerve he'd tried to turn off had turned up to its full, shuddering volume.

"You think yer gonna mess with me? Fuck you."

That voice. He spoke like Chris, and was around the same age too. He wouldn't look out of place on Chris's course.

Chris would always tell him tales about different uni-buddies' drunken confessions of bisexuality, and Josh's skin would crawl with envy at their experiences. All the scruffy boys he watched walk round college, all Chris's down-and-out mates who'd lie topless in the park on sunny days, swigging cider from black cans. All the men he felt he ought to hate, they were the men who'd never usually spare him the time of day. He spent so many mornings alone, fretting over his fantasies from the night before. What kind of person did it make him, to dream longingly about most people's worst nightmares? Someone pushing him down, making him yield, taking a hold over him.

Like a snake's wide jaw snapping forward, breezeblock fingers had suddenly sunk deep, and directly into the damp mess between Josh's thighs.

Josh had tried to believe that it really didn't matter if some scally found out you'd done a wet fart. "Sorry. Sorry," he'd muttered beneath a ball of phlegm.

The hand had slowly retracted. A puffa-jacket sleeve clogging Josh's mouth, those same fingertips were jammed beneath his nose. In shock, Josh gave a short, sharp intake of breath. The syringe had left his sight.

He had then felt himself being turned around to face the wall, trousers slipping to his knees.

It had been several seconds before he realised that he was now stood alone in the phone box.

⋆

Replaying Chris's message on his answerphone, Josh could already hear his friend's response to the incident.

"See, if that were me, I wouldn't've 'andled it as well as you, mate. Nah. Syringe or not, I'd just be so angry. Wouldn't 'ave been able to stop meself punchin' the git.

"I mean, you did right, like. Only an idiot *would've fought back. But I would've got so mad – so mad, Josh. I tell ya, 'e mighta cut me throat, but I'da broken 'is fuckin' neck. I'da fuckin' strung him by 'is nuts if e'da tried to touch mine. The queer cunt with 'is filthy AIDS blood. Sick. You did right, mate. You gotta control yer rage. That takes real strength, that does. Get mad later, eh? Get even."*

Josh had heard it all from Chris before, and it had nothing to do with having the strength to control your anger. Josh didn't know anger; all he felt was fear.

Josh began fantasising over the needle pressed to his throat; but this time, without a second thought, Josh would thrust his knee firmly into his attacker's groin.

And maybe it'd work.

Maybe Josh would be a hero like Chris.

Or maybe it wouldn't: so what?

Maybe he'd feel blood squirt through his neck and that'd be it. At least

Josh would die like a real man – not like a coward, not like a lifeless doll full of nothing but thick, emotionless stuffing. No nerves, no muscle, no dignity. He imagined his mind set in Chris's bulky, athletic body.

The angst built up against a part of him he couldn't change but couldn't deal with, couldn't confront but couldn't conceal. He rocked back and forward where he sat, yearning escape from the body that failed him time and time again. A giant wave of depression soaked his reasoning, and all he felt was a burning urge to break out, like an itch that kept building its intensity while someone was telling him he mustn't ever scratch. He beat the back of his head repeatedly against his wall, until he finally let himself sob, long and unrestrained.

⋆

"You're right. The weather has been bad."

Josh wiped his wrists against his eyelids. As usual, he let his father lead their conversation, and his response was never more than the natural follow-up to whatever awkward, irrelevant observation had last been made.

"Yeah. It's been raining a lot here too. Hasn't stopped this weekend, Dad. Last night was terrible."

JOHN JOSEPH BIBBY

Big Exit

I know that when the rain beats the ground I won't be busy, and I'm glad. I don't expect customers when the weather keeps tourists at home and locals at work. My windows fog up with the heat from inside as I watch mid-morning television and wait. It's one of the perks of the job; you can watch TV if you have no guests. There's a sex-trade special on one of those chat shows, which I watch with fascination, until it's swamped with girls from down south in cheap dresses and bleached hair, stripping. Stripping is hardly the sex trade. I fix my trousers (they're fitted, grey, and Donna Karan) so as to look respectable and I light up a cigarette, blowing rings of smoke in the air – my party piece. I have to keep up a standard, I've been told. "The men who patronise us" (or purchase us, as it seems to me) "do not want scruffy little bastards, but sophisticated boys." So, we keep smart. And accessible. No button flies – zips, and dark colours, only. With nothing to do, my mind's forgiven for wandering from work. TV and tobacco mingle with the noise of the city racing. I pick up a book and flick through it, remembering my days of studying. I had the brains, but brains don't pay the rent. That's the other perk of the job, you get paid regularly. I wonder, if I start at the beginning maybe I'll enjoy this book. *Captain Corelli's Mandolin* it's called, and soon I am engrossed. No longer am I waiting all forever in an empty room on a rainy day, Carlo is fast becoming my hero. It is all to the good that he is as he is, he tells me, for God made him that way. Of course, I have to be interrupted. I can hear the impatient knocks on my door. Someone comes in, I can hear him but I pretend I can't. I don't scramble to hide the book from the man standing there, I take a liberty and pretend I don't notice, hope he'll go away. He doesn't, he taps my shoulder and gives me a note. I smile. But I can't even see what he looks like. Same as the rest I suppose. Older, well off, horny. I lock the door. Lube up. And let him push it into me. I groan. Let him kiss me. Though he tastes like sick. And say Yes. Though I've never wanted anything less in my life. Fake pleasure. Though it borders on agony. "You like it", he keeps telling me, "You like it". I can't make out anything else he's saying at me. He pushes it in too deep. I nearly have to take it out. He comes and then goes. I light my last cigarette folding up the money, feeling sore. I'm glad I have the money but I'm in pain. I don't know how other boys take it all day without being addicted to painkillers; some of them are. I wish they weren't so rough sometimes. All the money I earn goes on the fucking clothes and cigarettes anyway. You can't get punters in a place like this unless you've got good gear. You can't pass a dreary day in a place like this without smoking. I inhale deeply. I have problems though, with smoking, now that I'm hooked. You can't smoke anywhere. If I have to eat out I spend two hours craving and even the bars are phasing it out now. It's just not socially acceptable to smoke. Out of the window I can see that man go. I wonder what he sees in me. I don't even see them as people. To me they are just a part of the room. But to them I must be something special, or else they wouldn't bother would they? Would they? I suppose they see me as a pricey way to have a wank. Easy maybe. I remind them of the boy next door. I remind them of who they thought of when they were fucking their wives last night. I remind them of that sexy indie student they see everyday, but can't pluck up the courage to talk to. To them I am inconsequential. Not one has ever asked me my name. Some of them shout "OH YOU'RE GONNA LOVE THIS. I'M FUCKING YOU SO HARD KEVIN/MARK/JONATHON" but that's never my name so it doesn't count. I don't want a fucking life history but it pisses me off how I go through so much for their few minutes of fun. The crap I've put up with. Some people are really dirty. They almost stick to you. People force you to do stuff you don't want to. Men who make you, to anyone else it's rape. The rank smell of someone being sick on you. And the feeling of its warmth. Have you ever fucked a stranger? A total stranger and the condom splits? Or how about being robbed by a man with a syringe? Didn't think so. Just being in this room unnerves me. "Pretend you're eight for me". And this is all because they don't have the balls to tell the truth, get out in the real world and get cock the way everyone else does. In clubs, or bars, or toilets or saunas. Makes no difference to me. Completely and utterly I hate it. I JUST WANT TO BE LEFT ALONE. Iftheysortedouttheirfuckinlivestheywouldntprojectheirshitonme. Literally. I pace the floor breathing blue spirals of smoke and calming down. I'm here with these walls, fucking men I don't know because it was easy money. I swear that if I could change things I'd never have cruised the parks for older men. "Just a suck, go on, I'll give you a tenner." I was into it and they were into me and I was the richest boy at school. "How'd you afford that?" Of course: soon I wanted everything my body could buy, expensive clothes and my own flashy place. And now I'm stuck with it all and my future looks as bleak as my past. Stuck here in Paul Smith and Ralph Lauren. Stuck here in this place, in this luxurious apartment overlooking the city's parks – ideal for boys on the game. I laugh to myself and suppose I'm lucky to be up here, not down there. I can see waif boys – dangerously thin – walking to afford deadlier habits than mine. Nasty pimps and pushers down there, too. They all have gaunt faces and hollow eyes, which dart in their heads watching for coppers and waiting for custom. On the other side of this block are the new cool cafés that rich intellectuals and socialites haunt. They click with the city's best heels and tingle with gossip. That they're on the back of *this* block makes them edgy and dangerous. The buzz of the day usually stops if one of us goes in. We seem to be instantly recognisable. I drink macchiato with hazelnut, because it leaves a nice taste in my mouth, and it seems to have become synonymous with whore. It's a different planet there. Even if I only ever get my coffee to take out, I feel like I should be *there*. For now they're the only place to be, but the appeal'll wear off. Sometimes café people in a hurry short-cut around the block. This is called stupidity. Once daylight is gone *I* wouldn't even chance it. The boys at night are that desperate or out of it, they aren't rational. If you're not a paying customer then you're in trouble. A month never goes by without an attack on an idiot kid with so much money he thinks he's invincible. You can't imagine the fear when he realises he isn't. Catcalls from the shadows and soft moanings from the trade. Skeleton faces appearing in the dim streetlights. The boys appear at their most ghoulish as they circle in the street, looking hungry and vying for the attention of prospective customers. Knowing you're ten minutes from a cab. I've seen it happen. Every time it does there's a bit of a fuss and a few of the boys lose their licences. Then it's back to normal. There's never even a threat of anything more severe, everyone of importance seems to have connections with this part of the economy. Corruption seems to be standard practice. For now, though, I console myself with another anonymous gentleman caller. He's very tall. He pays. I suck him off. I'm completely detached. I'm still thinking of corporate prostitution. He comes violently in my mouth. Thick, sharp semen. It makes me baulk. He leaves. I spit it out. Now I really need my coffee. The rain has stopped and the room feels a whole lot smaller. I feel deprived of a friend. The boys below move about more, now they have a whole dry street to roam. I've got this one room. My landlord, who rents me this apartment and directs my tricks (and all for only 40% of what I make) is talking loudly outside. He's straight in to have the money. I don't think now is the best time to renegotiate. As he leaves I return to the TV but it won't come on. Neither will the light. Fuck. I guess the electricity is off again. So, it's just me and the setting sun now. I can't even hear the boys down below. I watch in despair as the light dies. By the time it's gone the street will be full. Full of people, full of sex, full of noise. I'll be full. But I don't want to be. The darkness will suffocate me. I'm feeling panicked. Why? The dark terrifies me. It's more than that. It's not just tonight. I'VE GOT TO GET OUT. Theideaofanotherhornydirtyblokegettinmeonmykneesistoomuch. Even if I get through tonight, aren't there thousands more ahead of me? And once they're finished, t§here'll never be an easy way out. I have to go. Now I have light, in my head and in this room. Outside the noise grows and a clap of summer thunder rolls. Life seems to have been restored with my fuse box. Or maybe it was just on hold. Either way, I've got now to deal with, and I can hear footsteps approach, above the music of Sheryl Crow. A man with a huge smile appears and the song grows. He's looking casually nervous and passes me £50. I do my best to look shy, so he passes me another £20 from his fat little wallet. Before he puts it away though I take it into my hands and smile coquettishly. Thank you. I'm smiling, I'm standing, I'm leaving. He does look flustered, and I do feel sorry for him. It's probably his first paying visit, and maybe his last, which is no bad thing. My landlord (let's cut the crap – my pimp) is looking surprised that I'm done so quickly. My heart is pounding. He reaches for his money but gets my fist in his face. The force knocks him off his feet and I'm free, surrounded by 'Run Baby Run'. As fast as I can I run down and out, through the building and into the street. The cold night air hits me hard but my freedom hits me harder. Without stopping I run into two boys and a punter. And straight on. And laugh. I'm sure no one will follow me now, I count the cash. £500! I can leave for anywhere, now. The air and the night and cold and my sweat all mingle and it's fantastic. I need to keep running I'VE GOT TO KEEP THIS FEELING. It feels like waves. I could go to Brighton, or Spain, or even America, and have an ordinary, free of charge boyfriend who'd know how to calm me in the night. I'll never be anyone else's property but my own now. I'm overjoyed that I punched him and my laughing makes me almost fall over as I run. Tonight is kindly and cooling and refreshing to me as I pass through dark and light, dark and light, working and broken streetlights. I sweat out four years of cigarettes and decide to toss my packet aside into the gutter. IfIhurryIcouldgetmycoffeetotakeawaythebadtasteinmymouth. Permanently. Plastered with sweat and half-exhausted, I bet I look a picture. I burst into a coffee house and up to the counter. No one turns a head as I order. I won't stay here with my coffee though. I leave for the nearest taxi rank and leave prostitution behind me and leave the past in the past.

MICHAEL BOYNTON

Learning To Swim

Let's get these lessons started, huh?

Coming out is kind of like learning to swim. Sometimes you've just got to put the fear aside, close your eyes, and jump on in. The trick to it is realising you need to do it in the first place. I guess some people realise it gradually. Now, mine came to me like an epiphany a couple of months ago. You know, a sudden insight, when you finally get something and it makes sense? Something that changes you instantly?

Hey, don't laugh. Trust me, it can happen. You can change just like that. I read somewhere, probably one of my lifeguarding manuals, that if a person stops breathing, they have about two minutes until brain damage sets in. Permanent brain damage, that is. That's all it takes. Two minutes and you're changed, literally changed. Your brain, your personality, everything. Just like that. In two minutes you're a different person. Of course it's probably a change for the worse. I mean, not breathing is generally not a good thing, right?

Now an epiphany, that's the opposite. That's a personality change for the better. A realisation. In my case, I realised that I can't hide who I am from everyone. There is a world out there, and I can't avoid it, no matter how hard I try. We are all linked together, like a chain.

I have another book, I think it's a CPR one, that says the very same thing. It says that we are part of an important chain, and have certain social obligations rooted in peace, love, and understanding. Some kinda Hallmark card crap like that. Yeah, those books are pretty cheesy. In case I haven't made it obvious enough, I'm a lifeguard and a Water Safety Instructor. I teach kids how to swim. Well, I used to.

Let me just tell you what happened. From the beginning.

*

"Come on, Brad! Drag queens! You gotta love drag queens," Matt joked, pouring me a glass of water. Then he added, "God knows, I do!"

For some reason, Matt loved dating drag queens.

"I thought you were trying to get me to go," I replied.

Matt handed me the glass, chuckling. We had this argument every week.

"I am. And you are."

Matt plopped himself down on his couch and grabbed a remote off the coffee table. Soon the stereo came on and some wild techno dance music came blaring out of the huge Bose speakers that line our living room.

I sipped my water.

"I have to be at work at seven, Matt. If I go with you to some club we'll be out until God knows when and I won't get any sleep."

"Oh, yes. And you can't disappoint the little kiddies."

Matt then playfully mimed vomiting until I started to laugh. He then melodramatically sprawled himself across the couch, taking up the entire piece of furniture as if he were dead, head and feet hanging off the opposite ends.

"*Children*," he said with incredible disgust, "the most common sexually transmitted disease."

Matt and I were about as physically different as people could be, let alone best friends. He's an extremely tall, thin, dark-haired club kid with piercings over his entire body. And he says that I look like the really cute boy on *Dawson's Creek*, knowing how much I hate that comparison.

I tried to change the subject. "So, who is this?" I asked, referring to the music.

"For God's sake, man, it's Sonique! What kind of gay boy are you?"

"Not a very good one, I guess."

"Well that cinches it. You are definitely coming to the rave tonight," he said firmly.

"No, Matt. I can't. Someone might see me."

Matt looked up at me very seriously. I realised that what I had just let slip out was a little too honest for our playful conversation.

"Brad," he said in a very pensive tone, "we've been friends since when? Third grade? And I probably know you, the *real* you, better than anyone, am I right?"

I nodded, so he continued.

"You're never gonna be happy pretending you're something you're not. You know what I mean?"

I bowed my head and sadly said, "Yeah."

"Look, if you don't like the clubs and the bars, that's fine. But you need to get out there. Meet people, you know?"

"I know."

"So promise me that you are going to at least go with me to the Gay Pride march after you get off work tomorrow."

"Oh, I don't know."

"You really *need* to, Brad. Especially if you aren't coming tonight. So, promise me."

I looked up at Matt and saw the sincerity and concern in his eyes. And I think that is why I said, "OK."

★

I sometimes wonder what my life would be like now if I hadn't gone to that Pride march. Would I be here right now? Would I have ever had that epiphany? But I'm getting ahead of myself. Let me tell you about work that morning, the swim lessons I taught at the Bel Air Athletic Club.

★

"Hey, Brad! Brad!" all the children gleefully squealed, splashing around in the water, trying to get my attention. Level Twos are always a handful, but it's great to see them get used to the water and eventually learn how to swim.

"OK, OK. Everyone get ready for the lesson," I laughed, "and put your magic listening ears on now."

We all mimed putting on our magic ears and zipping our lips, myself included.

I know Matt would have laughed at me endlessly if he ever saw me teaching these swim lessons. Yeah, the games were silly and you had to pander to the kids, but I enjoyed it. Actually, while I was teaching was one of the rare times when I could say I was really happy. That I made a difference.

After a good session with the kids, we played some water games until it was time to leave. Once the lessons were over and I was drying off alongside the pool, I remembered that I needed to hurry and meet Matt to go to the

Gay Pride march. But as soon as I started for the locker room, Melanie, one of the little girls in my class, approached me along with her mother. For the life of me I still can't remember her mother's name.

"Look, Mr Brad, I drew you a picture!" Melanie handed me a sheet of white paper with a huge blob of purple scribbling. I couldn't help but smile.

"Thanks, sweetie." I gave her a big hug.

"You know, Brad," started Melanie's mother, "you do a great job with these kids. All the other parents agree. And I just wanted to let you know that we put in some great evaluations for you."

Now, I love teaching the kids, but I sometimes have problems putting up with the parents. Especially at the Bel Air Athletic Club. These bored, bossy, suburbanite, soccer-moms would perch themselves by the pool to gossip and tell us instructors how to do our jobs. Matt would bitterly call them 'Breeders' whenever we talked about them.

I glanced over to Melanie's mother, who was looking me over with a smirk on her face, and simply said, "Thanks."

"I hear you offer private lessons," she said, perhaps just a little flirtatiously. "Are you interested?"

I suddenly became very aware of the fact that I was still standing there, somewhat exposed in only my Speedo.

"Uh, sure." I said.

I quickly got her number, hurried through our goodbyes, and made for the locker room.

Now Matt always said that he was going to try and sneak into the locker room someday and see all those young, sweaty lifeguards.

"It's every gay boy's fantasy," he would say. But it wasn't mine. I always felt so scared and uncomfortable. I don't know why. I always zipped in and out as quickly and uneventfully as I could. But again I was stopped, this time by Pablo, one of my fellow instructors.

"Saw that mom looking you over, man. That's some funny shit," he said, picking up his sports bag to leave. Pablo was attractive, but so much the gruff, crude, frat boy that it totally killed any good qualities he might have had.

"Yeah," I replied.

"Hey, I say go for it. I hear lonely old housewives can really fuck. She might even pay to play. You know what I mean?"

"Never really thought about it," I said, quickly getting dressed and desperately wanting to get out of there.

"And that one is probably pretty starved for action. I hear her husband's a fag."

I flinched when he said that final word.

"Stupid queers. Don'tcha just hate 'em?" he said, looking straight at me.

I thought about what an inarticulate asshole he was for a second, but finally caved in. "Yeah, stupid queers."

I grabbed my bag and took off for the Gay Pride march.

*

To make a long story short, I'll skip ahead. Oh, don't get me wrong, the march was OK, I guess. But much like the clubs and the bars, I just felt out of place.

Matt was having a blast, cruising guys and dancing down the streets in his leathers, but I just couldn't get into it. I wanted to, but I was so concerned about being seen by someone I knew, I spent the whole day a nervous wreck. Especially in the '2QT2BSTR8' T-shirt which Matt made me wear.

Well, I guess my fear of being seen wasn't so paranoid, because guess who was on the local news? The clip of footage used by every station had me right up front.

The next day we were even joking about it. But that Sunday evening, I got a call from the personnel manager of the Club. And just like that, I was fired.

"Sorry there, Brad. Lots of parents called in complaining. It's not good for the club, you see. Kinda shot yourself in the foot, there, didn'tcha?"

I wasn't even given the chance to try and explain myself. And I was all set to lie and make up some sort of excuse. He just told me to come and pick up my last paycheque on Friday.

I spent the whole week depressed, moping around the house. Matt tried to cheer me up, but nothing seemed to work. Then Friday came.

★

"Hey, isn't that Brad?"

"Yeah, that gay guy they fired."

"No way, really?"

"Stupid queers."

I recognised that last whisper as Pablo. I didn't know who everyone else was. I just wanted to grab my cheque and get out of there. I could feel everyone's eyes on me. And their disgust. Or was that my own? I knew I shouldn't have even come back for the cheque.

"That sick little perv. Lord only knows what he got up to with the kids."

This one hit me like a ton of bricks. The very same parents who loved me, who wanted me to come over to their homes and spend time with their kids, looked at me like I was some kind of freak.

I finally got to the office, grabbed my cheque, and was out the door.

"Why does Mr Brad have to go?" I heard a little voice say behind me on my way out.

★

All of this is beside the point. The point was that even though I was upset, I wasn't mad. At least not yet. I had accepted it, like it was something understood. But that was about to change in an instant.

★

While walking back to my GEO Prism, cheque in hand, I commented to myself how incredibly hot it was. It was a really hazy, humid summer day. While I was thinking how crowded it was going to be at the pool that day and how glad I was I didn't have to work, that's when I saw him. Some guy on the ground. Something was wrong.

Time seemed to freeze or at least slow down.

My mind began going a mile a minute. All those stupid lifeguard manuals began flashing before my eyes. He wasn't breathing, and the longest two minutes of my life began ticking away.

By the time I got to the guy, I saw that he was about forty and out like a light. It was as if I was operating on instinct at that point.

He had a faint pulse but no sign of respiration, so I started in on rescue breathing, calling out for help every chance I got.

So much crap was going through my head. He was burning hot and sweaty, so I hypothesised that it might have been heat-stroke or heat exhaustion. The guy was in a suit with his collar and tie tight around his neck like a noose.

"Stupid business type," I thought as I took his jacket off and used it to prop his legs to prevent shock. It was then that I couldn't find a pulse, so I started doing CPR as well as rescue breathing.

At this point, I had no idea how much time had gone by. It seemed like forever. And despite my constant yelling, no one had shown up. A guy passed out in a parking lot and me screaming for help at the top of my lungs. You would think a crowd would have been there like a shot. I mean, in the middle of one of the busiest parts of Bel Air.

Finally, after what seemed like an eternity, people started to show up. The first person there was some guy about my age. I told him to get inside and call an ambulance. He was off like a shot.

At that moment, I felt like it was going to work. I was hopeful. But the next chance that I got to glance around sucked that right out of me. I looked up and saw that a small crowd, about ten, were gathering to watch.

Now I've seen it on TV and read about it in the books, but it really creeped me out. And pissed me off. You see, in an emergency situation where there is a number of people, a certain percentage of the crowd will help, I think it's ten percent. Seventy percent will do nothing. Nothing but stand there and look on blindly, completely useless. I was prepared for this, but actually seeing it scared the shit out of me. All of those brain-dead, helpless people not lifting a finger, waiting for the show to be over or someone to tell them what to do because they can't think for themselves. The majority can't think for themselves. Saying it is one thing. But seeing it blatantly in action is quite another.

★

So if ten percent helps, and seventy percent is idle, what about the other twenty percent? Well, that's the kicker. The remaining twenty percent of the crowd actually impedes the help and hurts the situation. This is usually out of stupidity or saving their own hides. Like those panicky assholes that will trample over kids to get off a sinking ship. Twice as many people will make things worse as will make them better.

★

So there I was, trying to save some guy's life, surrounded by on-lookers, when through the almost deafening silence in my ears I simply heard...

"Hey, he's that faggot."

For a fraction of a second, I paused. It was Melanie's mother. And there was her daughter right beside her. Little Melanie. I taught her how to do the front crawl by making her hands into big spoons and pushing the water like a windmill. And there was Melanie's mom, teaching her girl a new word.

In that brief second of slowed time, I could envision Melanie looking up at her mother with those big brown eyes and asking her mom what a faggot was. I didn't even want to think about what her answer would be.

My blood started to boil. I didn't know how to react or what else to do except keep going, keep putting air in this stranger's lungs, keep the blood in the stranger's veins moving.

That's when someone kicked me in the stomach. Knocked me down to the ground. Before I knew what hit me someone else kicked me in the back, so hard it knocked the wind right out of me. And you know that horrible feeling, that fear you get when you can't breathe? I was overwhelmed by it. And despite the assault, despite the fact that I couldn't breathe, I quickly got back up and scurried to the man on the ground. I think at that point it was like an instinct, my mind was in that mode where it only comprehended one goal.

But when I made my way back to the man and tried to give him a breath, I realised I couldn't. I still couldn't take a solid breath of my own yet.

I saw the crowd just standing there. Doing absolutely nothing.

Then I saw two guys, about my age, rearing back to take another swipe at me. That twenty percent. And while they beat the shit out of me in front of a crowd, in front of children, in front of a dying man, I had my epiphany. Right before I passed out. Right before they shattered both of my legs.

★

I accepted getting fired. I wasn't angry. It wasn't until I was bleeding on the ground that I realised I had every right to be pissed off. I guess I thought that I would be OK if I didn't make waves, if I kept my sexuality a secret. It wasn't until my bones were broken for being gay that I realised I should have been out beforehand. I mean *really* out.

I went to the Pride march and the bars, but I wasn't out. Not projecting a positive gay image. I mean, maybe if all those parents had known that I was gay while I was teaching their kids they'd have been like, "Wow, maybe gay people aren't so bad after all." I don't know. But it was then that I finally realised that the world is a piece of shit, especially Bel Air, and I can't avoid myself and what the world thinks of me. I can't avoid it, but I sure as hell can do something about it.

★

Lucky for me an ambulance was already on the way because I'm not sure if anyone there would have called one for me. They picked up the stranger and me and whisked us to the hospital. I never met the stranger again. Never really found out anything about him, except that he made it. Never even got his name. I'd like to think he's somewhere out there knowing a gay man saved his life. That would be neat.

So that's how I wound up here in this place. And when they said these water aerobics you have me doing would be part of my physical rehabilitation, I just laughed. I mean, here I am, the teacher now the student, learning to swim all over again. Thanks to those two eternal minutes, I've had to start over, from scratch. But I'm glad I did. I think I'm better for it. I mean, here I am talking to you, a complete stranger, about being gay. Openly. Relieved and without apprehension. It's like a brand new me.

DAVID BREWIN

Double Life

HEAVENLY EXPERIENCE • ***Slim, good-looking, M, 32, 5'11", GSOH. Caring & Christian. Seeking similar straight acting guy, 25-35 for friendship+. Yorkshire area. Discretion assured. (14902)***

Andrew recalled the advert from *Gay Times* whilst in the shower. Mmm, this could be Mr Right. He was Christian, which was good news, plus Andrew fitted what he was looking for. He started humming 'Pure and Simple' by Hear'Say and stopped. He mulled it over again. Perhaps it was too good to be true. Perhaps this guy would have no personality or be a real Jesus freak, one of the God squad.

He dried himself off, put on his Polo Sport trunks, a present, and looked at the magazine. He was still wondering. A slim guy in combats and a dark striped jumper looked back at him from the bedroom mirror in his Dales cottage.

"Daddy?"

Andrew was startled. He quickly hid the magazine as he heard his young daughter run up the stairs. She was clutching her Bob the Builder figure and wearing a tracksuit that matched her blonde hair. She threw herself at her father with a mischievous giggle and buried herself into his chest.

He gave her a hug and could smell the Dr Pepper she'd just guzzled.

She rubbed her sticky hands on his neck and he started tickling her. He really loved his daughter and was torn with the hurt it would cause his family, friends, let alone the Church, if his secret ever got out.

★

Andrew was Mr Respectable. He was a typically nice guy. He had a young family: one daughter, Nicola; a loving wife, Sarah (mad on Robbie Williams), to whom he'd been married for five years. They were both strong Christians and had abided by their beliefs, not having sex before getting married.

Andrew worked as an accountant, having done his training after leaving university, and was already beginning to move up the corporate career ladder. He went to church on Sundays with his family, although over the past few months he felt he wasn't fully engaging with the sermon or his friends there. His parents also went to St Matthew's, an Anglican church, and many people respected and looked up to him. To them he had it all – career, family, security, roses around the door.

He had managed to keep his wife unaware of his gay inclinations. He had no one to talk to. He couldn't talk to anyone at work, as he was sure his professional image would be shattered if he discussed anything too personal. He couldn't talk to his closest friend Greg, as he was the vicar of his church and would be likely to condemn him. He couldn't talk to any of his close friends, as they were all believers and probably wouldn't cope with the idea that he might be gay. He couldn't pray to God, as *He* wouldn't understand. After all, God hates homosexuals, doesn't He? And he certainly couldn't talk to his wife.

Andrew had tried to find a release from this burden through the Internet. Whilst Sarah had taken Nicola to the park one afternoon, he had surfed around and logged into a chat room on rainbownetwork.com. He had got talking to a guy and been quite aroused, but hadn't gone so far as to meet up.

Then he managed to find details of a nearby cruising ground whilst surfing. Careful to wipe the evidence from his computer, he decided to make a visit.

Over recent months, he had found a release through anonymous sex at this haunt. He drove the twenty miles there at least once a week. At first he had just watched, getting a buzz from looking and imagining what it would be like. But then he had wanted a piece of the action and let one guy suck him off. Andrew had tried to fuck one guy, but he couldn't. Fear, danger, the atmosphere. It would turn others on, but for him the pressure was too much and when it came to it, he was aroused in mind but not in body. He had lost his erection. So, he kept to what he thought was just about OK with the Church, a bit of sucking.

He often felt cheap and dirty afterwards, not to mention the guilt and betrayal. He felt he'd let everyone down. What if he were caught by the police? What if his wife found out? Supposing he saw someone he knew? There were far too many things that could go wrong – not to mention the threat of being beaten up or catching some STI. It had to stop.

Andrew had seen the contact ad in *Gay Times* one day by chance and it had been on his mind ever since. Surely another Christian would understand where he was coming from? They might be in similar circumstances. If nothing else, at least he would have someone to talk to.

He churned over the idea of making contact again in his mind. He knew it conflicted with all he had been brought up to believe. When he was cruising it was a one-off. He could confess to God, repent and appease his conscience afterwards. Contacting the guy from the advert would be taking things a stage further, making things more real.

He toyed with the idea of calling and listening to the guy's voicemail. He'd have to use his mobile so no one would find out. He looked for the number and dialled it, but didn't press CALL. He couldn't. Something was holding him back.

It was *wrong*. It went against everything he'd been brought up to believe. Andrew took his personal morality from the Bible. He'd been taught homosexuality was inherently sinful. He knew the story of Sodom and Gomorrah, better than the person in the next pew. He'd been over it many times, trying to determine what it really meant. But he was caught over a barrel.

He had heard of organisations that could 'heal' you from the 'disease' of homosexuality – even psychologists had tried it in the past. If it was *natural*, then these types of movements wouldn't have sprung up, would they? Perhaps he could contact one and they'd be able to 'cure' him. But the guy in the advert seemed to be OK being both gay and a Christian – and must have thought there'd be others, or else he wouldn't have placed the advert. He might have tried one of these 'ex-gay' groups and been through this struggle himself. Andrew had to contact him.

Andrew had read snippets in the papers that the gay community all led immoral lives. Having sex with everyone they met, constant drinking, drugs, boys. Gay pubs, clubs, drag queens, hanky codes. The piercings, tattoos, designer tops, the noise. It was all too much for him – not to mention the threat of HIV and other sexually transmitted infections that seemed to be prolific in the gay world. What did God think of all that? He didn't know. The guy in the advert would have had to deal with similar divided loyalties, Andrew thought, and it would help him to get another angle on such issues.

Still, it felt wrong. What about his wedding vows? He had made commitments to Sarah and he felt that he had to follow them through. He felt that he had to fulfil his responsibilities as a father and bring Nicola up in the best possible way.

Deep down, way down in his heart, Andrew was sure that what he felt compelled to do went against everything he believed. But there was another part of him, nudging away, urging him on.

He dialled the number. His hand was trembling as he held the mobile to his ear. There was an automated male voice which he found reassuring.

"Welcome to Chat and Date with personal ads for gay men. If you have a touch-tone phone please press the star key twice now.

"Thank you. Your phone is compatible with our service.

"Here is the main menu. To listen to an ad, please press 1. To browse through recent and new ads, please press 2. To collect your messages, please press 3. For further information about this service please press 4 now.

"Thank you. Please enter the five-digit message box number now."

Andrew nervously tapped in the appropriate number.

"You have selected Box Number 14902. There are four other profile matches."

This was it. He would hear the guy he had only imagined up till now.

The guy's message tallied with his advert and he had a gentle Lancashire accent. He didn't sound camp, which was a relief to Andrew, whose imagination was running.

"To listen to this message again, please press 1. To leave a message, please press 2. To hear the next message, please press 3. To return to the main menu, please press 4 now."

After the message, Andrew hesitated and listened to it again. What would he say? He came back round to the options menu.

"To listen to this message again, please press 1. To leave a message, please press 2. To hear the next message, please press 3. To return to the main menu, please press 4 now."

Andrew selected to leave a message. Another automated voice, a woman this time, gave instructions.

"Thank you. Please record your message after the tone. Please speak clearly and press the hash key once you have finished your message."

Beep.

He panicked and put the phone down. He felt hot and nervous. He couldn't leave a message, he didn't know what to say. What if the guy had already received plenty of messages? How would he make *his* stand out? Did he really want to be picked? Andrew decided to get his thoughts together and ring later.

Andrew had a restless night. At work the following day, he felt shattered and took a break. As he left the building, the fresh air of the morning hit him like a hangover. In the park nearby, he found a quiet corner with a bench where he psyched himself up. Ready to make the call he listened to the familiar menus.

"To listen to this message again, please press 1. To leave a message, please press 2. To hear the next message, please press 3. To return to the main menu, please press 4 now."

Andrew carried on with determination.

"Thank you. Please record your message after the tone. Please speak clearly and press the hash key once you have finished your message."

It came to leaving a message. He inhaled deeply. This time he was prepared.

Beep.

He left his message, trying to sound relaxed and confident. Underneath, he felt like a kid with the deep sense of anguish which filled him on the rare occasions he'd been called before the Headmaster.

"Thank you for your message. To listen to your message, please press 1. To save your message and listen to the next message, please press 2. To save your message and return to the main menu, please press 3. To re-record your message please press 4 now."

Andrew replayed the message and was satisfied with it. He saved it and ended the call.

His thoughts turned to what might happen next. When would the guy call? *If* he called. Would he meet him, or would they just chat on the phone? He didn't know what to expect. He was abruptly brought back by his mobile ringing. In a panic he answered to find it was Sarah, wondering what time he would be home from work. He had been brought back to everyday life with a bump. That was his nudge to get back to work. Life goes on.

⋆

The following Sunday there was a christening at church. Andrew was admiring the happy family, all together around the child. It was a time of new beginnings and always a joyous time for the church. Andrew was with his wife and daughter. As he looked around the congregation, he saw God's flock with all its diversity.

There were a couple from the PCC who liked to do everything by the book, very bureaucratic. They had to agenda, motion and vote on everything.

Gail, a busybody, sat in the front pew. She seemed nice enough, but when she asked if you needed praying for, you knew it would become common knowledge.

Right at the front in the stalls were the choir. They saw themselves as being higher in the hierarchy than the rest because of their special status and robes.

At the very back (for they'd arrived late) were the bell-ringers. They liked their alcohol and were loud and common. Andrew kept away from them, they were a bad influence on Nicola.

A couple of pews in front, Andrew saw Derek, one of the 'holier-than-thou' types, quick to point out everyone else's faults. Andrew steered well clear of them. They conveniently neglected the 'Let him who is without sin cast the first stone' verse from the Bible.

Andrew's mind began to wander to events of the previous week. He hadn't received a call from the guy whose ad he had responded to, four days back. He still held hope, however, that he'd be contacted, although he prayed it would be a time when he was able to take the call and certainly not when he was with his family.

He thought again about the familiarity of the voice but couldn't quite place it. No one he knew was gay and it certainly wouldn't be anyone from the church, but why was it so familiar? It couldn't have been anyone from the cruising ground – could it? Andrew put the thoughts to the back of his mind, aware that he was a little worried. Paranoid, even.

Andrew looked around the church. It was a very old building with stained glass windows, lavish pillars and carvings. Also very cold and unwelcoming. A bit distant, like the people who were seated in the pews. He looked at them now. They were quite a cross-section of the town in which he lived. Old, young, married, single, happy, not. They all had their faith, choosing to express it in various ways. Some were in the choir, or the music group, or part of the outreaching army.

This church didn't possess the smells and bells that some churches had, it was less formal and the people's faith was more grounded. In some ways Andrew was envious of the vicar, Greg, who seemed to have life sorted and was always in control of things. Greg was a good close friend to Andrew and they saw each other most weeks. He was in his early thirties, single and completely devoted to the church. A real live wire who gave it his all.

Andrew concentrated on the week's theme of conflict. What Greg was saying seemed to be making sense, everyone being equal in the sight of God and how Jesus had love for all – outcasts, sinners, lepers and those who were deemed spiritually 'unclean'.

Afterwards, Andrew thanked Greg for the sermon and shook his hand. As he left, he wondered what the coming week would hold and if the contact ad guy would ring back – and what he would do in such an event.

The following day at work, Andrew's mobile rang. He looked at the screen and saw it was a number he recognised. He glanced nervously round the office, then at the phone. He answered it to find Greg quite flustered and on edge. After a pause, Greg mentioned an advert. From the way he was talking it was clear he hadn't a clue who he was speaking to. Andrew tried desperately to recall what adverts had been in the last church magazine, but couldn't think of anything. Greg mentioned *Gay Times* and it all fell into place.

⋆

Greg and Andrew had met a few times since the ad, and they got on well as a couple. It had taken a while to get physical, but gradually Andrew had relaxed. Initially he stuck to what he was OK with – sucking – and would dive straight in and give Greg a blow if the mood took him. Then Greg began to lead him on to other things.

But meeting up was often difficult. Andrew was paranoid as to what Sarah might be thinking, and Greg always had some PCC meeting or church thing on. So, Greg made the most of it when he could. With the car parked in some secluded lay-by, Andrew got stuck in… and Greg became tense with excitement thinking about these times.

Greg had a great respect for Andrew. He was different to the other men he had met at Rainbows, a calmer bar in the city's village. Although Greg had to take the lead in their relationship it was worth it, as there was something about Andrew which was a challenge. Greg could see the relationship developing into something more. Perhaps a committed, full-on relationship. Sure, Greg knew about Sarah and little Nicola. He was jealous, as Andrew always ran home to play happy families. If Sarah really knew, he thought…

With Andrew's car parked at the roadside, they had gone into the woods for a quick shag. It was the only place where they could be alone. As Greg was holding Andrew close, he thought about his HIV diagnosis. When should he tell Andrew? Would Andrew freak and run back to wifey, or would he accept Greg and his explanation that he'd caught it from a previous lover?

Andrew was pulling up his Levi's over the firm, smooth cheeks that Greg loved.

Fuck! The condom had broken. What now?

Greg kept quiet and joined Andrew in the car as they returned to their separate lives.

⋆

Andrew was in the waiting room with Sarah at the hospital. He was nervous. Sarah was pregnant and today was her first scan where the sex of the baby could be detected. Andrew paced up and down the waiting room.

Just then Greg arrived. Sarah was surprised to see him and so Andrew appeared to be, but it had been arranged. Just then a young nurse called them all in to the consulting room.

The scan showed that Sarah and Andrew were going to have a baby boy. Andrew looked at Sarah and then at Greg. What could he do? He had grown close to Greg in the three months they had been seeing each other. But the pregnancy was proof that Andrew and Sarah were still very much husband and wife – something Greg was having a problem with.

Greg's eyes were beginning to well up and he left the room.

Andrew let him go. He would deal with him later. Right now he had to stay with Sarah and little Nicola – and he wasn't going to be leaving. Not for the foreseeable future. They were going to be the perfect family. For a while, anyway.

NATHAN BUCK

8

You press your palms to her belly as she lifts her shirt. You splay your fingers and gently touch them to the flesh, feeling for the pulse beneath the stretched and swollen skin. She runs a finger through your fine hair, brushing several strands from in front of your eyes, and you look up into her face, smiling, wanting to tell her that you can feel the kicking feet.

You lay your head against her and listen. There. The movement, the shifting in the waters of the womb.

"Mom?" you ask.

"Yes."

"Do unborn babies dream?"

She pauses only briefly. "I think so."

"What do they dream about? They're not even born yet."

"I don't know, Christian," she says. "I bet they dream about where they came from, and where they're going."

You lift your head but keep your hands on her stomach.

"How do they know, though? How do they know what the world is like?"

Adele chuckles at you, her eight-year-old son, and the crinkles around her eyes branch out on both sides. Her eyes have always been this deep green, like the centre of a forgotten forest. You got your eyes from your father. You can see your mother's eyes in yours, though, if you look close enough. If you lean into the mirror and look past the stormy blue, you are witness to her undercurrents.

You do not always like your mother's eyes. Sometimes they seem like ancient scars that have been sketched from shadows, reminders of some time when a woman was a girl. You think of playgrounds and if your mother preferred the swing set or the merry-go-round, turning, turning, spinning.

"Babies know," she replies. "They float in their mothers and dream of the angels that put them there."

"Why don't I remember the angels?"

Your mother pauses. She may wonder this about herself. "Maybe when we're born, as we grow up, we slowly forget where we came from. And it's our job to learn to remember."

You like this answer; it is evident by the way you take your arms from her stomach, stretch up, and wrap them around her torso. You hug her close, careful of the little brother or sister who waits to meet you in less than a month. Your head now leans against her breasts, and you become uncomfortable. You know that you once suckled them, took the nipples between your lips and drew milk-life from them. You remove your arms and sit back and look around the living room.

You have always loved this big, old house that you grew up in: the stucco walls on the outside, the Victorian antiques, the long, central hallway from which all the other rooms beckon you with their doorways. You even love the dusty basement and creepy attic with the arched ceiling and wooden beams. But you particularly love the walk-in closet in your bedroom. You often crawl through the darkness, past the wire hangers, and push your hands against the faded flower wallpaper of the back wall. You close your eyes tight, and when you open them you think you will be in a magical world. You never are. But your secret kingdom will be different when it arrives. You know there will be ice cream and unicorns, lollipops and fairy kings – although there is so much more you long for, whispering to you from beyond the waving clown.

"I love you, Mom," you say when you return your gaze to her.

"I love you too, honey. I love you like there's no tomorrow."

"When I grow up, you and Dad and the baby can move in with me. I'm going to take care of you."

She smiles wide, and you know you at least inherited your crooked teeth from her. You vaguely wonder why your mother never wears lipstick.

You continue: "I'm going to buy a castle, and you and Dad can have the biggest room. Adam or Ainslee can have the next biggest. I'll take the small one."

"Well, that's very thoughtful of you, Christian."

You shrug, but you are beaming inside because you know she is pleased. You want the biggest room, and maybe if you're nice she will let you have it. It will be your castle, after all.

"I'm going to write lots of famous books, you know," you say.

"I know," she answers. "You better dedicate the first one to me."

"Of *course*. You're my mom."

And you both giggle, and in the middle of laughing your father comes home from work. You hear the front door open and slam shut, the thudding of his shoes against the hardwood floor. You anticipate his arrival into the living room, as does your mother, and together you enter into silent expectance.

He pops through the doorway, dressed in his black suit and navy tie, his hair still slicked back after all these hours. You hate his suits. When he embraces you, as he does at the moment you dash into his open arms, all you can focus on is the slick material that reminds you of snakes and centipedes. You press your face instead into his white, crisp shirt that peeks out from the V of the tailored coat; this feels no better on your skin.

He releases you, pivots, and leans in to your mother, kissing first her left cheek, then her right.

"Adele," he says.

"John."

"I missed you."

"Dinner will be ready in an hour. I got a late start on defrosting the chicken."

He rubs her stomach, her shirt still pulled up. "If you get any bigger, Adele, you're going to burst."

You can see this hurts her. Your mother is overweight as it is, and she cannot help that day after day fingers and toes and elbows and knees finish their transformations within her. Your face burns red when he says things like this: Adele, you need to lose some weight; Adele, can't you try something else with that hair?; Christian, you're all bones, you need to get some muscles, buddy; Christian, why don't you put down that book and come outside and throw the football around with me. At these times, you hate yourself for waiting for his arrival home. You want to pinch yourself when he is late – which is often – and you and Adele are left sitting in the living room like weary puppets.

Your father stands. "Christian, do you want to go outside with me for a bit, while your mom finishes with supper?"

You would rather read the last chapter in the paperback that sits on the nightstand in your bedroom, and find out what happens to the princess. But you will go outside with him. You nod your head.

"That's my boy."

Your mother stands slowly and heads for the kitchen. Your father heads for their bedroom, to change. You go to the foyer and sit in the wicker chair. You pull on your gym shoes and mess up the first time when you tie them. You pull too hard on one of the laces, and it snaps. You frown and stick the broken lace in your pocket, trying a second time to get it right. You finally succeed – ahh, you correctly tuck the loop and pull it tight – but when you stand the shoe with the broken lace feels looser than the other. You walk, and the back rubs awkwardly into your heel. You hope it won't blister.

You wait by the front doorway for John to exit the bedroom down the hall. When he does, he is dressed in jeans, a chequered flannel, and boots. You like this father much better than the one who smells of late business dinners with clients, of photocopy machines and computer terminals.

"Come on, bud," he says, and he pats you on the back. That's my boy. That's my son.

He throws open the front door, and you both step out onto the porch in the early May evening. You breathe in the air, letting it curl down like clouds into your lungs. You suddenly feel giddy to be here with this big, strong man among the approaching night-time shadows.

As you and John walk down the stone steps, you are acutely aware of how much smaller you are than your father. He is muscles and chiselled jaw; you are anxious bones and timid smile. Sometimes when your father comes home from work, you will hop up onto the bed as he changes. You watch him strip to his underwear and put on his other, family-time clothes. You want to ask him why he has so much hair on his chest, or under his armpits, or trailing down from his belly button. But you don't want to sound strange. You know you already talk funny, and this is why the boys at school laugh at you.

At the bottom of the steps, John leaves you and jogs around the corner of the house, to retrieve the football from the shed. You swivel with awkward hips and walk out into your front yard, vaguely aware of your shoe rubbing past your sock into your skin. You look out over the long gravel driveway that slithers away into the woods and fields that surround the property. You let the breeze tickle your face, and watch as it moves among the sycamore trees. You fantasise that you live in a jungle, not on thirty acres outside Chicago, where monster-buildings stare with thousands of window-eyes over polluted streets and rushed city dwellers.

You bend down and run your fingers through the grass, press your palms to the soil. You think of your mother and the life growing within her, and if the baby dreams of grass and blue sky and trees that sway as if they are listening to secret drummers. You think of your mother's tomato garden and the way the green leaves twist and turn, and of the mourning cloak butterflies that flutter in and out of the shadows of the shed.

John returns.

"Ready?" he asks.

"Yes."

"OK, now I'll throw it gently."

He spreads his legs and stands upright, several yards from you. You square your shoulders and centre your hips, hoping your father doesn't tell you that you look like a girl again, the way you like to stand with your weight shifted to one side.

He raises his arm, and instead of watching the worn and tattered ball you watch the way his biceps flex, the way his thick, strong fingers tense and release.

The ball sails into the air, and at the last moment you see it descend from its arc in the sky. It spins, spins, hurls towards your face.

You reach out your hands halfway, afraid, then return them to your sides and step to your left. The football slams into the grass, bounces, and rests.

You quickly look at him. He frowns at you with thin lips. He does not shake his head, which you thank God for; that is the *worst.* You run to the ball and scoop it up in your gangly arms. You hold it to your chest. You want to rip it apart and throw its pieces down, but you know the man here with you worships this thing.

You turn, raise the ball in one hand, hesitate.

"Come on, Christian," he says. "You can do it."

"No, I can't."

"Yes, you can. Just like I showed you."

You feel it slipping from your grip, then you toss it. But you don't put enough momentum into your release, and the ball almost comically dances a jig, then falls three or four feet from you. Your face burns red again and you reach for the ball, painfully aware of your long fingers/stick-legs/bouncy hips/fragile lips.

John walks up to you and crouches down. He picks up the football and holds it in front of your face. You centre your frame and hold your chin high. You want to sweep the loose curl from in front of his eyes – eyes that echo your eyes like twins – as your mother does with you, but you keep your clammy hands pressed to your pants.

"Hey, son. Wake up."

"Sorry, Dad. I didn't mean to mess up." You feel the tears coming, but these are strictly forbidden. You swallow them behind your eyes.

"We don't have to come out here, if you don't like it."

"No. I like it. I do."

"We can go inside, and you can finish reading that book of yours. What's it about?"

You shrug.

"What's it about?" he persists.

"It's about a prince and a princess."

"And?"

"And the prince saves her. He rescues her from the evil sorcerer."

"Hm." He twirls the ball in his hands.

"I'll try harder, Dad, I really will." But you know you want to be talking about the prince and princess instead, about babies' dreams, about kingdoms that can only be entered through the back walls of walk-in closets.

"Maybe football just isn't your thing. Maybe we need to try baseball. I can give you my old mitt, just like my father gave it to me." He chuckles, but you know it is forced.

You nod your head quickly, wanting him to know you'll do anything to make him forget about your high, airy voice or the way you stand. You want him to forget how your mother worries about you at school because you come home shaking, with your head downcast. You will not allow him to think you are different, or know that Patrick Bales and Trevor Doyle jab you in the back during recess. You will not hint to him that these two boys and their friends call you 'girl' and 'sissy' and 'faggot', and that they like to corner you in the bathroom and force you into a stall and shove your head into the toilet. They make you drink the urine, but you will gladly do this if only your father will not find out.

You sit alone, always, during the lunch hours, and you wrap your arms over your knees, and watch as Susie Richardson and Debbie Parker play tetherball. Debbie can be nice, and once in a while she will come up to you, sit down, and ask how you are. She'll lean in with her red curls and green eyes and pat your arm. But Susie always calls her back, laughing at her to stay away from the weird boy, and Debbie obliges, but not before she gives you a final smile.

You do not want your father to know any more about all this than he already does.

"Do you want to go in for now?" he continues, defeated by your silence.

You nod your head, but not too vigorously, and you curl your toes.

John smiles at you and stands up, turning so he can walk back into the house. You follow behind him, slowly, and you forget about the fresh air dancing in your lungs. You think about your shoe rubbing on your heel; you don't mind the feel of it.

Your father tosses the ball to the side, and it lands beneath the canopy of a sycamore, whose arms reach like newly skinned skeletons yearning for the middle of summer. You walk behind him into the house and immediately kick off your shoes.

Dinner is quiet, as usual. You, Adele, and John pass each other the green beans and the mashed potatoes. You eat your chicken, and are careful not to scrape your fork and knife together because you hate the screeching sound of it. After you finish, you ask to be excused. Your father grumbles, and you scrape your chair back across the floor, avoiding your mother's stare. You go to your room and read the final chapter of your book. The princess is rescued at the last second. The prince destroys the evil sorcerer with an ancient family curse and carries her away into an intangible ever after.

You fall asleep with the book on your chest, and dream.

Your mother is giving birth to your brother or sister underneath the sycamore, alongside the football. Something is wrong. Adele is screaming, and the tree is crying. Sap-tears slide down the bark for her, forming a thick waterfall behind her naked body. Leaves cascade to the ground to cover her and protect her in a museum of memory. Your father is running in place, several feet from the tree, but he never gets any closer. He keeps looking over his shoulder, then snapping his head around, as if he's remembered that some things are more important than whatever he keeps staring at.

You see your mother and father from every angle; it's as if your body is pure iris and pupil. You do not know where you stand in the dream. The sun and the moon dance together; the clouds kiss; the blue of heaven ripples like an infinite ocean. The stars form a stairway for the baby's soul to come down and claim its body. You see wings and halos and white robes skipping down the concrete sky, but you do not know if this is the baby or its guardian angel.

Your mother screams one final time, and then Ainslee lies between her legs on the soil. Ainslee is dead. Her palms and feet are punctured, and blood pools out around her, forming a halo of regret. She is still attached to Adele by the umbilical cord, but the cord is wrapped around her little neck.

You are suddenly standing there, also naked, holding a long sewing needle. Blood drips from its tip. Your hand is raised high, and you know where you were all this time. You were in the womb, with the child. But you became jealous because the baby still knows where it came from, and you have no idea of time before your conception. You have no idea why the boys at school want to return you there, or why your father wonders if the angels made a mistake and put a girl's soul inside a boy's body.

You drop the needle, but not before your mother looks into your eyes. She cries red tears, and the leaves are falling on her, the sap comforting her, and you pick up Ainslee. You uncoil the umbilical cord from her neck and hand the child to your mother. She takes the child into her arms, brings her to her chest, and begins to breastfeed. Red-pink milk seeps from her nipples and trickles over the corners of Ainslee's lips. It flows into her small mouth, and the baby coughs. Breathes. She awakens. The tree stops crying, the sun and moon part from their eclipse-embrace, and the stars melt away into a settled blue sky. You quickly bury the football beneath the hard earth.

You awake, sweating, in your pajamas. Your mother must have come in and changed you and tucked you beneath the comforter. Pre-dawn night rules the planet outside the window. You sit up in bed and see a slant of light peeking out from beneath the door. You throw off your comforter – teddy bear pattern until age seven, now Superman – and you gently find the floor in the dark and stand with bare feet. You creep towards the door and grab the handle, turning it slowly. You hate it when it creaks and echoes. When the door is open a crack, you peek your head out into the long, narrow hallway. Your eyes trace the stretch of space, lingering on each doorframe.

Your mother stands in the middle of the hallway near the front door. She is facing away from you. Her nightgown clings to her back, and her legs are spread. You open the bedroom door and step into the hall. You can barely see as you walk towards her. The silence demands you to proceed. The doorways ask you to hurry. The whole of the house itself slinks through your ears and whispers to the corridors of your brain that you will no longer be welcome in this womb if you do not repent. You will be forced to run out onto the porch and down the stairs, away from the centre of this conception.

You reach your mother and you want to touch her hair, massage her neck, wrap your arms around her and pull her close from behind, the way you've seen your father do it.

She senses you behind her, and she turns around. You stop mere inches from her, and because of your height you must look up if you don't want to stare directly at her breasts.

"Christian, honey, what are you doing up?" she asks.

"I had a bad dream."

She raises a hand and scoops your hair back over your left ear.

"We need to cut this," she says.

"I know." You pause, then, "Mom, what are *you* doing up?"

When she smiles you know that she means her lips to be upside down.

"Never kiss a woman with too much lipstick, honey. That's the best advice I can give you."

"What do you mean, Mom?"

"If you love someone, and you kiss someone else, make sure she is careful with her lips when she teases your neck. Make sure, if she must wear it, that it is pink, at the most. This way, when your wife goes to wash your shirt, she will not notice the stains before she tosses it into the machine. She will be able to go about her business, rushing to get the clothes done so she can start on dinner. If she's busy enough, dusting the shelves and making the bed and vacuuming, she won't have time for anything as silly as a light stain. She'll just pick up the bundle, stuff it down, pour in the detergent, and slam the lid. She'll never know."

You look at her hand, the one that did not just sweep away a curl from in front of your eyes; you wonder if, in this blackness, she holds a white, crisp shirt in it.

She does not.

She kneels down – to pray? – and you kneel with her. You take her hands, as if you two were lovers in a past life and now must figure out how to survive together in this new existence as mother and son. You pull her the rest of the way to the ground, and she settles against your chest while you sit with your legs folded. She curls into a ball, and you wrap your arms around her, careful of the baby. You gently rest one hand on the lower curve of her stomach. You know now that it does not matter if these hands can throw a football or clench into shaking fists.

"Mom?" you ask.

"Yes, Christian?"

"Is it true that you have a chance to make a baby once a month? That it has something to do with you bleeding from your private place?"

"Yes, honey. Where did you hear that?"

"You told me. Dad has something to do with it too, right? I mean, I know he's my dad, but if I'm coming from inside you, how does he help?"

Your mother sighs. "Let's just say you were chosen out of a million little choices. God chose you."

You think of how you can't throw the football and how, when you grow up, your penis will get larger and you'll get hair in strange places, but you won't grow rounded breasts. You won't bleed once a month. You wonder if God made a mistake with you, or was too busy that day to care if He gave the right soul to the right sex. Somewhere, in the synapses of your brain, you know that babies are brought by naked bodies dancing and trying to become one person so they can create this perfect, breathing thing. You think about the time you walked into your parents' bedroom, and your mother was lying beneath your father with her legs wrapped around him.

You are jealous of her.

You realise your hand is wet. You remove it from below her swollen stomach and bring it to your face. Thick, dark liquid trails down your fingers, caresses your palm, and slides down to your wrist. You bring your hand to your nose and smell. You are reminded of the copper wiring behind your father's workbench in the basement.

"Mom, you're bleeding."

"I know, honey."

"What?"

"I know."

You hesitate. "But I thought you couldn't make another baby if one was already inside you."

"You can't, Christian."

You look down and in the dark of the hallway you see a puddle spreading out from beneath her.

"Should I get Dad?"

"No. Let your father sleep."

"But –"

"Stay here with me. Soon we can go outside and watch the sun rise."

"Dad!" you scream. "Hurry up, Mom's hurt!"

Your mother sits up and releases her grip on you and slaps you in the face. You gasp as the stingers of pain spread out over your cheek. She has never done that before.

"I told you to let him rest," she hisses.

"You're hurt, Mom. Adam or Ainslee could be in trouble."

Your mother stands, wobbling.

"Dad!" you scream again, scrambling up next to her.

The blood gently flows down her legs and pools out around her. You cannot believe you did not notice this before, your little brother or sister turning into liquid and trying to escape your family.

Your mother turns towards the front door. Your father nervously steps into the hallway, dressed in only a pair of sweatpants.

"Adele. Christian. What's going on?" he asks loudly, and he sees your face, and maybe he can see the blood. He runs towards the two of you, past the other doorways, which must also be telling him to hurry. He tries to slow down as he reaches you, but he has picked up too much momentum, and he doesn't see the pool of blood, after all. He runs right into it. He slips, throws his arms into the air, and then he falls and lands hard on his tailbone. His skull cracks into the wood panelling that runs along the corridor.

For a moment, all is still. Then your mother hurries to the front door, clutching her stomach, and she throws the door open and steps out into the pitch black of early day. You hear the cicadas and barn owls. You almost want to smile – Moon, call me, Sun, save me – but you remember that this is not a time for your own salvation.

Your father stirs, stands. He is covered in blood, both your mother's and his own. He holds a hand to a large gash in his head.

"Christian," he orders, "stay here. Do not leave the house."

Then John dashes after Adele. He slams the door closed behind him, and you can no longer linger on the chirping and singing that entices you from the grass and trees.

You want to cry, let your clear tears drip and fall into the tainted blood at your feet, but it seems to never be the time for this. Instead, you turn and walk down the hallway. The silence and the doorways do not reward or punish. They are deciding what to do next.

You enter your bedroom and without a single hesitation or pause you walk to your closet door and pull on the handle. You calmly open it and stand before the darkness; you do not pull the string for the bulb. You step into the portal and, with instinctive hands, you push aside your clothes and your wire hangers. Halfway there, you get down on your knees and slither through the heap of your dirty shirts, pants, and underwear.

You crawl, crawl, crawl until you reach the back wall. You slowly raise your hands. You splay your fingers, thinking of touching them to swollen skin, and instead press them against the back wall and the ugly, faded wallpaper that is hidden in the blackness. You feel the edge of a strip of the paper that has come off the wall, and you pull it back.

The paper rips easily, subtly letting go of the wood. Slow, slower. A part of you does not want your fingertips to reach past the paper. Because if they do, and you touch wood instead of the corner of your kingdom, you know that you will have to forget about lollipops and fairy kings and unicorns that will carry you. You will have to forget about your secret hope-thing that beckons to you from behind the clown – that girl's hollowed body and that boy's floating soul that are waiting for your choice. You will be forced, instead, to think about black holes that kill stars and steal unborn children.

And you reach past the wallpaper.

MILES DONOHOE

RU FREE 2MORO NITE?

Shit. I should've got off the bus with him, Mark thought as he broke the seal of a new vodka bottle. I could've been fucking his brains out right now.

Mark: young, single, attractive. He told his mates at university that he wanted a relationship, but all the pick-ups he found were just brief encounters in toilets, parks and clubs.

*

Mark had just spent another evening at work, waiting on tables at one of the many sushi-bars that had sprung up all over London. He'd been employed there for just over a year, and was now bored by the routine.

It was midnight when he finally left, after preparing the restaurant for the following day while Lincoln, his manager, was flicking through *Boyz*, trying to decide whether he'd have more luck in Heaven or Substation that week. For some reason no one had told Lincoln that in either case the likelihood of him finding a teenage boy with the mental age of thirty (Lincoln's own) was remote, to say the least.

As Mark ambled wearily down Islington High Street towards the bus stop, he started thinking of Kelvin once again.

Kelvin was a barman in Bar Fusion on Essex Road. It looked, with wrought-iron King Arthur–inspired chairs and bright garish colours, as if *Changing Rooms* had invaded for a weekend and transformed it with their own inimitable style.

Mark had met Kelvin almost simultaneously with starting work at the restaurant, spending every spare moment in the bar chatting with him. Despite this, it took Mark two full months to get his phone number and even then, although he had repressed this thought, it only happened after Kelvin had got pissed one night whilst celebrating a friend's birthday at the bar.

Mark had spoken to him a few times on the phone, but every time they had arranged to meet, Kelvin had – conveniently or otherwise – forgotten about the previous conversation and already made plans.

The plans never included Mark. He would've invited himself along to

Trade, Crash or DTPM, but he wanted to be asked by Kelvin.

Mark hadn't seen him now for close to six months, yet every time he passed the bar on the bus he felt a tinge of regret. Nothing had actually happened between them, but Mark found it very difficult to let go of what, he felt, could have been so good.

What was so good about Kelvin, was that he was drop-dead fucking gorgeous. But Mark preferred to believe that he wasn't so shallow.

Ironically, Mark found it much easier to end an actual relationship, always doing so in his mind before the inevitable happened. In this case, however, it was different. Kelvin was the kind of guy he'd dreamed of dating, but never had the audacity to do something about. He was funny. *Cute*, in a boy-band kind of way, and a similar age to Mark.

Mark's inability to accept that it was a relationship which would never happen meant that sporadically, and usually when drunk, he would test the waters by sending a text message to Kelvin on his phone. He rarely, if ever, received a reply, but Mark's mainstay was his inexhaustible ability to dream.

As he stood at the bus stop, more pissed off than usual at being kept waiting, Mark lit a Marlboro Light. As if by magic, as he knew it would, a 73 turned the corner and pulled in to the kerb.

Debating whether to chip his cigarette or throw it, he spent far too long deciding. He had no choice but to let it fall amongst its kin, of which a rather substantial pile had already been established, and then jump on the bus.

He climbed the stairs towards the upper deck and found what he was looking for, a space on the left-hand side. Mark sat down next to a rather Gothic-looking bloke, who – on closer inspection – was simply partial to black, rather than an extreme advocate of the colour.

Mark sat there wondering what the guy looked like, but the possibility of getting beaten up for staring forced him to look away instead. He gazed down at the man's black combats, pushed just low enough to see the waistband of some white Dolce & Gabbana trunks.

He wondered what the guy's thighs looked like under the dark cotton, but somehow managed to restrain himself from running a hand over them.

Mark reached into his CAT bag and whipped out his mobile. It was a new smaller model that he'd bought from a friend at university. No doubt stolen.

He started re-reading his old text messages, three of which were from Kelvin, all dated months ago. Then he tapped in a new message.

HOW U DOIN? STILL @ FUSION?
WAN2 MT UP 1NITE? SPK 2 U L8R M X

Unlikely, since he never calls me, Mark thought, as he erased the unsent message and stuffed the phone back in his bag.

The conductor, a miserable-looking, middle-aged woman, was hovering near Mark.

"Tickets and passes," she said loudly to all the passengers.

Mark fumbled in his back pocket for change to pay her, as she clearly expected everyone to have their money ready.

"A pound please," said Mark, as he held the money out to her.

"Where you going?" she asked, not wanting to relinquish what little power she had.

"Tottenham," Mark replied, abrasively.

"That's a pound."

Well, that would be why I said a pound in the first place, you stupid bitch, Mark thought, as he dropped the coin into the conductor's hand.

The bus swerved from Upper Street into Essex Road and Mark scanned the shops in search of Kelvin's bar. It was a habit he found hard to break, always sitting on the side of the bus adjacent to the bar, so he could indulge his vain hope of seeing Kelvin.

Mark passed the bar, and once again there was no sign of Kelvin. He slumped back in his seat, pondering over the thought of phoning him when the bus skidded to a stop.

People began squeezing along through the aisle to get off.

Mark edged himself further into his seat to avoid the mass of sweaty flesh heading towards him, and in doing so his leg gently brushed against the guy next to him.

There had been countless times over the years when Mark had been on various forms of public transport, wondering whether the man sitting next to him was gay or not. Many times they probably were, but how he was supposed to approach the fanciable ones, he didn't know.

He didn't think he'd bother spending another bus journey figuring out ways he could discover the bloke's sexuality, and then, if Mark thought he was queer, try and do something about it.

He breathed in deeply and amongst the overpowering smell of perfume from women on the bus he could smell aftershave in the air. Aqua di Gio, Armani. He remembered it from a brief fling last year, that and the odd shag being the only stuff he could remember about Mr October 00.

Before Mark had a chance to try and remember something else about that October, he felt his leg being gently pressed by the guy next to him.

He looked down and saw Combats' knee still pressing against him. Mark waited a few moments, and then – ever so slowly – pushed back. He felt a definite response. All thoughts of Kelvin vanished as he now entertained the idea of being picked up on the bus.

As Mark looked around him, everyone seemed exactly as they had been before. Nothing had changed. No one was staring at him, yet he could quite literally feel himself being cruised.

Strange, it occurred to Mark, how the various ways of finding a quick shag differed. Not only between the sexes, but sexualities as well. If this man had done the same thing to a woman it was more than likely she would have been a) pissed off, and b) bloody frightened. Change the gender of one of them and suddenly there is no fear, only the thought of a good fuck.

It was obviously exclusive to gay men that foreplay was the way to begin a conversation, this being a conversation without dialogue. A form of gay sign-language maybe, with only horny words being interpretable.

A movement next to him drew Mark back to the matter in hand, as opposed to the philosophy behind it.

Combats was lifting a bag off his lap and placing it on the floor. Mark assumed there was some reason for the action, and with the man's lap now visible, he saw what it was. Mark started wishing he was able to run his hands over this body, working his way down to where Combats had just drawn his attention.

Would he be hairy or smooth? Not that it mattered.

A quick glance, to see that no one had noticed what was happening, and Mark followed suit.

The man stretched his legs again, pushing one against Mark's, and then slowly his arm edged itself back behind Mark's own, pushing gently into his torso.

Mark felt his body shiver at the touch of him.

Both of their knees had begun a circular motion, caressing each other. Mark could feel the heat from Combats' body.

He felt himself getting harder. He wanted to lean over and lick the smell from Combats' body, to have his tongue feel the sensation of stubble as it roamed over his face, but wisely he let his leg do the talking.

Even in the crowded and sweaty atmosphere of the bus it all seemed so much more sexual and romantic than the usual groping Mark sought in clubs. Spending week after week at Substation didn't seem to register in his mind as lessening his chance of finding a boyfriend who would last longer than a few hours.

The driver slammed the brakes, jolting Mark back into the present again, and ground to a halt at Stamford Hill station.

It was then that the man started to shift a little in his seat.

Just five more minutes, please, thought Mark, then I'm home and you can come to mine. I'm too tired to wake up early in some alien place trying to find my way back.

Combats, unable to read Mark's mind, had a different idea, and moments later he moved to get off the bus.

Mark stood up to let him pass, and as he looked back the man stared into his eyes.

Fuck me, thought Mark, as the newly named Sexy Combats walked away.

The whole journey and I hadn't even looked at his face properly, Mark thought. Twat.

It was in that split second that Mark had to make his decision: stay on, or get off. And as the man descended the staircase, Mark's indecision took over again. He'd feel bloody stupid rushing off the bus now, seeing as he'd got up to let someone pass and just stood there instead of leaving as well.

He sat back down.

Decision made.

As he sat there waiting for the bus to move on, Mark had a vision of himself rising from the seat and making his way downstairs. It was a vision already confined to the past, along with all the possibilities that the vision could have entailed.

The bus pulled away. Through the window Mark saw Sexy Combats glance up at him.

Wrong choice.

The bus continued on its way, with overgrown branches smacking against the windows.

For the final few minutes of his journey, Mark argued with himself about whether he should have stayed on the bus or not, all to little avail. The decision had been made and there was nothing he could do about it now. The thought of getting off the bus at various stops and running back had occurred to him. But Mark wasn't *that* desperate. Apparently.

Finally the bus reached its destination and Mark began the walk home. Anyway, he thought to himself, I'm too busy at the moment to have a relationship with someone, I haven't got the time. Not that a relationship had been offered, but Mark liked to assume that every encounter held that possibility – especially as Sexy Combats only lived a short bus ride away. Ideal really.

As Mark unlocked his front door and kicked it open (it had been stiff for some time now) he sighed heavily. Once again he was home. Alone.

*

Shit. I should've got off the bus with him, Mark thought as he unscrewed a new bottle of vodka. I could've been fucking his brains out right now. Well, maybe I'll see him on the bus again.

What if he won't bother next time he sees me? I've probably put him off for life now.

A thousand and one meaningless thoughts flashed through Mark's mind as he poured some semi-sparkling tonic into his inch-deep vodka.

★

9.30. The alarm.

Mark stretched out his arm and turned it off.

As he dragged himself out of bed, grabbing his robe and heading for the shower, he remembered Sexy Combats from the night before.

Why am I such a twat, he thought, as he stood under the shower. He cleaned his nipples carefully, he'd only had them pierced a few months ago. He checked his balls, nothing different there, thank God.

Mark put his hand behind the shower curtain, pulled down the robe and placed it over his body, stepped out, and grabbed for a Marlboro Light.

As he left that morning to catch the bus back to work, he wondered if Sexy Combats might get on the bus as well.

Mark was staring at all the cheap-looking shops as the bus pulled into Stamford Hill. Lisa's Star Nails, for ladies and gentlemen. That might be a good place to find a gay boy, Mark thought. As the bus pulled away, he realised no one had come upstairs. Sexy Combats wasn't on the bus.

Mark sat there, feeling dejected. Out of the window he saw one of the bright yellow police signs, detailing yet another crime. An assault at two in the afternoon. Not even safe in the daytime now.

His attention quickly shifted.

The threat to his safety wasn't his main priority. There was a sexy guy. Tight jeans, leather jacket, tanned face. Italian probably, Mark thought.

The Latino was chatting away on a mobile. Was he an escort?

26 yo, Sexy Latino, Active, VGL, XVWE and thick.

Mark was still staring as the guy strolled away, oblivious to his penetrating gaze.

Mark scanned around for any other cute men. None. Fit arse, he thought, returning to the Latino, forgetting he was meant to be miserable.

The bus rolled on towards its destination, through Stoke Newington. He looked at the park outside, inhabited solely by pigeons, clumps of daffodils, and a few trees. And the odd traffic cone. Not a good cruising ground.

Eventually the bus pulled into Essex Road and Mark started searching for Bar Fusion again. The bus drove past all the monotonous, pale brick buildings: pubs, betting shops, offices. Eventually it arrived at Bar Fusion, and no, Kelvin was not there.

The thought dawned on Mark that maybe this wasn't a good bus to catch any more, the whole journey being spent looking for missed fucks at either end, and only one cute Latino in the middle.

He got off the bus and walked down Islington High Street towards the restaurant, promising himself that he would forget about both Kelvin and Sexy Combats. He'd get a different bus home tonight. Fuck it.

When the time came to head home, however, Mark found himself back at the 73 bus stop, eager for a re-run of last night's journey.

He rushed up the stairs before the bus lurched off, and as he got to the top he saw Sexy Combats sitting there, just a few feet away. Mark walked past to sit a few seats in front of him, looked back and caught his eye.

Mark was just thinking about all the things he'd do to him tonight, when he saw Sexy Combats put his arm around the girl next to him. She looked up at Sexy Combats and smiled.

Fuck. They're together. The cunt.

Mark sat back in his seat, pissed off. So fucking what, Combats wasn't as cute as Sexy Latino, anyway. If he wasn't going to get a shag from Combats then he'd get one somewhere else.

Chariots?

Pleasuredrome?

The Cruise Club?

One last try, Mark thought. He pulled his phone out of his jacket pocket.

HI KELVIN U OK? WOT U UP 2?

RU FREE 2MORO NITE?

DEAN M DRINKEL

The Child Fucker

"Is this love?" I hear someone ask, imagining I was dancing for him.

Then I open my eyes.

Bob lies bleeding. He's not dead, but he's dying. The life ebbing right out of him.

He's there on the bed. Now. His throat cut from ear to ear. A red smile. Smiling at me. Like he always does. Or did. No, does. He's not quite dead yet.

Almost.

I don't do anything. I mean, what can I do? Trussed up in this chair? I have no choice. Just sit back and watch him go.

His blood is spilling onto the white sheets we bought together, a couple of months back. Satin has become velvet. A red wave reaching out for me.

I've never been able to swim, and I doubt I'll be able to learn now. I expect I'll drown in the scarlet ocean. Not for the first time, I'll have drowned in Bob.

This isn't happening.

There's no point in kidding myself, of course it's happening. I thought the worst of it was over. How wrong I am. Windows through windows.

A nightmare that's been going on all my life. Once, it was a good dream – but how could I have been sucked in? So easily.

It won't be long. And the truth will be out. I can't believe we haven't been discovered before now. Not that it matters, I suppose.

Bob's clock strikes twelve. Noon or night-time, I have no idea. It's only been twenty minutes since we were left alone, together, in peace. Well-travelled roads, unravelling until now.

It's a lot to take in: the blood on the walls, the bed and the floor; the mess of what has been our home for the last few months, out here, by the beach.

I think I'm going to be sick. The sight of him, that man, the man I loved: Bob. There on the bed, naked. The sheets ripped, tied round his wrists and ankles.

The furniture is everywhere. Most of it broken, smashed into thousands of pieces, but I'm not bothered about that anymore. All I want to know is, who will love me now? Who will cry for me, when I am gone? I'm all alone.

All alone in this world.

Who would have believed me if I'd told them it was all going to end like this? The golden dildo shoved so far up his arse he could probably taste it. Not for the first time, I know. We were old friends. The barbed wire wrapped around it, that was an interesting extra – something that neither Bob nor I had thought of before. But then, I suppose, we had never thought something like this would ever happen to us. Nobody's perfect.

I'm trying hard to concentrate, which is almost impossible. My mind shifts from one memory to another. Back again and fast forward, rewind and slow motion. Pause. Still. Funny really, because that's where all this started: the video films. At first, I thought it was the photographs, but later, when I asked Bob what it was all about, he said that the films convinced him. I was special.

Something black leaks out of Bob's mouth. I don't like the look of that.

The light flickers on and off.

I look up at the ceiling, a bubble is forming in the plaster there. The bath water must still be running. I'd forgotten all about it. Ironic, that was the first room where Bob and I got it together, but also where Bob was first attacked.

That queen, here only last week, maybe the week before, I'm not sure now. She wanted me to be involved, but Bob said no. I could watch, that wasn't a problem, but I wasn't allowed to be touched by anyone except Bob. She said she'd pay plenty, but Bob wasn't having any of it. Once Bob had taken her in his mouth, she'd forgotten all about me.

I did sit there for a bit, in this very chair, but it didn't turn me on. There was something I didn't like about that weirdo – not just the devil tattoo above his dick, so I just went upstairs to watch the Pumpkins on MTV.

The cold is making my teeth chatter. It was me that caused this hurricane. All this is my fault.

I so want to cry now, but I can't. There are no tears left in me,

I'm trying to take my eyes from Bob, I don't want to see him like this, but I'm scared that if I do, he'll die and I won't get to see it. I should be angry, so fucking angry, but I can't be that either. Weird.

Out of the corner of my eye, I can see that she's left the front door open, there's blood on the wood and the wall. I know it's Bob's, and that can't be helped, but some of it also belongs to her.

Bob gave a good account of himself, did what he could with the blade stuck in his belly, smacked her in the mouth, knocked one or two teeth out, but she was too quick for him, grabbed the blade, twisted and turned it like fuck and when he fell down on the bed, she was at his throat. Back, forward, a glint in the light. I think I screamed. Already tied to the chair, there was nothing I could do, and that was that.

All over.

Well almost.

The water starts dripping through the ceiling. It's running down the light cord, onto the floor.

Shit, I looked away then. Just for a second.

No. He's not dead yet. There was a flicker in his eye. I wonder how much pain he's in? Maybe he's getting off on it. We used to enjoy tying each other up now and again.

One of the first times he did it to me, he filmed it. Then invited some people round to watch. They paid a lot of money. So much that the next time we were able to buy a bigger television. Ten of them, sitting there, salivating, but then two walked out. Bob wasn't too bothered, they had paid their dues. If they didn't want to stay, well that was up to them. No refund.

Bob introduced me first. I had been hiding on the stairs. Though they didn't know what they were going to see, they applauded me anyway. They wanted to touch me, to see me naked, but it didn't matter how much they implored Bob, begged him with more money, it just wasn't happening.

I was all knotted up inside, shit scared. I didn't want others seeing Bob and me together – our love. But he kissed me, whispered in my ear that he loved me. I tried to smile and went upstairs. Played with my toys.

All through it, he knew I was watching. Not what was on the screen, I had relived those moments thousands of times. No, I was more interested in the others. Their eyes didn't leave the TV set, even when they unbuttoned their trousers and played with their dicks. They were transfixed. Bob, standing there, an erection in his pants, but rubbing his hands instead. He knew he was onto a winner. Me. Lovely little me.

I suppose that's how we ended up in this mess. We wouldn't be able to show anything on that TV now. Most of it's on the floor. Where it sat by the wall, the queen had painted CHILD FUCKER right across it. Bob's blood.

But the men came. Over and over again. We made different films, tried to cater for what they wanted. The money was flowing. I'd never seen so much cash. And truly, we were happy. We really were. Not that the money was important, not really. It was our love that mattered. And we had so much of that. Bob said so.

There's something here that's not quite right. In all the time I've known Bob, I've never known him to be so quiet. I can't remember a time when I couldn't hear his voice. Always there in my ear, whispering, kissing, telling me it was OK, promising to be gentle. And I believed him. Why wouldn't I? Here I am though, trussed to the chair, and I so want to be with him on the bed, under the sheets, in his arms, being loved.

To the rhythm of the dripping water, I relax and hear the other voice, singing to me, yanking me back to reality.

I want him to die. I want this to be over.

Only now, I remember someone else. Someone who said they loved me. I know they were lying. This voice was also called Bob.

"Father knows best."

Bob's eyes moved. I'm positive. He's looking out at that framed photograph. That picture I hated. A man, a woman, a child.

Him, me and the bitch that fucked us both. His words. Time and time again, his words.

The ceiling explodes, water flies everywhere. The light flickers off. And a gurgle from Bob. That's it then.

I don't need the light to see now. The image is burnt into my retinas, where it will forever remain. I cough, spit out the phlegm. Shit, it's more blood.

I look down at the smile carved into my flesh. The queen got me good too. I don't know why though, what had I ever done to her?

"I'm the one who was born to save you."

After she did Bob, she played with me. But I didn't like her games. She made me kiss that tattoo. Tried to get me to leave with her, said that Bob was evil. Bob was the devil. "Come to Daddy!" She mocked him, teasing him. She spat at him, then at me. "Was I Daddy's little angel?" Why would I believe her, when she had the tattoo? How could I leave Bob?

He loved me. She hit me again, reckoned she was going to knock some sense into me. The cunt.

Lies. And liars.

I'd thought I'd won. Just when I thought I was king, I should have guessed there was more than this that met the eye. She hurt me bad. All because I wasn't interested. So she took me upstairs, tried to drown me, then relented for a bit. That wasn't the right way for me to go, she said. So she cut me up, brought me downstairs and tied me back up. If someone finds you, you'll pray I killed you.

She was crying when she left. Don't know why.

I hear voices. Metallic. Someone coming down the corridor. The door opens. Two men, dressed in black, enter. Shining torches. I want to tell them to come back some other time, when the next film is ready, when Bob's better, but I don't think they're going to listen to me.

One of them whispers "Fuck!" I'm not sure why, or what for. Is it Bob, deceased, lying on the bed – or me, more in the next world than this, naked and bleeding? Or is it something worse?

I think my body is shutting down, one sense at a time. I haven't had any feeling in my legs for ages, and that shadow is creeping up my body.

My sight is fixed and back on Bob. I pray there is some life locked in those old bones.

I try moving my head. My ears are giving up.

One of the guys has fallen to his knees, is wailing.

Ah, I knew I was king. Come to anoint themselves at the altar. The other tries to help him to his feet, but it's no good. I'm sure they are shouting things at Bob, about us.

No, they've got it all wrong. I can't believe they are saying those things.

Now, they're spitting on him, smacking him with their sticks.

Please. Don't hurt him. You don't understand. He's not the villain of this piece. He loved me. Is this how he's going to go down in history?

How wrong they are. All they have to do is ask me, "Who is this man? Who is this bastard that did those things to you?"

And I would reply, "This man, he was my father."

But they don't. They've formed their own conclusions. None of this was my fault. What did I ever do? Oh yeah, I had the misfortune of being born. I remember now.

Before I close my eyes and sleep, I think back to a time when I was happy. Me, a woman and a man. A summer's day.

Bob lifted me up onto his shoulders. "Stick with me son, I've got so many sights to show you." He kissed my leg. "You're Daddy's special little boy."

MAT DUNNE

When A Smile Is All It Takes

HAYDN, 19 *5'11, 30" waist, enjoys going out, clubs and pubs. WLTM anyone, anytime.*

SCOTT, 20 *6'1, 32" waist, into the scene, dance music and cinema. Looking for no strings sex with attractive guy.*

JAKE, 18 *Student, 5'11 $^{1}/_{2}$, 30" waist, likes Steps, Kylie, and Noel from Hear'Say but not Danny.*

PAOLO, 22 *6'2, VWE, slim build, smooth, brown eyes, black hair. Italian.*

TOP TOM, 22 *Toned, out for a good time. Adventurous and versatile.*

BEN, 19 *Cute, thin, looking for fun, friends and whatever else comes along.*

ALEX & **MARK** 29 and 27, *into sports gear and poppers. Enjoy threesomes or group sex.*

ROBERT XXL *35, 42" chest, muscular, likes going to the gym, looking for sporting partner for fun and games.*

PHIL JANSEN, 23 *Trainee accountant. Not out, lives alone, looking for new friends and the right guy to broaden my life. Genuine and caring.*

HORNY H, 19 *5'11, 30" waist. Any excited solos out there with a webcam?*

WATCH-ME-WANK *8 $^{1}/_{2}$" uncut. Cum, turn me on…*

The cosmos was vibrant, matter and antimatter were waging war. The shining white stars ricocheted around the centre, illuminating each other while the black holes hung on the horizon, hungrily waiting for any chance to pull in a victim.

In the middle of the cluster, flying high above the rest, was Haydn.

HAYDN, 19 *5'11, 30" waist, enjoys going out, clubs and pubs. WLTM anyone, anytime.*

With their light behind him, Haydn eclipsed them all. He was the Northern Star, everyone was drawn to him. There he was, up on the podium, arms rotating around in perfect rhythm, preaching to his followers below.

The eyes of every man over thirty in the club were on Haydn, watching him, wanting him. Of course, each time Haydn's eyes rolled in their direction they looked away, back to their drinks, or to one of the over–forty-year-olds in the corner who'd been eyeing them up all night, who would suddenly think their luck was in.

They all knew better than to look for too long.

With a boy like Haydn it was far better to watch and hold onto the faint hope that you could have him if only he would see you, than to actually let him see you and realise you never stood a chance.

In this gay boy world where everyone was wearing all the colours of the great queer rainbow with no imagination and very little taste, it was a rally for attention and Haydn was at the front of the runway. He knew men were watching him, as always, and he loved it. He felt wanted.

Haydn had that cute, boy-next-door quality, blue eyes, enough blond hair to run your fingers through in a style depending on his mood and what day it was, with a super-slim body, not crowded with muscles, yet perfectly toned.

Haydn was attractive, much more so than he realised, which only added to his charm. There was no arrogance about him, just a mischievous smile that let the object of his attention know that they had his interest.

As the cringingly infectious Maria Rubia played yet again, Haydn swooped around.

Below him, the glitter-gel–coated heads were laid out like lights to guide him to his target, the guy Haydn had been orbiting on the dance floor for the past hour.

SCOTT, 20 *6'1, 32" waist, into the scene, dance music and cinema. Looking for no strings sex with attractive guy.*

He was only wearing a pair of white leather trousers, which looked expensive. Probably Warren Kade, Haydn thought, soft and silky to touch all at once. Scott was dark-skinned, and buff, with a cross-weave gold chain around his neck that Haydn could slide his fingers under to pull Scott closer to him.

Haydn shuffled on the podium, trying to get into Scott's zone of vision, and caught the reeling arm of some queen beside him.

JAKE, 18 *Student, 5'11, 30" waist, likes Steps, Kylie, and Noel from Hear'Say but not Danny.*

Haydn's attention wandered to Jake for a second. Grey trousers, reasonable bulge, blue Born To Ride T-shirt, all from George Man – all cheap. Flat stomach, nipples unpierced as yet and one of those sexy barbed-wire tattoos wrapped around his left bicep. The colour was still deep, Haydn felt it must be new.

Jake looked like he was having a fab time. He'd tell you he was having a fab time if he could stop having a fab time for long enough.

Jake was fab.

Fab was all there was to Jake.

Haydn spun right back to Scott. He'd read a survey in *Attitude* the other month that said 47% of men preferred guys who were straight-acting, 2% those who were excessively masculine and 51% were comfortable with some campness. Yet 0% went for out and out camp. Haydn had no problem with camp boys, he knew the moves to all the Steps songs just like everyone else, but he did remember another part of the survey – that 55% were most turned on by a partner's face. On this point Haydn totally agreed, and that is why he left Jake and started looking for…

Damn.

Scott had gone. Whatever Haydn could have had with him was gone. And so had the club's taste in music. It must have been getting closer to closing time because this was the third time Haydn had heard Sonique's 'Put A Spell On You' tonight, although the first time might've been in the bar earlier, not that he could remember that far back.

His throat was starting to feel dry now, too, and as he was on the podium with Jake, who was getting way too close, Haydn swung himself under the railing and down onto the dancefloor.

For a second he stumbled as his eyes adjusted. He always lost his way a little when he first came back down. On the podium he was above everyone else, even above the stars, but back on the dancefloor he was just another asteroid spinning along and bumping into other rocks as they vied for attention.

He wandered along, brushing against one guy by accident and a few others on purpose, all with no noticeable response. Haydn's throat had really dried up, after flying for over two hours, it was a steep descent. Luckily, there was an air steward close at hand.

PAOLO, 22 *6'2, VWE, slim build, smooth, brown eyes, black hair. Italian.*

Paolo smelled fantastic. Before Haydn even reached the bar, the scent of Jean Paul Gaultier's Le Male was wrapping itself around him. A sweet, sensual wave – strong enough to attract without drowning him.

Paolo handed Haydn a bottle of water without being asked. Haydn flashed a smile at Paolo. He'd shagged Paolo thirty or so fucks back: all it had taken was that same smile back at Essential and they were down each other's trousers an hour later in the subway – neither of them wanted to wait to get to Paolo's flat off Canal Street.

The smile was not going to work this time, though. Paolo went to the other end of his drinks trolley to serve another passenger – no Mile High Club for them tonight.

Haydn unscrewed the bottle, opened his mouth, tilted his head back, and gulped the chilled contents down in no time at all. The water soon assimilated, his body was so desperate for it.

He banged the bottle down onto the bar and turned to scan the passengers.

Contact established.

Haydn was offered a seat.

TOP TOM, 22 *Toned, out for a good time. Adventurous and versatile.*

Other players were queued up on standby, fingers on their joypads, eager to strike. But Haydn was the top scorer – they could have a go when he'd finished.

Haydn snaked his way through the crowd, keeping his head tilted down and his eyes rolled up like a doll, all the time focused on Tom.

Tom waited, not moving, not dancing.

Haydn didn't have a clue as to what Tom was wearing, all he could look at were the sculptured pecs and arms that seemed to bulge from Tom's red splattered, leather-look sleeveless top from Plein Sud, that made Haydn just want to be held down and taken.

He had to force himself to look up from Tom's chest as he reached him.

Haydn let Tom speak first, not that he was really listening, there was just so much to look at. He thought he heard Tom ask if he fancied a shower.

Haydn smiled a bit, tried not to seem like he was totally in love. Then Tom said he liked to be showered while wanking.

Game over. Haydn bolted. Tom could find himself another bath buddy.

*

Haydn had another drink. Paolo was busy so he was served by some fat barman who worked there because it was the only way he could meet men without them running away before buying a drink.

He walked around the side of the dancefloor and noticed Jake had left the podium and taken half the crowd with him.

What time was it?

The question flickered through Haydn's mind, he'd booked a taxi for some time, but without knowing what the time now was, he had no way of knowing if *now* was the time or not. It must've been late, since people were coupling up – the queue for the cloakroom was full of playful pairs.

Haydn reached the toilets and headed in. He liked it in there, a central washroom full of mirrors that led into the separate male and female rooms. He found a mirror and checked his hair. It'd been a rough flight and his messy indie look looked *messy.* He dampened his fingers and brushed his eyebrows, then caught Scott's reflection staring over at him.

Haydn flashed a smile at Scott, and Scott's face seemed to light up just as some twat shoved past Haydn and blocked his view.

BEN, 19 *Cute, thin, looking for fun, friends and whatever else comes along.*

Ben had one of those pink cowboy hats that had been all the rage up until a few months ago but were now so out of date only the first-time flyers wore them until they were told how crap they looked.

Haydn was pissed off. Ben was hot and so was Scott and now they were necking away right there behind him. All he could do was watch. That might have been fun for a while but Haydn bored easily and went to the gents.

All the cabins were full, as usual, though no one else was waiting except for Haydn. A door swung open and a couple of ageing beauties staggered out.

ALEX & **MARK** *29 and 27, into sports gear and poppers. Enjoy threesomes or group sex.*

No prizes for guessing what they'd been up to.

As Haydn stood there, he could feel himself gliding back down. He was no longer soaring above the clouds, he wasn't even among them anymore. Now he was just gently floating to the ground. His feet were almost there, he could sense the earth beneath him, knew he was close, he had just a few more seconds of airtime left before the bang at the door.

The landing was signalled by the next passenger wanting to use the cubicle. Haydn unlocked the door and was dwarfed by the impatient waiter.

ROBERT XXL *35, 42" chest, muscular, likes going to the gym, looking for sporting partner for fun and games.*

Robert barely gave Haydn time to get out the door, he just barged straight inside and, as they collided, Haydn saw the reason why Robert spent hour after hour in the gym to build up his body – the guy's face was in serious need of a Clinique makeover.

Putting one foot in front of the other in a wavy fashion as he found his land legs again, Haydn meandered back out onto the dancefloor. Hardly anybody was left now, certainly no one worth worrying about even at this time of night. All the first-class passengers had departed and Haydn was left with the economy tickets, one of whom had locked on to Haydn as soon as he walked back out.

<u>**PHIL JANSEN, 23**</u> *Trainee accountant. Not out, lives alone, looking for new friends and the right guy to broaden my life. Genuine and caring.*

Of course, genuine and caring meant desperate and dull, so Haydn quickly moved away from Phil's gaze. Even all the cute barmen were too busy rushing around so they could get off home to notice Haydn.

There were no good men left.

He hated this sort of night.

He'd been so preoccupied with flying high that he hadn't looked around for someone, and was now left solo.

He'd have stayed at home and watched *Ally McBeal* except, lately, even fictional losers were getting laid.

Haydn headed for the door, pushed it open and nearly died. Cabin pressure had been lost, a thousand freezing icicles lunged at his chest and his whole body convulsed with that first wispy breath – that would teach him to come out without his life jacket on.

Bracing himself, he pushed on through the unlit streets. Haydn could hear the faint thumping of the engines still droning on in his head. It was a bitter night, but he'd loved this top from the moment he saw it in the shop window and was not going to cover it up with some jacket, even if that did mean his arms were now goosepimpled.

There was a guy leant round a lamppost down the road. Haydn stopped in his tracks. Nice arse. Just big enough to get a good grip on and still nice and tight. How had he missed this guy inside? Or was he straight and in need of turning? Haydn liked a challenge.

The next second the guy threw up all over the path. It splashed onto the kerb and down his mashed trainers.

Haydn started walking. Away. Fast.

There was no way he was spending another Sunday afternoon in a choccie frenzy listening to all the voicemails from his friends about how they'd scored.

He knew exactly where to go, it was only a ten-minute walk away, seven if he slid along some of the frost that had begun to form on the path.

★

At this point in the night, in those few hours where Saturday blurs into Sunday and you don't know where the hell you are, there was one last hope for pulling – the Internet Café. Easy Everything.

It was so warm inside, it had to be deliberate, to attract all the lonely, desperately freezing and plain sad people who were on their way home, to come in and warm up for a while and spend some money while they were there, too.

Haydn had plenty left, he'd only needed one boarding pass in the club as when the first one had expired he was ready to leave anyway.

With all the terminals on this floor taken, Haydn went down to the basement, his black side-laced Kickers echoing on the polished pine stairs.

This was the dregs area. Over in the corner a forty-something man in a trenchcoat was making like Napoleon over some chat screen he was reading. There was a kid Haydn guessed to be about fifteen, his skin pockmarked by meteorites and sniffing some after-flight amyl, taking zero notice of the screen.

Haydn spied a secluded screen at the back, sandwiched between two grotty architectural posts, and knew he could sit there with only the top of his head being visible to anyone who might look over.

He accessed gay.com straight away, went to the UK chat rooms and logged himself in.

HORNY H, 19 *5'11, 30" waist. Any excited solos out there with a webcam?*

No point in being coy, not at this time in the morning. Besides, anyone on here would be looking for the same thing he was. Haydn opened about five different chat rooms and started looking around. Most of the profiles were full of people offering their phone numbers or wanting cybersex, both of which Haydn was happy to consider as a last resort – but he wanted something that little more substantial. Finally he came across one in his local room.

<u>**WATCH-ME-WANK**</u> *8 1/2" uncut. Cum, turn me on...*

With such an enticing invitation, how was Haydn to refuse? He clicked on Watch-Me-Wank and started typing. He got an immediate response. Seems Watch-Me-Wank was about to log off, but Haydn had just caught him. Haydn asked for his webcam address straight away – no sense in wasting time.

True to his profile, Watch-Me-Wank was there waiting, jeans undone and joystick in hand. It was only a body shot. Haydn couldn't see his head, but that didn't exactly bother him too much.

Watch-Me-Wank was a bit disappointed that Haydn hadn't got a webcam, but Haydn described himself in intricate detail and that got Watch-Me-Wank on track.

As he pounded away on the screen in glorious refresh, Haydn looked around the room. There were only a few people, most of them supping cappuccinos and facing away from him so there was little danger of anyone noticing anything dodgy. Haydn really wanted to get back in the air again, he was pretty confident he wouldn't be seen, so he slipped a hand into his trousers and took hold of his own flight controller.

He kept Watch-Me-Wank informed of his progress – pre-flight checks complete, landing wheels rolling faster and faster, thundering along the runway.

They were both airborne now, soaring steadily. The people around Haydn seemed so far away, just little black ants in the distance. He felt himself enter the clouds, knew he was about to break cover.

Watch-Me-Wank got there first and gave Haydn the encouragement to pursue.

For a few brief seconds Haydn was there again. Above them all. No one could touch him, he was flying so high. Then his wings were cut from under him as Watch-Me-Wank leaned forward.

Haydn saw the tattoo first.

Jake.

If there were life on Mars, it would look like Jake.

His face was frozen there on the screen, waiting for the next refresh, beaming out at Haydn in orgasmic aftershock.

A droplet of sweat ran down Jake's forehead, weaving over his spot-riddled cheek before falling to the carpet.

Downed at once, Haydn struck 'Esc' and shut all the windows.

That old adage about closing your eyes and just getting on with it seemed appropriate.

Poor Jake, he must have been one of the first to disembark, running off home so he could get on his webcam straight away. Haydn couldn't help but feel sorry for him. After all, if Jake had waited around a little longer he could've copped off with someone like Phil and they could have gone on the webcam together.

Thinking that those two could have got it on and Haydn would still be left alone started to depress him, so he got up and tried to avoid treading on the ants as he passed them.

*

It was still cold as Haydn walked home. He had to go back past the club to reach the taxi rank and it looked so empty from the outside. No lights blazing, no passengers inside jumping to the engine beat.

Now the wheels were down and the engines were cold. But in just a few days it would be taking off again and Haydn would be back to board it.

That much went without saying.

In fact, Haydn thought, why bother saying it at all. Some things didn't need saying, but some things did, only if you didn't say certain things, you forgot how to say other things, and then ended up saying nothing, or not saying what you should, and sometimes what you shouldn't say you did say because you couldn't remember what things did need saying and what didn't as some things really didn't need saying.

It all confused Haydn, in a world with so many ways of communicating, why bother saying anything at all? Surely that had to be the better option?

A bleep startled Haydn as he was about to step off the kerb. A jet-black Ford Puma pulled up alongside him, twin headlights casting dancing shadows across the morning mist.

Nice car. And nice guy looking out at him from the window.

Paolo.

He flashed a smile at Haydn and opened the passenger door. Haydn didn't say a word, just kept smiling that smile of his as he boarded – he was airborne again.

ALEX FÍNEAN-LIÁNG

Blue Eyes In Green Park

He had the bluest eyes I have ever seen. Contact-lens blue, almost neon. When I looked into those eyes of his, I felt as if nothing else mattered. His short blond hair, natural blond that is, you can tell from the eyebrows and eyelashes, was combed neatly and parted at the centre of his head.

I imagined him to be in his late twenties, maybe thirty-one or thirty-two at most. I had never seen him out of a suit, often pinstriped and expensive looking, probably something from Savile Row, perhaps Richard James. And glasses, on some days he wore glasses, with a thin silvery frame, which made him look intellectual, if not a little geeky. With a look like that, I'd imagine he'd be a banker, an accountant or a lawyer, perhaps a management consultant.

His dick is cut, which makes him American, or Jewish. Maybe even Muslim – or just a guy born with a really tight foreskin. It's not too big, kind of pinkish. Healthy. The kind the good Lord made for guys like me to suck on for hours and hours. And I could never have too much, it was always over too soon, too quick, and he would zip up and walk out on me before I'd had enough.

★

"And you don't even know his name?" Anne-Marie, my fag-hag mate, asked.

"Erm... well, no," I answered, somewhat embarrassed.

"And you've shagged *five* times over the last three weeks?" Anne-Marie yelled at me across the table at Starbucks. I looked around and thought the woman seated behind us was stifling an embarrassed giggle.

"Uh-huh, yeah."

"This is *so* unfair, why don't women get such privileges?" she moaned. "Fucking hell, I wanna have a sex change and be a gay man."

★

My name is Kyle, but most people on the scene call me Kylie. I've been seeing this guy – well – I keep running into the guy with the most beautiful blue eyes in the Green Park cottage.

I used to find the whole idea of toilet sex quite distasteful. My earliest memory of my parents ever talking about anything 'queer' was when I was about seven or eight. Some Tory MP literally got caught with his pants down in a London loo, doing a George Michael. My parents were – and still are – convinced that all homosexuals are sick perverts who hang around public toilets waiting to molest young boys.

On a visit to London when I was nine, my father refused to let me go to the public toilets alone – and we were in the *British Museum*.

"It's a big bad city. Loads of wicked people out there. You don't want to go running off on your own or else they'll kidnap you and do nasty things to you, understand?" my father warned me sternly. A keen reader and believer in the *News of The World*.

*

I grew up in a little village called Cheston in the Lake District, a place so minuscule that it rarely appears on maps. Civilisation was a two-hour drive away in Newcastle, Leeds or Manchester. In Cheston, there was nothing but sheep and green fields.

I stumbled upon the joys of cottaging when I first popped into the gents at Charing Cross station when I was about sixteen years old on a school trip to London. And, oh my God, guess what I saw? All these men, some old, some young, some black, some white, some rough-looking, some dressed for boardroom meetings, all at the urinals: wanking. Some were even jerking each other off. There was this old guy, an amputee, perching himself with one hand on a crutch, the other hand shaking away as if his life depended on that impending orgasm. I was shocked. I had never ever seen anything like that before. I was too terrified to join in. I just ran out of there without even having a pee.

I spent the next year back in Cheston thinking about that, the stench of those toilets. Every time I had a wank, I conjured up snapshot visions of all those men standing at the urinals, cocks unashamedly on show. I simply could not get it out of my mind.

★

When I moved down to London last autumn to begin university, I could not keep myself away from the cottage. It started with one nostalgic visit back to Charing Cross, and it just went on from there. Every time I walked past a public toilet in London, I would pop in, hoping that it would turn out to be a cottage. Most of them were not, but the ones in Oxford Circus, Liverpool Street, Tower Bridge, Marble Arch, and Baker Street did not disappoint.

On those afternoons when I had nothing to do, I would run around London with a travelcard and my A-Z, looking for cottages. I tried the toilets in every train station, every department store, every pub, and even every fast-food restaurant. I had a tourist map of London pinned on my wall, and I would mark every cottage I found with a gold star. I spent hours surfing the Internet for all the sites on cottaging. It became my new hobby. Once, I even saw a skinhead in a leather jacket who was obviously cottaging strike up a conversation with a homeless bum who was having a wash there. And they were talking about Arsenal FC.

There were messages scribbled on the toilet doors or tissue paper dispensers like 'Horny guy, 33, VGL, most days after work at 6pm, will suck any cock' and 'Older guy will pay white boy 16-24 £50 to fuck him, leave time and place'. Others were just rude for the sake of being rude (often complete with anatomically detailed diagrams). Sometimes the toilet attendants would use really strong bleach to clean off the graffiti, but new messages would appear almost instantly. Do people really respond to these messages? I don't know.

★

My first encounter with poppers was also in a cottage – I used to think it was some kind of disinfectant. After all, I came across the smell all the time in the cottages and naturally associated it with public toilets. It was only when a guy standing next to me at the urinal took out a small brown bottle and snorted from it whilst wanking that I realised the powerful smell which filled the whole toilet actually came from such a tiny bottle. He took a last snort and shot his load against the white porcelain urinal before throwing the bottle away. I almost dived into the litter bin after it.

I nipped into a cubicle and read the instructions on the side of the bottle. *'Remove the cap, and allow it to stand in a room and aroma will develop.'* Aroma? It stank like some kind of ammonia cleaning fluid gone off. *'Avoid contact with eyes and skin, avoid prolonged breathing.'* What? *'In case of eye contact flush with water and get medical attention. If swallowed, give one or two glasses of water or milk and induce vomiting. Keep out of sunlight and away from heat, sparks or flame. Keep out of reach of children.'* This could have been the warning label on a shipment of radioactive waste from a nuclear power station.

*

My favourite cottage quickly turned out to be Green Park because of its size and quality. Sure, there are old and ugly men who will not leave you alone, but quite often there are also some really cute young guys.

In the winter when it got dark early, the men would leave the cottage in pairs after picking up and disappear into the night in Green Park. I suppose that beats risking getting caught in the toilet, but on some nights when it was so freezing cold I could not take my hands out of my pockets, an *al fresco* fuck under the stars was not an attractive option.

In the spring, the grassy fields outside the entrance to the toilet were covered in daffodils. There would be guys lingering around outside, smoking or composing text messages on their mobiles, but I knew they were having a breather from the stench of the toilets or waiting for the talent in there to improve before popping back in.

It's a matter of convenience, I suppose. Go to a gay bar or club and you have to chat someone up, maybe buy him a drink and talk crap for a while before asking for his phone number. Invite him back and there's the worry that he might nick your CDs or turn out to be a very cute psychopath into genital mutilation. In the cottage it's simple and straightforward: just spot the guy you fancy, sidle up next to him, inspect the goods and make eye contact. If he's up for it, off you go into a cubicle together for some action.

If not, move on to the next guy. Entire operation: fifteen minutes max. What could be easier?

Most of these men are probably married, with kids. Poor sods. Guys who cannot bring themselves to step into a gay bar. Perhaps they can't afford to be spotted, always ashamed, hiding away, pretending to be straight. The anonymity of the cottage is perfect for them. No talk, no bullshit, just fast sex. Work, cottage, home. Sure, everyone knows about Hampstead Heath or Clapham Common, but who wants to go out there and get their shoes all muddy? It's cold, dark, out of the way and dangerous. I've heard horror stories about anything from metre-long grass snakes to demented fisters. But as for cottages, they are en route to home sweet home, active at a convenient time. The ones at Oxford Circus and Hyde Park Corner even play classical music and have potted plastic ivy greeting you at the entrance.

At eighteen, I have youth on my side. So what am I doing, hanging round public toilets evening after evening? Waiting. For him. Blue Eyes.

Before I met him, I was always on the periphery, too afraid to join in but too curious to stay away. I would visit the cottages, linger around the urinals, looking at the other men playing with themselves and each other, but never really doing anything else for fear of getting into trouble. Then one day Blue Eyes marched up beside me in the Green Park urinals and whipped out his dick. He then reached over and held my dick firmly, taking me by surprise. Eye contact made, he then winked me towards a cubicle. He led, I followed. I never thought sex this good could take place in a public toilet. I always imagined this kind of sex took place to the setting of soft music, by a roaring fireplace, on a bed of pale pink rose petals – not pushed up against a stained wall of cracked broken formica in a wet, mucky public toilet which stank of piss and bleach.

*

I saw him again that Friday, two days after the first fuck. And the following Tuesday. Then Thursday. There was a routine, a pattern. He would appear after work, between 6.15 and 6.30pm. I began waiting for him, hopes high. On those evenings when he didn't pop in, I'd be pissed off, even worried. Why wasn't he there? I would wait till 8.30 when I would be the last idiot left lingering there. Then I would pop into a cubicle and have a wank, fantasising about him, wishing he was beside me.

I learnt to recognise the fine dress shoes he wore – American brogues – and would peer under the cubicle doors to check if he was getting off with someone else. The others there would glare at me – that is unacceptable behaviour in a cottage. I even turned down advances from some incredibly good-looking guys because I was waiting for Blue Eyes.

And I didn't even know his name, stupid or what? I spent nights awake thinking about who he was, my angel with the Blue Eyes – American or Jewish? Banker or accountant? Who? What? I had fantasies, I had dreams. I wanted to have so much more of him. I've had a tiny bite, now I want to eat the whole cake. This was driving me out of my fucking skull.

*

"Just talk to him, you idiot," Anne-Marie told me assertively. "Ask him out for coffee, maybe a movie or Heaven. Ask him what he's doing this weekend. Make plans and invite him along."

She was always so full of inventive schemes for catching a man, which makes me wonder why she chooses to hang around gay boys like me instead of getting herself a guy.

"But… nobody, I mean, like *nobody* talks in a cottage. To do so would attract attention. No, people just don't do it. I'd just scare him away like that."

Anne-Marie puzzled over this, plotting the next move like some kind of SAS operation. "OK – compromise then. Write your phone number on a piece of paper and slip it into his coat next time you see him. Mm?"

*

I spent the next few days and nights wondering what should go on that note, how to play it. Even during my lectures at college, I spent my time trying to select the right ten or fifteen words instead of listening to my lecturer go on and on about the eastward expansion of the European Union. The decision made: 1) a plain white postcard, 2) with these words: Hi I'm Kyle. Would like to see you again. Call me on…

Not too tarty, not too desperate, just enough – I thought. I even put up one of those ads in *Boyz*. You know, those contact ads under the category 'In Touch'. It read something like:

> **Blue Eyes In Green Park** *6pm. 21st March. You were great, would like to see you again. Please call me. Kyle. ML 27058*

I waited for him every day for the rest of the week. No sign.

I went back again the following Monday and, sure enough, at approximately 6.15pm in walked Blue Eyes. He performed the usual ritual, casually strode up to the urinal and unzipped. I went up next to him. Our eyes met and we went into a cubicle.

Even before we started kissing, I quickly stuffed the note into his shirt pocket. I felt every hair on my body charge up as he slipped his hand under my shirt and ran his fingers across my chest. He lifted my shirt and licked my nipples, nibbling gently. I wanted to scream, to holler. I longed to bring him home and do this every day, every hour, every minute. This had become what I was living for – that rushed five or six magical minutes a week in a public toilet with Blue Eyes.

When we were done, I pointed to the note in his shirt pocket to remind him. "Call me," I half-whispered.

He instinctively put his forefinger to my lips in a gesture that silenced me. He then calmly picked up his briefcase and opened the door of the cubicle, just enough to let himself out.

And he was gone.

I looked at his thick white milky jism slowly dripping down the toilet door. I ran my fingers across it, feeling the warm stickiness of all that was left of him. His rich musky aftershave lingered a little longer than him. Then, even that was gone. I missed him already.

⋆

Over the next few days, I kept my mobile on all day and night, even during lectures. My classmates were extremely annoyed when Anne-Marie called up during our tutorial debate on Britain's refusal to sign up to the Euro. I made some excuse that my mother was very ill and I needed to keep in constant contact with my family in Cheston. All this while I was wondering why Blue Eyes had not called.

I stared at the phone, craving for it to ring. Three days passed. A week. It was soon quite clear even to myself that Blue Eyes was not going to call.

No reply to my *Boyz* ad either. Maybe he dropped the note. Maybe the dry-cleaner destroyed it. Maybe he doesn't read *Boyz*. I must find him again.

★

The following Thursday afternoon I was sitting in the library writing an essay that was due in the next day. I was trying hard to focus but all I could think of was Blue Eyes. The blank screen on my computer reminded me of the pressing need to get my essay finished. All around me, university students were in a mad end-of-term rush to finish projects and coursework assignments. I sighed and looked back down at the stack of photocopied notes I had, trying to make sense of them and somehow turn them into a three thousand word essay.

I spotted a hair on the keyboard, not a long one, but it was definitely not mine. It belonged to a blond, and it was just the right shade of blond. It didn't take much for me to conjure up those Blue Eyes again and soon I was no longer staring at a blank Word document but into the Blue Eyes in my mind. I looked at my watch. 5.35pm. This was a sign. I had to go. I grabbed my bag and dashed out of the library.

I arrived at Green Park at about 6.10pm. Just as I rushed down the stairs towards the toilets, there he was – *leaving.* Shit, why is he early today? I felt angry, I felt confused. I felt like crying. I felt like running up to him and asking him why he didn't wait for me today. He saw me, and quickly turned away, blending into the rush-hour human traffic. I had to follow him. Just had to. First through the ticket barriers, then down the escalator.

He got on the westbound Piccadilly line. The train was really packed and as it was a Heathrow train, it was full of tourists with large suitcases. He was at one end of the carriage, me at the other.

I hid behind a fat black woman who was wearing a big hat. From under the brim of the hat I kept a constant lookout at Blue Eyes. He didn't notice me. I didn't know what I was going to do if he did, or if he didn't. But I had to follow him, just *had* to.

Perhaps I would find out where he lived, so I could bump into him in his local supermarket or off-licence and casually ask him if he shopped there often. Perhaps I could even follow him to work and run into him at the Prêt-A-Manger near his office and ask him for his recommendations on sandwiches. I didn't know what I was doing. But this time I was not letting him out of my sight.

He got off at Earl's Court and I tried to keep my distance as I got off the train. As bad luck would have it, I got stuck behind a group of Japanese tourists lugging big Harrods shopping bags and typically, they were ignoring the sign that said 'STAND TO THE RIGHT'.

I elbowed up the escalator and spotted Blue Eyes making his way towards the Earl's Court Road exit. I ran down the platform after him. He took a right out of the station and walked in the direction of Brompton Road, oblivious to being tailed. I was quite pleased with myself. It felt exciting, bizarre, even dangerous.

As Blue Eyes got to the junction of Earl's Court Road and Brompton Road, the lights changed. There he stood. So close. I tried to imagine what kind of apartment Blue Eyes might have. A studio? Chic, modern, filled with tropical plants, or maybe continental antiques? Perhaps it would have a sunny balcony with a small herb garden, and a big hall with wall-to-wall mirrors. I pictured seeing six, eight, ten reflections of Blue Eyes on the walls.

The lights changed. Blue Eyes already advanced across the road. I sprinted towards the junction. I thought I was just about going to make it across the road before the lights turned red again.

I didn't even see that motorbike. All I heard was the rider's scream.

★

Sprawled across the side of the road, blood running down the side of my face, stunned. I tried to get up but couldn't. I tasted fresh blood in my mouth.

A passer-by came over but she just stood and stared.

"Don't move him," someone said.

That was when I realised I was seriously hurt. I looked up – there were several people standing around me, some were trying to help.

Then I saw him – Blue Eyes – there he was. But there was no compassion in his eyes. Just a bored, curious look, staring back at me. I struggled to speak but no words came out, only a hoarse croak as I gurgled blood in my throat. Then I passed out.

★

When Anne-Marie came to visit me in hospital, I could have had all the sympathy in the world from her if I'd played the poor accident victim. But I couldn't stand it any longer. I confessed it all. Everything, I left no detail untold. I cried and I cried. I couldn't stop crying.

"You sad, sick, depraved boy, you," she sighed. "Kylie, look, he doesn't want to talk to you. And that's it. You've tried. He's obviously not interested in anything more. Can't you bloody understand? I've nothing against you cottaging, OK? But look at what you've become. What the fuck do you think you were doing, stalking him like that? If not for the accident, what would you be doing for the next few weeks? Following him to work? Waiting outside his flat? Boiling his pet rabbit? You wanna be a Stan, huh?"

"But… I *love* him," I said. I was not lying. There was nothing in the world I wouldn't do for Blue Eyes, nothing I wouldn't do for another moment with him.

"Give it up, matey – he doesn't even have a name. Blue Eyes. Puhlease. You met him in a public toilet. Get real! Stop torturing yourself and for fuck's sake, grow up!"

★

I could never bring myself to go near the Green Park cottage again, for fear of running into Blue Eyes. That it might bring back all the pain. Or simply remind me just how foolish I was.

I spend most of my evenings now with Anne-Marie and gang at Ku Bar or splash about with Out To Swim on other evenings and weekends. I am even seeing someone else now. Someone real. He's a Scottish journalist I met at Out To Swim and I think I am in love again.

But every time I look into the mirror and see the ugly scar running across my left cheek, or when I find a stray hair on the keyboard, or even just sitting on the tube, looking at the route map, seeing the Jubilee, Victoria and Piccadilly lines cross each other at Green Park, I see those big, beautiful, Blue Eyes again.

GEEZER
Bloke

"Hey Mum, where are my school trousers?" I shout from upstairs.

Damn. I'm already dead late. Can't believe she's hidden my *trousers* as well.

"Mum," I shout again from the top of the stairs, "I can't find 'em."

"Stop yelling!" she yells. "They're in the wash."

Panic hits me. I only own one pair of school trousers and an old skirt I've not worn for over two years.

"They were filthy dirty," my mother continues matter-of-factly.

I go back into my room and consider my options. It's now half eight. Shit. No time to think.

I rummage through my wardrobe and find the awful grey skirt right there at the back, crumpled on the floor underneath my football shorts. I stare at the dusty skirt and feel sick. Should I bunk off today, or face the imminent ridicule of my peers? Christ, why did I have to go for that sliding tackle when playing footy in those trousers last night?

Mum calls up. "Do you want a lift in today, love?"

Now, pressurised to make a decision.

"Yeah, great. Thanks," I reluctantly shout back.

"Right, I'll go and get the car started. Be quick."

In seconds I'm stripping off my boxer shorts and putting knickers on instead, then I'm sprinting to my mother's room to borrow tights.

"*Urgh!*" I groan as I pull them on. How do 'girls' wear this stuff?

Finally I yank that skirt up. God, it makes me feel vulnerable and nakedly airy!

My mother's ready to go, beeping the horn, so I've no time to check my appearance in the mirror – thank the Lord.

"Ooh," Mum exclaims after a smiling glance at the skirt, "you *do* look nice."

Yeah? Then why do I feel more uncomfortable than a pig in a bacon factory?

I moodily switch the radio on to hear the DJ announce it's 8.50. Arghh. So, *so* late. Then we hit rush-hour traffic and it has taken fifteen minutes to do half a mile. Pissin' excellent. Another 'L' in the register. Last thing I need.

★

So, it's five past nine and I'm sprint-walking into school, yanking that skirt down and trying to remember how to walk with my legs together. I'm so late there's no one around. Just as well, 'cos these knickers are doing my head in and I'm constantly retrieving them from wedgie world.

I practically burst through the classroom door, making everyone in 11A look up at once. Slowly the realisation that I'm wearing a skirt dawns on the group, followed by a ripple of giggles and gasps of astonishment. I feel like a deer caught in the sight of a hunter's gun.

For a moment I'm totally paralysed with embarrassment, then I see my tutor and snap back to life. Quickly I apologise to her for being late and, head down, I shuffle over to my seat.

"Don't even say a word," I warn Andy firmly as I sit down at the shared desk. Too late. He's already off, rocking back on his chair in a fit of hysterics.

"Sorry Geezer, it's just…" he trails off, his flabby body shaking like jelly as he takes in the sight of my muscular, unshaven legs clad in unflattering 'tan' nylon. His twittering giggles are annoying me now, so I slap him round the back of his big ginger head.

"Mother only went and put my bleedin' trousers in the wash," I explain angrily as Mrs Taylor reminds us all for the fiftieth time that all coursework must be in on Friday – *or else.*

"I've not worn this thing since it was made non-compulsory back in Year 9."

"Nah," Andy whispers back, "suits you. Maybe you'll discover your feminine side." He grins sarcastically. I'm about to remind him that *he* is my feminine side when I notice Mrs Taylor is glaring right at us with her sucking sour lemons face. I nudge Andy hard in the ribs and he instantly stops laughing and crosses his arms like we did in primary. Strange boy.

Mrs T nods and calls out the last three names on the register.

"Yoseff, Yuan, Zander."

★

First lesson is double PE. I love PE, but no matter how much I beg, they won't let me do football or rugby and I have to settle for poncy netball or the ultimate horror of *dance* with Ms Leahy.

Andy can't stand PE and every Monday you'll hear him whinge, "My body just isn't made for confrontation, Geez, I'd rather do double maths!"

I walk to the sports hall with Louise and Shaz, they're popular and really pretty. I think they only talk to me 'cos I make 'em laugh. I notice that when I'm with them more people are nice to me, calling me 'Geezer' instead of 'Bloke' – which I prefer. I know it's only because they want to be mates with the 'in group' as well, but it feels good while it lasts.

"Nice skirt Geez," Shaz remarks. "What's the deal? Thought you hated looking like a girl."

"I do," I reply, "thing is... right now my only pair of school trousers are being intensely interrogated by Mr Persil and are up to their waist in water, spinning round and round."

Shaz takes a minute to work that out. Simple – but stunning with it – so who cares?

"You... you look so *weird*," Louise comments just as we enter the changing room, and I have to agree, with a hollow laugh.

I must be the only girl (God, I hate that word) in Year 11 who hasn't had her legs and bikini line waxed or bleached. The *only* one.

I get my tracksuit on in record time. Phew, that's better.

I'm relaxed now and sit back to discreetly watch the girls getting changed. It's not that I'm perving or anything – well, maybe, just a bit – I'm just always amazed to observe their natural, girly ways. They pray for their breasts to grow, I pray for mine to disappear. And God, when I got *my* period it felt like the punchline in a very sick, unstoppable joke.

Those girls... they chat about make-up, the boys from Hear'Say and the latest clubs, whilst prancing around in lacy underwear, doing each other's hair in new styles 'n' stuff. I know I really belong in the boys' changing room, talking about footy and *FHM* girls.

Thwack!

A shoe comes flying towards me and hits me right in the face. I look up furiously.

"Who the fuck did that?" I scream, jumping to my feet.

Kirsty Ray (Year 11's unpaid whore) steps forward, all hairspray and cherry-flavoured lip gloss and I know exactly who. She's had a problem with me since I walked in on her snogging that student art teacher back in the spring term. He changed schools the following week, terrified I'd spill the beans on him, leaving Kirsty blaming me for the end of her little affair. Stupid slag.

"You were staring at my tits, Bloke," Kirsty sneers, saying my nickname like it's shit.

Slowly she saunters up to me.

We now have an audience and I'm turning red at her accusation.

"As *if!*" I roar, perhaps sounding just a *bit* unconvincing.

"Bloke was gawping at all our tits," she declares loudly to the other girls. Oh, this day just gets better! It's like a scene from *Bad Girls* as heads turn my way in disgust. I try and look hard and stare Kirsty dead in the eye. She just tuts and turns her back on me. Chicken shit.

Rescue comes in the form of Miss Halgate who walks in, senses something is up and orders us all into the gym immediately. Miss Halgate's wicked, doesn't take any shit. And, for a teacher, quite sexy in shorts.

⋆

Andy's waiting outside the dining hall, as per usual.

"Thank God that's over," he gasps, looking like he has just run twenty miles in a fur coat. His chubby face is still shimmering sweat and there's pinky-red blotches all up his neck. Poor sod.

"For once I agree with you," I tell him, "I've just had two hours of Kirsty Ray telling me I'm a dyke and I fancy her."

Andy grins at me.

"I can't imagine what gives her that impression," he teases, touching my arm in a campy, limp-wristed fashion.

"Oh, shut yer face, ya fat poof," I reply, dragging him by his blazer into the dining hall. "Come on, let's go eat chips 'n' donuts!"

Andy's my bestest friend ever, we've been mates since primary and

know everything about each other. *Everything.* Andy complete
I should have been born a boy. He's the only person I feel I ca
it all to.

The giggles and comments continue while we're queuing for lunch. Everywhere I turn someone is staring or pointing at me. "Blimey," they're all saying, "Bloke's wearin' a friggin' skirt!"

The queue is so slow. One long moment of torture: the humiliation. I want to tell them all to fuck off and get a life, but I don't. Ever.

"Bloody hell, Geez," Andy groans once we have been served and found a seat, "this place is *so sad*. Look at 'em."

He takes a swig of his Coke.

"You wear a skirt for one day and it's flippin' headline news."

I nod, but don't know what to say. I stare at all the gender-definite pupils of Wood Hill Secondary and feel that familiar lurch of confusion. Like someone's shaking my brain vigorously, leaving me with no answers, just millions of questions.

Brrinnnggg!

That's the bell. Back to class.

★

The second I walk into class things get even worse. Jay (resident psycho) Wilson starts ranting at me for upsetting his so-called girlfriend Kirsty in PE. Yeah, right. Poor, sweet, delicate Kirsty.

I try and ignore the twat but next thing he's grabbing me by the arms and yelling in my face.

"Oi, Bangkok Chick Boy, where'd'ya think yer goin'?" he jeers, backing me into a wall. With survival instincts activated, I scan the class. Uh-oh. I'm alone in this. Andy's in the loo, checking to see if he's lost any weight since PE, so there's not even him around for support. It's obvious that no one wants to stand up to this maniac – 90% of the class are his sad cronies, anyway. Morons.

He starts poking me in the stomach and I feel his nails piercing my skin.

"Fuck off, Jay," I protest, trying to smack his hands away, but it's no use.

"Knock her out, Jay," some bastard pipes up. Matt Ryan, who eats mice for fun.

Jay is loving this and his face contorts with pleasure.

"Don't ever tell me to eff-off, you dickless, transie piece of shit!" he screams, spitting all over my face.

My legs start to shake and my heart's about to burst out of my chest. I sheepishly glance up at my tormentor. Face scarred by acne, eyes grey and cold. Six foot of living evil now tragically all centred on me.

Out of nowhere, tears start welling up in my eyes. This really pisses me off. I've never cried at school before and I tell myself I'm not about to start now, not in front of this knob.

Fear builds up and somehow froths over into anger. Something powerful clicks inside me. All the terror, frustration and pain explodes at once.

I snatch Jay's tie and yank it up, then knee him with all my strength in the groin. Only hanging around long enough to see him double over in agony, I sprint out the door at lightning speed.

*

I run as fast as possible out over the fields and I don't stop until I reach the line of shops in the housing estate. Blinded by tears and gasping for air, I collapse against the video store window.

God, did that really just happen?

I'm in shock at my actions but feel empowered as well. Jay and his sad muppet friends make living in this body so much harder than it has to be. Maybe it's because I intimidate his so-called *masculinity*. But that's no reason to punish me.

I know I can never go back there now, and I don't want to anyway. All that small-mindedness. Fuck 'em. Fuck 'em all – except Andy, of course. There's always other schools, I console myself, and I imagine the freedom of maybe leaving Devon altogether.

As I light up a cigarette and take a few deep, calming pulls, I feel the slow gradations of calm descend.

I catch my reflection in a shop front window: a tall MALE – but those mammary glands on the chest and the bloody skirt say FEMALE. It's no wonder my life's one difficult situation after another.

My mobile rings. I quickly grab it out of my bag. A text message from Andy.

CAN'T TALK NOW. IN LESSON.
RU OK? HEARD WOT U DID 2 J.
NICE 1 M8. RING U LATER. A

God, gossip doesn't half travel quickly. I smile when I remember the way Jay's eyes almost burst out of his skull when my knee made contact with his sweaty balls. On the long walk home I replay that victorious moment in my mind and it becomes funnier every time. Like a cartoon. The look on his face: *Ahhh!*

*

Back at home, all is quiet. No one in, just me. I figure I've got a couple of hours before my mother sticks her key in the front door. I go up to my bedroom and just stand in front of the full-length mirror, staring at myself.

Once I've closed the curtains, I take off all my clothes and throw the skirt in the bin. History.

I stand in front of the mirror, totally naked. I see the body of a woman and yet feel like it isn't mine. I pray it will disappear before my eyes, but it doesn't.

My mind starts to run through all the double-take looks, the insults, the embarrassing situations and – mostly – the confusion that I've experienced since birth. People have never understood me and it's not like I know how to explain what I am, either.

I hold my breasts and wish they'd just fall off. Vanish. Just like that.

I remember adult neighbours asking me what I'd do when I grew up and got boobs. I said I'd flower-press them – huh. So young, so stupid.

I put my hands between my legs and imagine having male genitals.

I squeeze my eyes tight shut and if I think really, really hard… I can almost feel them.

Jay's voice is booming in my ears. I see the sniggering faces from school and just gaze into that mirror at the 'dickless, transie piece of shit' who looks back at me.

Then I have a new idea. I dash to my brother's room and pick out a pair of his Calvins. Back in my room I slip them on.

No, something is missing.

There. I stuff a Reebok sock down the front.

"That's better."

Next, I hunt around my First Aid box and find five big roll bandages. I know this might be wrong, but I want to be what I should have been for a while.

I go up to the mirror and slowly wrap the bandages around my breasts, watching the transformation as they magically disappear under cloth.

Yeah, it hurts, but I don't care. Looks brill!

Then I put my clean clothes on over the top and look at the new me, I can hardly breathe with anticipation.

Wow! This is it. I look and feel fantastic. I'm dancing round my room in this temporary escape from the prison that is my body.

The suppressed movements and expressions flow out like water from a burst pipe. Too long I've been struggling to control them in order to fit in – not that it's ever worked. I can't believe how right this feels and I've never been so satisfied with my reflection.

Finally my eyes see what my brain feels: MALE.

I caress my fake penis and rub my almost flat chest.

I feel a slight twinge of guilt and wonder if this is good for me. Then I think I've spent fifteen years in the wrong body, what can be so bad about spending half an hour in the right one?

Shit. She's back already, I know the sound of that engine.

I check through the curtains and I'm brought back to reality with a thud.

Shit, better get this lot off sharpish. Good job I didn't Pritt-Stick on a moustache. People do. Drag kings. I've seen it done on telly. BBC2 it was, 'bout three years back. Mum turned over, though, after a bit, laughing uncomfortably at the 'freaks'.

I take one last, long look at myself in the mirror.

I smile at the new me and tell him, "Maybe, one day."

LEWIS GILL

A Picture Of James

The ones you find in public toilets are usually there because no one knows their secret. That makes them harder to trace.

The ones you find in clubs usually only have friends, not families. That means fewer people are likely to care.

The ones you find on street corners… well, they are beneath society so they are usually forgotten.

Another has been found. This one has been left longer than the first one they found, so it should take them longer to identify. I do not imagine that a ditch in the woods is the most preserving of places, especially at this time of year.

The last one they found was in bin liners and left in a deserted house in the countryside. I only remembered where I'd left that one when I saw the description in the newspaper. It was claimed within a fortnight.

★

"Our little James," Jim and Margaret said. Not so little, as I remember. Not theirs anymore, either.

A BRUTAL KILLING it said in the papers.

The news simply described it as a murder. They showed a picture as well. False smile, combed hair and school uniform. A clip of Jim and Margaret was shown on the news, too. They were stood outside their house, crying and asking for people to help with any information they might have.

They looked a fairly ordinary couple, a little bland to be on TV.

I was interested by the concern they were showing. Loving parents, out to avenge their son's murder.

That's not the picture I had been painted. Only one side was shown on the news. Only one view expressed in the press, too.

A schoolboy gone missing and found murdered. How awful for the parents. From what I had been told that wasn't really the case.

They were oh so loving and caring on the news when they didn't have to face what they didn't like. When they didn't have to face what they didn't understand or, more likely, what they didn't *try* to understand.

They were grieving for a dead son. Dead. R.I.P. Funeral. Flowers. That was all the press and the news and the police needed to know about little Jamie. They didn't have to admit to any other part of him. Nothing else had to be acknowledged. Nothing for them to try and understand anymore.

A raped and tortured son was easier to face up to than a gay son.

*

I went to see them because I had a curious and nagging interest as to why they appeared so concerned. Maybe they appealed to me in some way, maybe they just annoyed me. Whatever the reason, it overcame me and I went.

I figured out where they lived from the clip on the news and what information the papers had printed. I drove to their house on one of those warm, clammy summer nights. The kind of night when boys walk the streets with their shirts off. I passed a few like that, on the way. I was tempted to stop, but didn't.

When I got there it was just what I expected, really. Like them, a little dull. An open-plan garden that housed a small fountain with free-flowing water was enclosed in a carefully constructed rockery. A garage locked and bolted and a big bay window. Some things proudly on display, others hidden from sight.

The man whose troubled face had flickered on my TV screen a few nights before answered the door. He looked puzzled, but I explained myself away as someone whose own child had also gone missing years earlier and after being touched by their appeal I had come to offer some advice and emotional support. He was pleased at that and summoned Margaret to the door. Within minutes I was seated in the lounge with a glass of iced lemonade in my hand.

They told me how completely distraught they were and how they were struggling to cope.

Jim lit a cigarette. Not a way he had found to cope, just a filthy habit he'd always had.

"*We wish he was here with us now,*" they bleated.

I wondered which James they wanted here right now. Was it their little Jamie, or James as himself? Little Jamie, the well-groomed son who was always polite to his mother's guests or James the sexy, independent young lad that was happiest in the arms of a man? The polite one I guessed.

The James as himself wouldn't have been here with us now anyway. He suffered from asthma and had to leave the room whenever a cigarette was lit. He told me that. I remembered.

What should have been Jim and Margaret's harrowing story seemed to flow easily. Apparently, James had left for school one morning and not come home that evening. That was the last they had seen or heard of him. No reason for him not to come home, they said.

I had been told there was a reason, but that wasn't mentioned. The reason was rejection, yet that wasn't spoken of. Maybe they were embarrassed. Maybe they were just wallowing in self-pity. Maybe it was easier to ignore that part. It might make them feel guilty. Might make them partly to blame.

There was a picture of James above the fireplace. I looked at it and remembered. It made me hard. He was younger in the picture. School uniform again. No dirty denim, no baseball cap, not the image I faintly remembered. This was their innocent, little Jamie – safe behind the glass. Shut up in the frame, preserved.

⋆

I didn't have to talk much. I said it helped to have someone listen more than anything else, so they told me their version of everything. Did they believe they were telling me the truth? Had they blocked things out of their minds so much that they couldn't even remember them? They wouldn't have been able to block things out if James had still been around to remind them of the things they tried to forget.

He was gone now though, no need to remember the bits they didn't want to.

★

I asked if I could use the toilet and was directed to the first door at the top of the stairs.

As I started to climb the stairs I noticed that there were more pictures of James. They went up the wall in a step fashion, correlating with the stairs.

At the bottom of the stairs there were younger pictures of Jamie, then at the top of the stairs there were older versions of James. Up on the landing there was what seemed a very recent picture of him. Well, from what I can remember anyway.

Their young and innocent Jamie was downstairs for everyone to coo at and admire, while the James who grew up and started to become his own person was left up here, out of sight.

When I reached the top I passed the first door and went on to the second. I opened the door slowly and looked inside. This was James' room. I felt hard again. I went in.

On the wall there were no pictures, no posters. It wasn't how I imagined. When you see the bedrooms of dead kids in films and on the news, the parents have always kept them preserved. But this one had been altered. Where there should have been posters, there were just bare walls with a faint outline, bleached by the sun, of where one had once been. These nonexistent posters obviously weren't the kind Jim and Margaret wanted to preserve.

There was still a teenage smell in the air, though. I breathed it in deep and remembered where those smells came from. Glistenings of sweat in his lovely little regions, which I savoured with my tongue.

That thought and the room turned me on.

I went to the bathroom and flushed the chain, so Jim and Margaret would hear it, then went back down the stairs, passing a reversing time line of James, James, Jamie.

★

When I returned to the living-room, Margaret was stood by the window. She told me that the police were on their way, with a few more questions. I froze inside.

I said that I hoped it had helped talking to me and that I should be off so they could help the police.

As Jim escorted me into the hall I saw, through the window in the door, a police car pulling into the close. My body went from cold to hot in a second. Sweat appeared on my brow.

I tried to act calm as Jim opened the door and the patrol car pulled onto the drive.

I walked slowly out of the house. Then down the path to where I'd parked.

A policewoman nodded at me as she got out of the vehicle. I forced a smile and nodded back.

For the first time I felt real fear. Fear of being found out.

Jim waved from the house as I stepped into my car and pulled out of the close.

I was OK again as soon as they were out of sight.

⋆

I remembered that as I left they thanked me.

Service rendered.

I had rid them of what they regarded as an embarrassment. They owed me that thank you.

DAVID GUE

Men At Work

Once I'd left there, I didn't want to go back. The invitation from the guy in the bar the other night was just enough to complicate things.

That guy was Aidan. I had just finished up working with him at this little recruiting firm in downtown Philadelphia, and the invitation was for the annual Christmas office party. When my boss had invited me to that same party on my last day in the office a few weeks ago, I didn't think I'd go. Seeing Aidan on Saturday night changed that.

Aidan was a few years older than me, but at thirty-five, he honestly didn't look a day over twenty-seven. Because his mother was Hawaiian and his father was Irish-American, he had a bit of an exotic quality. His chocolaty skin was complemented by his cool, calm, serene blue eyes. He was the stuff adverts in *GQ* are made of: a thick-sculpted torso, that V-shape which guys – gay and straight alike – would kill for, and that devil-may-care–style hair, coal black and tight all the way round, except for that curiously spiked part right up front.

In contrast to him, I was a bit taller and less stocky. Pushing thirty, and losing whatever shape I had managed to keep myself in since college, I could never seem to put an outfit together like Aidan. I think he had Tom Ford come in and dress him every day before work, the bastard. Mom's German and French, Dad's pure Italian, and I am your classic American mutt. No amount of gym time during the holidays was going to put me in fighting form again, but this would have to do until I had time to sort out a new routine after the big move.

We'd worked together for almost three years but neither of us knew that the other was gay for the whole first year I was there. After a few flubbed words, the realisation that being picky was not the reason I was still single, and the discovery of a key mutual friend (in no particular order), things were different, and not necessarily better.

We got to be fast friends at the office before we had found out. It was the best working relationship I'd had with anybody. Although that was great, the best part was that we would go to the gym together after some gruelling days on the job, which allowed us to spend a good bit of time outside of work together.

I tried to fight an attraction to him for months, but it was a losing battle.

I always seemed to like the straight guys. Because he often mentioned his girlfriend when we worked out, that was enough to keep my straight-dude fantasy going, while squelching any real-world hopes of a relationship, beyond spotting his bench presses and going out for beers during the Friday happy hour.

He was always a private guy at work, and it's really not the climate for spilling all the details of your personal life, although the girls in the office managed to. That made his silences at the conference table during lunch all the more palpable.

I was only just coming out myself, and it had been a long, slow process. I didn't need the added pressure of telling anyone at work.

It hasn't been much better the last couple of years. After Aidan and I realised that working for the same firm was not all we had in common, it actually put a strain on our friendship, in work and out.

The first day at the office after we found out about each other, I ignored him most of the day. When I saw him and Hugh, our boss, coming at me in the morning, I said a casual hello to Hugh and didn't even acknowledge Aidan.

It got to be mid-afternoon and pretty tense. After a few hours of near misses and averted glances, he called me into his office to discuss the Monday morning meeting.

"What are we going to do about this?"

"I don't know."

"Well, we can't just go around not talking to each other forever."

"I don't know what to say."

It was fun to have another buddy to go out clubbing with on the weekend, but I really didn't need another buddy like that. It became too tough to keep it all out of work. It wasn't an ideal situation, only because he was so paranoid about anyone finding out. Sometimes Aidan couldn't even refer to us hanging out, in friendly conversation, even though everyone in the office knew we had been going to the gym together for over a year.

I respected his decision to stay with the company for the long haul, and even though he was out to most of the people in his personal life, he felt it had no business in the business, so I kept my mouth shut. I never could understand, though, how he kept the spheres of his personal and work lives so separate.

At times it made me feel so isolated. It felt like we were in our own little existence.

All the guys we would see when we went out knew that we worked together. They didn't think it was too big a deal, but would make jokes about us hooking up in the male staff toilets during coffee breaks. They were hoping it was more exciting than it actually was.

The girls at work knew we were friends, but assumed that we were both straight. They had no idea what was going on.

We had accumulated so many mutual friends from both worlds over the years, but they could never manage to co-exist with each other. We were the only ones who could keep them all straight. And it was even a struggle for us.

If there were tensions at work, they spilled over to the weekend, along with too many beers and the all-night clubbing. If I knew he was cheating on his boyfriend or he found out I got dumped by mine, it came into the office with us, right there with our briefcases and work porfolios on Monday morning.

I was always pissed at him for something and it seemed like I could never talk to him about it.

"*Shhh!* We can't talk about that here." That became the party line.

There were some fun times, but the amount of secrecy and tension that was involved far outweighed them. Even when I wanted to come out at work, I felt like my hands were tied because of him.

After a while I had enough. That was one of the reasons I thought I needed to leave.

Things were so stale by the end that, aside from last Saturday night when he asked if I was going to the party, I hadn't seen him since the last day of work, and I didn't plan to before the move to Brussels.

★

"Hey, Paul, glad you could make it."

My old boss, Hugh, was a big-time stud as well. Straight as an arrow, though, with a wife and four kids to back it up. Apart from Aidan and me, Hugh was the only other man in the office, and he had no clue that Aidan and I were gay.

"Tell me about this big move to Brussels."

He was the first of many that day to ask me about my new job. I was going to be running the sales division of a slightly larger company in Belgium. I couldn't wait. On my last day at the firm, I hadn't secured the new job yet, so Hugh was excited to hear about the trip.

"That sounds really solid. Oh yeah, thanks for the Christmas card, too."

Running into Aidan had reminded me to send out Christmas cards to everyone in the office, but the one that he got also had a few lines scribbled on it at the bottom.

Hey, was fun working with you. I'm going to be hard-pressed to find a better gym partner! It'd be great if we could keep in touch.
Merry Christmas and Happy New Year.
Paul

"So, when are you headed to Brussels?" I heard over and over. There wasn't too much to talk to everyone about.

"Right after Christmas. I want to get settled before I have to start work."

"That's great," one of the older secretaries said. "Sounds like you'll have a prime spot over there for a while."

"Yeah, well, at least two years," I said, not wanting to come off as pompous or arrogant. "We'll see how it goes."

Throughout all of the mindless chatter that ensued over the next few minutes, I kept an eye out for Aidan, walking by, spreading cheer, holiday or otherwise. I felt slightly awkward there in just a pair of jeans, a big grey Polo T-shirt and an old pair of Adidas, when all the old co-workers were wearing what they had worn to the office that day. I didn't exactly fit in with the holiday atmosphere. I had just woken up a few hours before and thrown on the first thing I could find.

Just then I saw Aidan, bursting through the door. The size of his biceps made the two cases of beer he was carrying look like footballs.

He knew he was the favourite of the office.

He walked by, nodding and smiling as he went. I received a special wink.

I think he loved to tease me. That fucker. Even after he broke up with that girlfriend who was a boyfriend, we never got beyond platonic.

"Paul, you're obviously very queer and I'm obviously very lovable," he'd always say. "What's going to happen when you eventually fall in love with me and we have to work together every day?"

"Uhh, no worry of that happening, buddy. Sorry. Besides, we have the responsibility to be *pro-fes-sion-al*."

Professional. That became the buzzword. Whenever we were after the same guy on a Saturday night, I'd tell him we had to be professional about it.

When the boys would tease us about groping each other in the office, he'd just give them a blank stare and say, slowly, "Professionals." It came in handy whenever he wanted a favour, like a ride to the airport or help with moving into his new house. "Gee, Aidan, I'm not sure that would be professional."

Nobody else noticed him wink at me. They never did. Sometimes it was exciting hiding it from everyone else, but the novelty wore off. They were all sad fucks and I was thrilled I wasn't working there anymore.

It didn't help that he was gorgeous. He knew it, though, which was a slight turn-off. Slight.

As he came in from outside wearing his sporty Calvin Klein suit pants, a crisp white J Crew dress shirt with the sleeves rolled up, and a dirty white baseball cap turned around backwards, I inadvertently followed him to his destination: the drinks table. The old hat on backwards trick was sexy. Yeah. A remembrance of the college glory days gone by and a rebellious bucking of the corporate world at the same time.

I managed to detect the Issey Miyake that I had bought him for his last birthday when he walked by.

When he turned around, he caught me staring. He always managed to. I couldn't count the number of times he'd knelt down to look at the bottom drawer of the file cabinet or stretched out over the photocopier, only to catch me sneaking a peek. Every time, though, it was as if it were a surprise to him. He'd get a smile on his face like he'd just found twenty bucks in his pocket, and roll his eyes at me.

After a few beers, the atmosphere seemed kind of chill, and I was actually starting to enjoy myself. People were pouring in from other departments and the place was filling up. It was dark outside, but the Christmas lights from the building across from us lit up the street. Patty, the giddy girl from the cubicle in the corner, was running around and terrorising everyone there with a disposable camera with shots that were sure to bring embarassment and awkward smiles come New Year. The radio was set to some Christmas hits countdown and the songs were interspersed by the announcer reading off traffic reports and a forecast of cold winds and a dusting of snow for the night.

I felt a tap on my shoulder, and knew who it was before I turned around.

After politely excusing myself from talking with Agnes, one of the secretaries, about her gall bladder surgeries (plural), I went up to the second floor storage area to grab two more cases with Aidan.

It was a small office to begin with, and there was already enough beer and wine down there to float a boat. Aidan could have taken care of both cases himself and didn't need help carrying only one case downstairs, but I went anyway.

The closet was about 6'x10' and crammed from wall to wall with file cabinets that stretched almost to the ceiling. There was one light bulb in the middle of the ceiling. It was kind of tight in this oversized closet, which held an odd mix of outdated recruiting information, all of the holiday decorations for the year (minus Christmas), six cases of beer, and now, two guys who were lugging around a couple of crowded closets themselves.

The door creaked shut, and Aidan reached up to turn on the light bulb. Our eyes made contact after what seemed to be a yearlong blink.

"So what's up? How are you?" he asked.

"I'm good, yeah. Just trying to get everything together for the move."

"How's that going?"

"Fine."

This chitchat could have gone on forever. In fact, I think it did. This is the kind of conversation I was getting sick of downstairs.

"Hey, Aidan, did you get the Christmas card?"

"Yeah. I meant to tell you."

An uncomfortable silence.

"So. Brussels," he said.

"Mm."

"When did all this come up? I mean, you weren't even sure when you left here. The next thing I hear you're up 'n' moving. Where did this come from?"

"I don't know. It seemed like a great opportunity."

"I can't believe you'd be ready to get outta Philly so quickly, Paul. I mean, you never even told me you were thinking about taking it."

"And I can't believe you're saying that. Are you saying I should have cleared it with you? We don't talk about this kind of stuff with each other, remember?"

"What does that mean?"

"It means we just go out and get sloshed and then we don't talk about anything on Monday morning because we're always trying to be fuckin' *professional.* Chitchat at the water cooler. Bullshitting in some club. Banter at the conference table. Not checking with each other on major life decisions."

And then he kissed me.

It happened so fast. I caught a glimpse of his eyes dancing around as they came at me. I can't say I expected it, but we had never had this heated a discussion before.

It felt like he hadn't shaved that morning. His thirty-six-hour stubble excited my chin as it scraped slowly like a piece of sandpaper.

I was angry at him for putting me on the defensive. I didn't pull away, though. My frustration with him only made me want him more.

Whenever I thought about the two of us getting together, it was never like this.

The next few moments seemed to rush past us. A grab at his dick. Panting. A lunge for my ass. Wet, moist kisses.

We knocked around between the file cabinets, and I was sure one of the thirsty partygoers would be able to hear the noise from outside. But they couldn't have been as thirsty as I was. They were all downstairs and I didn't really care anymore.

"Thanks for the card," he growled.

"Mmm. Welcome."

There wasn't any mistletoe in that closet, or anywhere else in the office, for that matter. Must not've made the decoration budget that year, but that didn't stop us.

As we wrestled back and forth, balancing ourselves between piles of brochures and creaky shelves, my heart raced even faster than my mind. At any moment, everything could have come crashing down, which only added to the excitement.

I forgot all about the beer we had gone up there for, but I knew we had been away from the party for too long.

"Aidan, we should go."

"*Shhh*," he said, as his fingertips plucked at my nipples. My T-shirt began to feel wet with perspiration as he lifted it off me. His breath wandered across my face and neck, and I couldn't get enough. His mouth soon followed there – kissing and biting, wanting and having.

"Don't go."

ROBIN IBBESON

Crabs

I've got crabs. Got in the bath, looked down, began to think about the creation of new moles. Didn't even know I had one there. Or there. Or there. Oh, I got it. They were insects, my hairs tower blocks to them, my skin their city, my blood their food. Remembered a guy from a couple of Saturdays back, was glad I didn't ring him. But it should all be over soon. I have the means to cause death to my plague. Tonight I am committing genocide. And I'll only be using a shampoo.

*

Didn't work. It was quiet for a day, maybe, and then they were back. They were smaller in number at first, but definitely back. And this time they talked.

Zor-at is on my fingertip (he has limited language skills, but an expressive face) praising me, deferential, calling me Master, having elevated me from the level of mysterious but destructive nature to that of angry deity. A priest-king to his people, one of the few survivors of the cataclysm that befell his brothers and sisters. His subjects, a new race of worshippers, are somewhere near my balls, ready to commit sacrifice. There are seven new-borns, eggs to be given to qualm my death-need.

I lower Zor-at and watch the brutal minutiae, the life let in exchange for immortality.

My crabs are singing hymns to me.

I think about going to the doctor's and wonder whether to say that my problem has returned or that I have become a religion. I decide to do neither and instead turn, once more, to the shampoo.

*

Aughüst is telepathic. Son of Zor-at, he has overthrown his father's spiritual notions, instead becoming a student of society, politics and science. He appears to be a genius.

There is an army near my anus.

Having learnt from historical mistakes, Aughüst bred his people quickly, although we are fortunately still undergoing peace talks. Aughüst broadcasts for an hour a day, his mental agility far surpassing any human's. I no longer have to see him to hear him. He talks while reorganising his government or patenting another of his fantastic inventions.

Aughüst is an interesting conversationalist, well-read and intellectual, as one might imagine Churchill to have been. Aughüst holds a desperate need for the continuation of his life and his people's. He calls it co-existence, but I can recognise whitewashing political wordplay when I hear it.

It has been an entertaining few days but I can't rid myself of the feeling that it is essentially disgusting to let parasites live off your body, no matter how well you get on with them.

⋆

I woke up to shouting. Aughüst is on my nose. Though blurred, through one eye he is scarred and has apparently lost several legs.

"Once more there is chaos amongst us. Once more we have died."

His voice is phlegm-ridden, European.

"Our cities, societies, *families* destroyed. Without warning, without mercy, ignoring all attempts to find mid-ground."

Aughüst pauses, to cough.

"But we are not our fathers and mothers. And we will not so easily be washed away."

There is a cheer from down below. The speech is as much a rallying cry for the remnants of Aughüst's nation as it is a warning for me.

"A gift, my old friend."

Aughüst begins hobbling away down my face.

"Something I kept secret from our daily interactions."

For the very first time I feel action in my crotch hairs, as if all of my invaders had joined together and moved at once. I hear several clicks and then up it shoots.

Lawlock has a body like silver, is propelled by little flames out of his feet. He whirrs his chainsaw teeth in a grimace as he moves to hover behind his master. Aughüstia, it seems has entered the arms race.

Too quick for my snatching hand, Lawlock flies onto my scalp, putting spikes immediately into my skin. I yank out my hair to no effect except to cause myself pain. Aughüst laughs movie villain guffaws, mad with dictatorship as he scuttles away.

"A sample, my friend. Of what we are now capable of."

There is buzzing in my head. The outlook is agonising, everything is pink then black. When I come round, Aughüst is in hiding. He has one more statement to make.

"Are you fully aware now, my friend, my enemy, my world? Because I have plans for us both, human. Oh human, do I have plans."

More and more laughter. Uncontrolled – at least, not controlled by me – my bowels convulse. For the next hour in pain, I am lying in a duvet that is messy with shit.

*

The guy keeps touching me, my collar, my chest. When he laughs, I get mouthfuls of his sour breath. I tried to leave but couldn't. Lawlock's teeth pincered too far into my skull.

This bar is too hot for Gareth and as he lunges he emits a claustrophobic reek. He breaks the kiss to smile at me and I take the moment to suggest we leave.

I am blocking him out as he crawls all over me, thinking myself empty when he cuddles up to go to sleep. I have an insomniac's night, kept awake once more by the sound of insects giggling.

*

I'm spending long hours in toilets and saunas, all my money in bars and on whores. Aughüst's broadcasts are almost twenty-four-hourly now (he does sleep, though rarely) and his speeches are mainly concerned with his obsessive need to spread his kind. I think his scars and the ravages of war have sent him insane, but whatever his state of mind, I am still his slave.

★

I decided I couldn't take it any longer. Lawlock had just become too painful, so during a break in Aughüst's rants I went out onto the balcony of my eleventh-floor flat. I knew there wouldn't be enough time for a note.

I'd got one foot over the safety rail when the static began. It's Tura, Aughüst's daughter, desperate leader of a secret rebellious force. She says she's about to kill her sleeping father. The people are on the verge of revolt, she tells me, overworked, bred to the point of exhaustion by their cruel dictator. The only freedom left to them is death.

I ask about me. All Aughüstian machinery is linked to the despot's vast brainpower, Tura reveals. When he is removed then their objectives will be gone. She begs again, there is not much time. Fortunately, I still have the shampoo bottle. There is enough for one good application left, and despite my worries, my head remains OK, even when I am rinsing off.

★

Tura's plan worked. In a funny kind of way I miss being occupied, although sometimes at night when I hear the listless mechanical whine of Lawlock searching for his absent master, I take comfort in the fact that I am not so alone after all.

MORGAN MELHUISH

Like When You Swallow Ice Cream

Dickdickdickdickdick. That was all I could hear – the seconds on the clock, waiting for the bell. Detention on the last day of school – agony, right? How long until I'm finally free for an amazing six weeks?

My back's burning as sunlight hits my shirt through the classroom windows. Trapped in this place, this prison, a cage of sun.

Dickdickdickdick. Yep, it's pointing up and out through my grey trousers. Pointing at Dan. *Dickdickdick.* The back of his neck covered in short dark hairs. I can see his bare arms, a strip of alabaster torso where he's come untucked. How much longer to go? There's an itch I need to scratch. Something's got to be done.

★

This isn't some bit of yank wank in which the guys go through the same tired moves, grunting and groaning with 'authentic dialogue'. This is the bit they never film. This is taboo. It's about me, me as a kid.

No, not me. Not just me, anyway – me and my dick. This is about me with my dick in my hands. In the bath. Me, jerking off. First wank, first orgasm.

I suppose I'd better introduce myself, my name's Alex. Although I could be any one of you guys. We've all been there, the unforgettable first time. That's enough.

★

I was in the bath, shit day at school. Obviously. At least Dan was with me. Partners in crime, that's what we were. Head full of thoughts. All questions, no answers.

I knew I was gay. Twelve, nearly thirteen, and absolutely sure of that. No angst in my nearly teenage closet. It felt great knowing that about myself – admitting that. Being so sure. It felt like... like when you swallow ice cream. As it slides down your throat, freezing as it goes, slipping into your stomach. Like when you swallow ice cream, when you're pigging out, not caring if you get spots. That. That feeling rushing to your head, making you dizzy. Permanently. But no headache.

★

I can't get him out of my head, *DanDanDan*. So sexy, so very sexy. Dan on cross-country runs, watching his package bob up and down in tight black gym shorts. The smell of him, soap and sweat and something primal. Something exciting.

Dan and me, caught in the toilets. He was showing me how to wank, masturbate, choke the chicken, blow your load. We blagged the teacher off, but still got kept behind. Mr Gibson's so out of order, what a twat.

I suppose we were lucky to get away with just detention. I guess he was relieved we weren't smoking. If he'd phoned Mum, I'd be done for. She'd explode or something, just at the thought of something 'dirty' going on. Something she'll never understand.

I can still see him there, with his cock in his hands, playing around. It seems disgusting, but somehow there's an edge to all this. Something dangerous, alluring. I can't wait to suck on it.

But back to the bath...

I could feel myself becoming aroused, decided that now was the time. Time to copy Dan. My prick was reacting to the attention of five small fingers attached to one small hand. Mine. That hand was warm, that hand was soapy. One very wet hand, one very wet dick. To me there was nothing but my groin and my hand.

Guiltily, I kept checking the door to make sure it was locked. You know what I mean. Furtive glances.

Cock up and out of the water. Above the surface. Foreskin all rolled back, safely tucked away. Kind of nice, kind of weird.

My hands were on that swollen head. Cock there, breaking the surface of the water like a periscope. Or lighthouse. I wondered how many men I could snare on the rocks of this beacon. Water lapped around my thighs, waves crashing on my beach.

★

Doing everything wrong, wasn't I? Too young to know any better. No idea. Just feeling myself up. My wet white-blond hair, plastered to my head. Heart going *boomboomboom*. The scent of coconut soap, some rubbishy herbal shampoo my Mum had bought, and me, thick in the steamy bath-water air. Everything was magnified, intensified. But my little brother was at the door. Not understanding, but listening?

I guess he'll never understand. Not until he's older, at any rate. His winkie, that's what he calls it, it's just there for piss. Not pissing about with. Marks out who's a mummy, who's like daddy. He probably doesn't even get hard. Like on the bus, as you go over speed humps, or in the morning when you wake up and it's digging into you.

The lads talk about boners and stiffies, gawping at page-three models. Now that's something even more disgusting than a cock. It makes you want to heave. The girls reckon we talk shit, I suppose we do.

"Mum says you'd better get out of the bath, they'll be here soon."

Just a question of time, I thought, before she'd be banging on the door with a J-cloth and bottle of Domestos, ready to kill all known germs… *dead*. My Mum, what a headcase, 'sprucing up' the already immaculate house.

Can I really do this now? I'm not even sure I want to. Time to get out of the bath, anyway.

⋆

It was like that. Couldn't think of anything else. It was *cockcockcockcock*. It was almost shouting at me. The one-eyed monster gasping, begging for it, crying out *giveittomeGIVEITTOMEGIVEITTOME!*

Who could refuse?

⋆

Once across the landing in my own room, I put a track on, then locked the door. Casual like. Locking doors was new to me.

My own room. Safe from the outside. The thick blue carpet seems to ram itself between the gap of door and floor. Muffling any sounds. Feeder belt out a tune and I imagine Grant's singing just for me. I wouldn't mind any of that lot. The drummer's a bit of a troll, though. Still, I'd let Grant take me any day, as he stares down from posters, his hungry eyes boring into mine. Next, it's Damon's turn for some attention. He looks as though he wants to jump out from the magazine page and fuck me stupid. Horny, that's what we are.

And my cock's still in my hand. Straining to be unleashed, like some demon from a Ouija board.

Not long to go, I thought, they'll soon be here. Another downer to the day. My mother's sister plus her three crap kids. Nutters, the lot of them. Must be in the genes.

My brother was particularly excited, I remember, at the prospect of having three new victims to play with. Three new victims to beat on the Playstation.

*

My cock – penis. That's a more grown-up word. It's wet and dripping from the bath. That room, already looking a bit too childish, stupid. The duvet cover is too bright. Harry Potter books and *Star Wars* Airfix models, collecting dust on the shelves, they'll have to go as well.

I rub myself down, the sports towel absorbing water. My nipples stand out. Echoing my dick. They're hard, as if I've been cold too long. Just like a page-three girl. Perhaps I should be posing, perhaps I've missed my vocation.

I touch them and it feels good. So many new things to learn. It almost tickles, another time I might have laughed. Not now.

I sit, still damp, on my bed and look at my new-found friend. The colour of it is amazing: a rich, dark red – pulsating as my heart beats faster, wilder than some club mix. And it's all mine. And the sheer size, towering over my stomach, so big it casts a shadow. And it's all mine. Tougher than steel and ready for another touch. Yeah! It's all mine and I can do whatever I want with it.

I remember our sex education lessons. Giggling on the back row while labelling some diagram. We knew it all from covert chats in the classroom, the boasts from the sixth form. The graffiti at the bus stop. That's practically all we talk about, the straight stuff at least, don't they know anything?

Dan's brother's in the sixth form. He's been dumped by the school slapper. Her legs are open more often than an all-night store. At least me and Dan have each other.

I bring my hand around the base, just happy to feel the heat and the control and power. If I have power over just one thing, it's my body.

I close my eyes and all I can see is Dan. I move my hand up and down my cock, the way you wash up cutlery.

*

Just me and my dick in that room, me and Dan in my head, fooling around. Feeling, rubbing, stroking. Snuffling.

No, wait. That's not me snuffling, it was coming from the door. The dog was there. Dog at door. Dog at the door waiting to come in and see what's happening. Have I been making noises? I don't think so. Crazy mongrel, what does it want to do? Do I smell or something?

I can't stop now. Dan's still in my head.

"That's it. Now faster, *really* squeeze."

So I do.

My breath's all ragged now. Panting. Just like the dog, Lucy. Waiting outside, is it still there? Stupid bitch. Just like my mother, on the prowl. One causing mess, the other clearing it up. Vicious circle.

"Come on, Lucy, out my way. Can't you see I've got cleaning to do?"

Four paws pad down the stairs. She's given up. Fine. I can get back to the task in hand.

I feel as though I'm about to shiver, there's an energy building up in me. Like pins and needles, only better. Someone walking over your grave. I can't feel my feet any more. I'm stretching and stretching, I feel as though I'm going on forever. All that matters is that penis, this pleasure, this fantastic feeling.

"Are you in there, Alex?"

No response.

The handle twists. My guts freeze. Think of something. Oh my God, she knows. No, don't be stupid.

Ohmygodthinkofsomethingthinkofsomethingohmygodhelp!

"I'm just drying myself, Mum."

"Why's the door locked?" There's suspicion in her voice now.

Helphelphelphelp.

"Come off it, Mum, I'm *naked*."

I don't stop squeezing and pulling. I don't want to think about what she'd say if the door were open.

"They'll be here soon. I've just finished the bathroom, is your room tidy?"

"Yes, Mum." I kind of gasp, my voice is coming out all funny. Strained. I probably sound guilty.

"It better be."

I hear her stomp off downstairs, ready to put the kettle on and give the surfaces one final wipe. I change the CD to radio, Capital, just in time to catch the Friday night countdown.

*

That's when I noticed the smell, the liquid that I thought was sweat, lubricating my palms. It smelt a bit salty, tasted that way too. A bit like oil or bubble bath, it gave the same sheen to your skin. Is this what Dan'd taste like, or Grant or Damon? Cool.

Doctor Fox's mellow, calm voice. 'Not long to find out what London's chosen as tonight's number one…' A voice of reason in all this madness. I couldn't wait for the climax.

I was discovering things that I had never seen before. Nothing like the diagrams. There's no sensation in a picture is there?

I remember taking peeps at the big medical book in the front room. My mother's bible. Any hint of a symptom and she's flicking through those pages. I *nearly* had meningitis once. How can you nearly have something? Like I said, she's crazy.

But I remember the pictures, those unfamiliar words. And it's amazing that it's all going on inside me. Hormones and testosterone pumping around, miles at a time.

'This week, last week's winner drops two places to… number three.'

The corpora cavernosa and corpus spongiosum: my erectile tissues, stiff with pleasure.

'Engorged with blood,' the phrase had stuck with me, so clinical and yet seductive.

I wanted to memorise it all, but knew it couldn't last forever. The relatives were coming and I just had to put in an appearance.

There was sperm bubbling up inside my testes, coursing along the vasa efferentia, straight to the epididymis.

All those processes involved in one spinal reflex action. Erectile tissues, check. Prepuce back, check. Warp drive engaged.

Dan came to me in a flash. "Remember to have some bog roll nearby." I had asked why, but he had just winked and said, "You'll see."

Sod it, I thought. They'll all just have to wait. My brother, the cousins, my mother and Lucy. They would all just have to wait.

They were all so desperate to come in. To have a go, to see what big boys do, to join in. But as soon as I crossed that doorway, I was normal again. Here, in my room, I was safe, excited.

If I didn't have to, I'd never open that door again.

I pulled a handkerchief from my knickers drawer. A neatly folded square of material. God, I hate that word. Knickers. I wonder why my mum insisted on calling them that.

My hand pumped up and down faster. I squeezed my eyes shut. Dan was there, grinning in that way he always does when something good is going down.

That summer I was determined to have something good going down with Dan. I could see him tying up his laces, back to me. I could see that curve of flesh filling tight trousers. I could see his green eyes. His freckles. I could see every aspect of him at once. Like a Picasso painting. I could see his cock quivering in those toilets, excited as I was. Am.

★

'With number two a non-mover, we've got a brand new number one, but running up…' I couldn't wait.

Yeah. Sure, we know what's happening. Don't we?

And then I could feel it coming out. It hurts. Splurting out over my hands, over the shadowy hint of pubes. Wow! Orgasm at last.

Hey! Doctor Fox, can you take my pulse. I think it's going wild.

'The Capital's favourite this Friday evening is…'

I don't even care what they're saying. Yeah I'm number one.

It's a bit like pissing and bleeding at once, when you cut yourself and you don't actually realise. Relief. A dam bursting somewhere inside. A puddle of spunk, sperm, forms in my hands. Looking like pus, running like lava.

I didn't expect the heat. I suppose I thought it'd be cold, like hail. It's nice, though.

I wonder how much stuff a cock could hold. All those little wriggling sperms, thousands of tiny seeds. Are they flapping around like dying fish or what? Caught up in the rough cotton of the handkerchief.

★

I opened my eyes, audibly gasping. A stupid smile plastered across my face.

Bollocks! They're here. I can hear the car on the driveway.

But I don't care. That was amazing, all mine and amazing.

Scrunchscrunchcrunchcrunch. The car's stopped. Now doors are opening. I can hear my mother coo. The kettle's boiled already. They've arrived, but I can't get this smile off my face.

It was the fastest I've ever changed into new clothes in my life, ready to face all that 'Ooh, haven't you grown?' chit-chat.

That smile stuck all summer.

KEITH MUNRO

Pornography

I started writing a porno novel to try and earn some cash. I thought it might be an easy way of financing my more artistically justifiable literary aspirations. I would publish it under a pseudonym, of course. Something for my faithful biographers to unearth once I was dead and buried – a snippet of scandal to add some posthumous spice to my otherwise irreproachable existence. That was the plan, anyway.

★

When I told Dougan about my novel he was unimpressed.

"What the fuck dae *you* ken about pornography?" he sneered. "I know whit you're like. You'll end up putting folk off, no' turning them oan."

"Thanks. If it's *Prone* you're referring to, that was meant to be *shocking*, not arousing. I'd like to think I was capable of writing erotically if I chose."

"You huvnae hud enough sex tae ken how tae write pornography."

"For God's sake, it's fantasy I'm dealing with, not reality. What counts is imagination, not experience. And I've got a *very* vivid imagination."

"Aye right. You'd need tae wi' the luck you huv."

★

Dougan and I have a history, or make that a non-history. We've been best friends since childhood. We used to complement each other perfectly: I was the sensitive, artistic one and he was the football-mad little thug. For ten years we were blissfully inseparable. Opposites attract.

You can probably guess what's coming next, though. We hit puberty, our hormones went berserk, and I found myself sucked into a bottomless infatuation for him. I yearned for his body until it hurt. It actually *ached* to be near him. I would catch myself wanting to chew on his hair, gnaw at his nipples, suck the pus from his spots, prance around my bedroom late at night in his soiled, sweaty boxer shorts. You know the sort of thing. I wanted to crawl all over him. I wanted to curl up *inside* him, like that alien in John Hurt's stomach, living off his chewed-up food. It was full-on, full-blown obsession.

Dougan, of course, remained oblivious. Or, if he wasn't oblivious, he chose to ignore me, which is probably worse. He enthused about footballers and gawped at girls. He made the obligatory insensitive remarks about poofs and faggots. He seemed so unassailably straight. The whole thing lasted about nine months. I got over it. Eventually.

Picture my amazement, therefore, when I got home from university years later to discover that Dougan had transformed himself in my absence from a cocky little jock into the Designer Queen from Hell. From out of nowhere he was suddenly a screaming queer. He'd got the haircut, the highlights and the sunbed tan. He'd had himself strategically pierced. He knew the words to every Kylie Minogue song ever written. He was going out clubbing and not coming back till morning. He'd definitely done his homework. He was telling me I should read *Outcast* and *The Milkman's On His Way*. (I already had. I told him he should read *Frisk* and *Funeral Rites*. He ignored me.) He was taking the right drugs and he'd found out how to spell *promiscuous*. He was, he told me, and always had been, very, very gay.

This unexpected revelation of his true self was all the more astonishing since he obviously reckoned it would make me want to sleep with him. Much as I hate to admit it, I almost did. But in the end he was just too manufactured. This *thing* wasn't my Dougan, this was some bad Vengaboys clone masquerading as Dougan. The brash, loyal, lovable fifteen-year-old running about a football pitch in shorts and a Russell Athletics sweater on a foggy winter morning, cheeks flushed, bare legs splattered with mud and a communal shower awaiting him was *my* Dougan. The normal Dougan. The unattainable Dougan. This waxed, primped, plastic Dougan unnerved me by virtue of his very availability. I was no longer smitten.

Things have never been right between us since. Dougan says we're too alike. I say we're far too different. Either way, I could never shag him now without it feeling like a defeat. He's so much better at being gay than I am. It would be too much like giving in to my shy, sullen, besotted adolescent self, a ritual satiation of desires harboured silently as a boy but long since put to sleep. Teenage fantasies are always so much better than adult realities. Best left alone.

★

I went online to find some characters for my novel. I imagined it might be easier to describe the sex scenes if I had something concrete to work with. I roamed idly for a few hours, marvelling at the diversity of tastes catered for. Huge, muscled men with moustaches and hardhats did things to themselves and each other which defied their bulk, throwing their feet over their shoulders and spreading their butt cheeks in a manner that became faintly ludicrous after a while.

Elsewhere, thin young men divested themselves of their clothes and posed with strange mixtures of wantonness and mortification on anonymous beds or in front of hastily erected white sheets. These, I assumed, were the straight boys who were doing it for the money, the Russians and Eastern Europeans, the yoof of Berlin and Bangkok, jacking themselves off in a cheap hotel room while a digital camera recorded their exploitation for posterity.

I saved a few of the cuter boys, only noticing later that I seemed to have picked all the ones who looked most uncomfortable with the situation, or were the least capable of adequately hiding their misgivings. How curious.

★

When I told my feminist friend from university about my novel she got very excited, albeit reservedly. She rarely got excited about anything unreservedly.

"It's all so mechanical," I said. "So *savagely* sexual. It doesn't leave any room for *intimacy.* You know? I suppose what I'm saying is it doesn't leave any room for *love.*"

"But it's all sucking and fucking," she said, twisting a long strand of purple hair around her index finger. "It's not *meant* to be about love."

"I know, but most people still fuck out of love rather than lust, don't they? Or am I being naïve?"

"I can't speak for you gay guys. In fact, I can't speak for myself either. I haven't had a shag in months. But I do know what you mean."

"A porno novel in which the protagonists do what they do out of *love*, not lust. Porn with a sense of romance. Do you think it can be done?"

"Surely Mills & Boon have been doing it for years?"

"I'm not talking about that kind of stuff. I don't want to deal in metaphors. I want it to be *hardcore*, I suppose. Real. Honest. But romantic."

"Love and hardcore? I'm not sure they're compatible. I think your readers would rather have lust. Who are your protagonists, anyway? How old are they?"

"I don't know. Probably not very." I was flicking through the copy of *Fluid* she'd brought me, wondering why the hell a straight feminist would buy something like that. I mean, hadn't she noticed? "Like you say," I sighed, my eyes gliding over the parade of shapely flesh, "I've got to consider what my readers will want to read."

★

I continued logging on every night, running up huge phone bills in the name of research. I was becoming intrigued by the subtle delineations of dignity each boy was prepared to concede, recording and categorising them on a sliding scale:

those who simply posed naked;
those who displayed an erection;
those who wanked their erection;
those who wanked their erection to climax;
those who wanked someone else's erection;
those who allowed someone else to suck their erection;
those who allowed someone else to suck/lick other parts of their anatomy, excluding the anus;
those who allowed someone else to suck/lick other parts of their anatomy, including *the anus;*
those who sucked/licked other people's anatomy, both excluding and including the anus;
those who sucked someone else's erection;

> *those who were willing to fuck someone else but not be fucked themselves; and, at the very pinnacle of the pyramid, those who were willing to be fucked, or at least have some form of foreign body forcibly inserted into them.*

This last category seemed to be composed entirely of the prettier/smoother/skinnier/sluttier/girlier/gaunter/younger members of the pairing. Unlike the beefcakes with their leather caps and utility belts, who were so shaved and oiled and indistinguishable that it didn't really matter who was up top and who underneath, with these younger lads a strict sense of age hierarchy was preserved. Boy next door was the one bent over while big brother did the penetrating, roughly but reverentially.

What deep-rooted cultural obsessions with youth and purity caused this phenomenon? What ancient pederastic ideal did it represent? What notions of dominance and passivity, assertiveness and submission, teacher and pupil were being played out in these images? Or, given the choice, do we simply much prefer to see the fresh young thing getting fucked? Less chance of catching something nasty, more chance of them doing what they're told? Honest, perhaps, but hardly romantic.

And then, one night, in the midst of all the grimaces and groans and endless sweaty skin, I stumbled upon the ultimate younger brother.

★

I came across him on one of those sites you get to at three in the morning having followed links from site to site all night, utterly unable to remember where you started or what route you took to get there.

At first glance he looked like just another cute blond indie kid, all baggy cut-off jeans and wooden beads. He had the same air of cultivated scruffiness I'd always aspired to myself. You just looked at him and thought 'cheeky scamp'. Archetypal boy next door, skateboarder material.

> joe001.jpg shows him standing in someone's back yard, smiling… uh, knowingly? You can see over the fence into another garden, where one of those rickety climbing frames for children tediously rusts.

Perhaps he really *is* the boy from next door.

joe002.jpg: he unbuttons his shirt, still smiling.

joe003.jpg: the shirt comes off, revealing –

joe004.jpg: brownish nipples, not that big.

joe005.jpg: he stretches laboriously, exhibiting smooth chest;

joe006.jpg: long slim back, with prominent shoulder blades;

joe007.jpg: bald armpits;

joe008.jpg: *adorable* little belly button.

joe009.jpg–joe010.jpg: he unfastens his jeans, eyes downcast, grinning shyly.

joe011.jpg–joe012.jpg: the denim slides slowly down his thighs.

joe013.jpg: jeans bunched round his ankles, hampering escape, blue cotton boxer shorts, crushed, bulging interestingly.

joe014.jpg: front view.

joe015.jpg: rear view. *Very* cute bum.

And that was it. He didn't wank himself off on a settee or tentatively poke his arsehole with a dildo. He wasn't even nude. He didn't need to be. Fifteen jpegs was all it took for this blue-eyed, tousle-haired, snub-nosed, pouting pixie boy to work his magic. Scrawny-chested he might have been, and bony-backed and thin-limbed and pallid, but all this merely contributed to his charm. For that's what he was: thoroughly charming. Utterly, totally beguiling. Bewitching. Beautiful.

The site insisted all the models were over eighteen, but any fool could see this kid wasn't a day over sixteen. Who was he? Where was he from? What the hell did he think he was doing? Didn't he understand the effect he would have on people, posing like that? Didn't he realise how enticing he was?

I saved the complete set of pictures, fearing they wouldn't be there if I tried to find my way back to them later. I had located the hero of my novel. And his name was joe.jpg.

⋆

Next day I telephoned my friend Martin, who has spent some time living in Amsterdam and therefore knows more about pornography than most. He even spent a couple of weeks working in a sex shop as a favour to the owner (an old ex-shag), so he considers himself something of an expert on such matters. Having outlined the project to him, we arranged to meet in Edinburgh that weekend, giving us both time to collect our thoughts.

I spent the rest of the afternoon staring, trance-like, at the picture of joe.jpg taking off his shirt, doing the whole writerly thing, i.e. getting to know him: trying to imagine what that torso felt like, how hard the ribs, how soft the stomach, how warm the skin would be if I pressed my face to it, inhaling the subtlety of its odours. By the time I snapped out of it and closed the file, I could see the muscles flexing in his bare left shoulder wherever I looked.

I contemplated printing out a copy for Dougan, but I could already imagine the spite of his response. He'd say the kid looked about twelve, which isn't true; that I always go for blond sk8boarders and Gothy Nirvana types, which also isn't true (apart from the blond bit); that I was only allowing myself to fall in love with joe.jpg because he was just a picture-off-the-Internet-not-a-real-person and I knew there was no chance of actually meeting him or ever being in a position to act upon my desires.

Which, as it turned out, wasn't true either.

★

When we were maybe ten or eleven and the best of friends, Dougan and I found a page torn out of one of those glossy top-shelf porn mags in a field near my house, entangled – if I recall correctly – in the branches of a tree. The page was torn from the Readers' Wives section: dark, gloomy polaroids of ordinary-looking women on ordinary-looking beds with their legs akimbo and their M&S knickers pulled aside, accompanied by feverish commentaries from their husbands concerning *rogerings*, *fingerings* and *damn-good-fuckings*.

I can't quite remember how we reacted. I imagine we probably stared, then sniggered, then awkwardly stared some more, wondering why these sordid little snapshots didn't conform to the concepts of sex and femininity handed down to us by Society, or whether they *did* conform, and it was us who had got the wrong end of the stick.

If this was fiction, or a gay memoir, I'd have us whipping out our embryonic erections and satisfying the Kinsey-inspired need for an adolescent homoerotic experience. I'd give you the budding sweat on our brows and the milky smell of our mingled breaths as we panted together towards our first (dry) orgasm. But this was central Scotland in the late 1980s, and we'd never heard of Kinsey. So we hid the page in a place so public that any passing dog could have picked it up, and vowed to return later. Which we never did.

I returned on my own, though, and retrieved the page myself. I smuggled it into my bedroom and examined it for hours – or maybe minutes – wondering why I found it disgusting and vaguely disturbing when it should be turning me on; wondering what it was about these women – women who could quite easily be my friends' mothers – I was supposed to find so stimulating. Wondering what it must feel like to have a hole between the legs, if the absence was something they felt as keenly as I guessed I would if my willy wasn't there.

In the end, fearing the consequences of it being discovered, I smuggled the page back out of the house and set fire to it, just to make sure I was rid of the thing once and for all. That's the end of the story: make of it what you will. Maybe straight pornography turned me gay. Or maybe it didn't.

*

I met Martin in a café the following Saturday.

Martin fancies himself as a bit of a performance artist, transforming himself from one male stereotype into another on a weekly basis. One week he might be a skinhead with LOVE/HATE scrawled on his knuckles in biro, the next he might be Dale Winton with fake tan and limp wrists. These magical transformations are achieved with make-up, wigs and various other prosthetic attachments, which apparently elevates the whole thing above mere dressing-up into the realms of gender performance. Very Cindy

Sherman. That day he'd come as a sort of Italian gigolo, complete with leather trousers, hair in a ponytail and aftershave that followed him around like a cloud of flies on a hot day. He says it's art, although the DSS takes a dimmer view. I bought him one of those expensive beers with half a lime wedged in the neck of the bottle while he arranged himself artistically at a table.

"In porn," he informed me loftily, "all the power lies with the viewer. They're the ones who can take an image of two guys fucking and transform it into whatever they want. At the end of the day, a picture of some bloke tossing off is not inherently sexy. No more so than the label on this beer bottle. It's the *construction* the viewer places on the image, the ability of the viewer to make it *mean* whatever he likes, that transforms it into something arousing. It's the viewer who decides *who* this guy is, *where* he is, *why* he's there, *what* he's doing. It's the viewer who controls the story. The people in the picture are completely at the mercy of the viewer – they're powerless to control how they might be cast in the fantasy. *That's* what makes it so sexy."

"Oh," I said. "That's all very well, but I'm writing a novel."

"Same principles apply. Make your characters vague, leave the locations unclear. Concentrate on the sex. *That's* what your readers want. *That's* the deal: you supply the sex and they supply the rest. No one wants to read a book that keeps trying to insist the picture they've built up of the principal character is wrong. It's the *reader* who decides what he looks like. They'll resent you trying to tamper with that."

"Ah. I wanted to try and introduce the concept of love."

"Impossible. Love and porn can't co-exist. Porn is rough, forceful, abrupt. Love pacifies things too much. Love makes people take long walks and talk a lot. Avoid love at all costs. If they wanted love they'd be reading Armistead fuckin' Maupin. Anyway, have you got a scenario yet? Porn works with scenarios, not plots."

"Um, I thought I'd make it about a young skateboarder? Maybe he's run off to the big city in search of drugs and sex. At the moment he's just sort of skating from shag to shag in my mind."

"Good start. And skateboarders are sexy at the moment."

"I know."

"You said you'd found a picture of him?"

"Yeah," I muttered, sheepishly pulling a printout of joe.jpg from my bag and trying to slide it surreptitiously across the table as if it were a kilo of cocaine. "I found him on the Net. Isn't he gorgeous?"

"He certainly is. There's just one problem. This kid *is* a skater. And he *did* run off to the big city. And he *does* skate from shag to shag."

I do believe I actually felt my heart stop for a moment. "Wait a minute, you *know* him?"

"Sure I know him," Martin replied, beaming broadly to reveal a painted-on gold tooth – and only then did I notice how much like a pimp he looked. "That's Jeroen."

*

Two days later I was flying into Schiphol, Martin having made the necessary arrangements for me to meet with Jeroen in some bar called April. Although he claimed to have known nothing of the photos, Martin didn't seem particularly surprised that they existed. Nor was he entirely forthcoming about the precise nature of Jeroen's current activities, specifically whether he was or was not a card-carrying rent boy. One thing he did make clear was that those shots of joe.jpg in the garden were several years old.

"Jeroen's a big boy now," he said with a grin.

Dougan, of course, poured scorn on the whole enterprise, insisting I wouldn't have the nerve to go through with it. The more derisive he became, the more determined I was to get on that plane. And Martin assured me this was just the kind of ludicrous coincidence that makes great porn, so what choice did I have? Write from what you know, etc.

A thin, wet mist lingered over the city as I hurried through the streets, following Martin's hastily scribbled map. The bar was busy – I'd arrived during happy hour. Having fought my way through the crowds to procure a beer, I retreated to a table in the corner to wait. A detailed description of my appearance had been e-mailed to Jeroen, right down to the clothes I'd be wearing. It was all beginning to feel a bit cloak-and-dagger.

Five minutes. The beer was finished and the doubts were setting in. What in God's name was I doing in a bar in Amsterdam, waiting to meet a virtual stranger who was almost certainly a renter in a city full of renters and would almost certainly assume I'd come all this way for sex? And *had* I come for sex? Was that why I'd dropped everything and rushed over here? Did I really think I was about to fuck this guy? *Did* I actually have the nerve?

I heard a small cough behind me. I knew it was him the moment I saw him.

And that all this had been one dreadful, dreadful mistake.

The last few years had not been kind to Jeroen. He was a good six inches taller than me, easily 6'5", and impossibly thin. His hands and feet were out of all proportion to the rest of him, and his neck was so frail I couldn't understand how it supported such an enormous, spotty head.

His blond hair was no longer short and spiky but lank, floppy, making him look like a clumsy, lumbering hippy. He was wearing a hideous floral shirt under his denim jacket, which didn't help. He was also quite definitely on something, which caused him to sway unsteadily on his size 11 feet.

And not a skateboard in sight.

To my considerable alarm he sat beside me and insisted on trying to make conversation, despite his negligible grasp of English – a barrier I hadn't bargained on.

I tried not to pull away from the smell of – was it *diesel* oil? – saturating his clothes, or stare too blatantly at the worrying scars on his trembling hands. Having established that I was a friend of Martin's, whom he knew through the owner of the sex shop, I brought up the subject of the photos. He seemed genuinely disturbed when I mentioned them, and I sensed I'd committed some disastrous *faux pas*.

Things went from bad to worse after that, as I struggled to find words to explain Martin's theory about pictures supplying the stimulus to the fantasy and the viewer supplying the rest. For the story I had created, the charming reality I had constructed around those pixels bore no relation, absolutely no discernible relation whatsoever to this skeletal, rueful, borderline-suicidal young wreck sitting next to me. His actual reality contradicted the reality I had imagined so sharply, so totally, that I could see no way of ever reconciling the two. Especially since – and I didn't tell him this bit – the reality I had created for him was obviously so much better than the reality he was living.

The reality he was living scared the shit out of me.

I didn't make a good job of explaining myself. After a while he stopped pressing his leg against mine and got up to go to the toilet.

He never came back.

To be honest, I was glad.

*

When I got back to Scotland, Martin phoned to ask how I'd got on. I told him the whole sorry story.

Dougan also called. I told him joe.jpg and I had fucked through the night. Not that it made any difference. Dougan knows me better than that, fuck him.

ARDEN PRYOR

The Golden Mile

The Californian Café – Oxford Street, Sydney, Australia

They used to call it the Golden Mile, a mile-long stretch where anything could happen. Where your life was a gay urban legend just waiting to happen. I used to love the Golden Mile, and even this café.

No one calls it the Golden Mile anymore. There's nothing golden about it nowadays. The Mardi Gras is much more of a benefit for the straights than it is for the gay community. AIDS is just another word and all you need to be the centre of attention is enough ecstasy to knock out a kangaroo.

If you think I sound bitter, that's because I am. I've been on the scene since I was sixteen years old, when the only place to let me in was the Albury and I used to love having lunch at the Californian Café, back when the décor was green, the waiters Asian, and the music video player was still there.

New management took over and things changed. The décor became red, the Asians were fired, the stuck-up queen waiters introduced, and it became just another café on the Golden Mile. I really hate it now.

"Ready to order?"

"I'll just have a hot chocolate."

You won't find Amaretto, Lagavulin or Mocha in this place.

"Will you be eating anything?"

"No."

The waiter rolls his eyes.

If Matt were here, he would say the waiter was tragic. But he's not. So I can only think it. "You can dress it up all you want," he would say, "you can put a diamanté belt on it, but it's still trash."

I smile a little. Matt would have said it to his face, too. But he would be right. Judging by his accent and mannerisms, the waiter is still living in the western suburbs and still thinking his K-mart shirt is the hottest thing on the catwalk this season. Pushing thirty, but desperately trying to pass off those crow's feet as laugh lines.

I don't have to worry about that. Most people my age would stay inside, but I'm not about to hide away. Only twenty, yet I could so easily pass for someone of thirty.

Minutes pass by and my drink finally arrives. That's how things work around here. Even my diabetic grandmother could have done it faster, with or without insulin.

The hot chocolate, like the café smells stale. Just as it had that autumn. The smell of cakes as NutraSweet as ever, the smell of coffee as weak as ever. And though over two years have passed, the clientele cologne has not, the odd whiff of CK one and Eternity still lingering in the background.

I shift around in the booth to face the street. It's cloudy outside but still warm enough to wear just a T-shirt. Typical Sydney weather in April. One minute sunny and warm, the next windy and cold. Just like that stupid song, it's four seasons in one day.

I'm here looking for closure in a way. Nothing happens by chance. If that's true then I was supposed to meet Mark here that April.

It was the middle of autumn. There was a chill in the air and the leaves on the trees were beginning to fall. It used to be my favourite time of the year, just before the rain, when you could still enjoy a walk outside.

It was Friday – no – a Saturday afternoon, and extremely busy. The music video player was still there and I had selected a few songs, Britney Spears, Madonna and the obligatory Kylie. I was sitting by myself reading one of the trite local papers, *CapitalQ*.

Mark had come into the café, looking for a seat. Booth or table sharing was rarely done in Sydney, so you can imagine my surprise when he approached me.

"Do you mind if I take a seat?" he asked, pointing to the seat opposite me.

I paused. "No. That's OK."

"Thanks."

He leaned several shopping bags against the booth before sitting down. An assortment of bags ranging from SAX leather to Hound Dog and Pile Up.

What happened next can only be described as a miracle; if I wasn't there, I would never have believed it… he was served immediately.

As he ordered, I momentarily peeked over the paper to give him a once-over. He wasn't overly attractive, a nice body for sure but I've never been one to go for a thirty-something clone. It was the way he carried himself that really caught my attention, very confident and sure of himself.

He didn't fiddle with his hands the way most queens do, or even rely on exaggerated facial expressions. He was just there, living in the moment.

He caught me checking him out and smiled. I quickly changed pages and lifted the paper to cover my face. I was ridiculously shy at first, a modern day wallflower. Soon I heard footsteps, a cup being set down.

"Do you mind?" the guy opposite asked, waving a cigarette and his lighter at me. "Is it OK if I smoke?"

He looked me directly in the eyes. He was so stern and in control, like a headmaster with a cane. I really liked that about him.

"That's fine by me, but you're not allowed to smoke inside."

"Oh." He put the cigarette back in the packet and placed it with the lighter back in his shoulder bag.

When 'Baby One More Time' began playing on the music video player, Mark reacted immediately.

"I can't believe someone actually selected Britney Spears."

"You don't like Britney Spears?"

He took a look around the café. "Who in their right mind would actually pay money to listen to this crap?"

He was always outspoken like that, even if he was obviously wrong. He didn't care who he offended as long as he got to put his two cents in. I was not the same. "I have no idea. I really don't like her… that much."

He gave me a look and I wondered if he knew the truth.

"So what do you do?"

"I'm a student."

His eyes lit up and I could almost see him mouth the words 'young one'.

"Which university?"

"Sydney Uni."

"Good campus."

"Yeah, really big."

Emphasis on the 'big'. A little innuendo was needed, I thought. He didn't seem to notice.

"What are you studying?"

"Communication." I kicked the table as I crossed my legs, trying to look cool, when I blatantly was not. "With a major in journalism."

"The UTS is more in-depth. A friend of mine did it."

I tried drinking my hot chocolate and burnt my tongue. I set down the cup in agony and stood up. "I'll be right back."

I stormed up the stairs to the bathroom and slurped cold water from the tap, trying to soothe the pain. When I returned, he was gone.

I'll admit when I went to the counter and discovered he'd paid the tab, I started feeling better. Maybe he did like me, I thought to myself.

If left at that, things would have been much better. Still, chance as always intervened. Four nights later, at Mailbox at the Stonewall. A lot of good wearing a number did for me. I sat in the corner by myself tapping my foot to a ridiculously speeded-up version of Dannii's 'All I Wanna Do'. I didn't like Stonewall but it was where everyone was supposed to be on a Wednesday night.

I finished off my OJ and got up to leave. It was a mistake coming, I had decided. I shuffled along the perimeter of the ground floor and stormed outside past the bouncers, nearly head-butting Mark.

"Hey cutie."

'Cutie,' I thought, that's a good start.

"Fancy running into you. Sorry about running out on you at the Californian. It was later than I thought. I was supposed to meet someone for lunch."

I weighed it up a moment. "That's OK."

He paused. "Are you leaving already?'

Remembering his dislike of Britney: "Yeah, I don't really like Dannii Minogue."

"Really? I think she's a legend."

"Oh." I was such a sad individual.

He gave me a wink, "Come on, stay a bit longer. You'll have fun with me around."

I hesitated.

"Well?" Mark asked.

I paused. "OK."

"I don't think we've introduced ourselves..." he said as we walked back in, "I'm Mark."

"Jonathan."

We spent the rest of the night together at the bar area on the ground floor. He was very social and knew a lot of people, it seemed. He wasn't afraid to go up to someone and start talking to them. I was reserved and just stepped to the music. I didn't really click with his friends, a lack of cocaine on my part, I think.

He tried to kiss me a couple of times. I always pulled away. As silly as it sounds, I didn't want to be one of those guys who simulated soft-core porn at clubs. I wasn't about to put on a show unless I was getting paid for it.

Towards closing, he invited me to his place and I accepted. We went to his lavish loft in Paddington. White walls, timber floors, windows draped with rich red curtains – minimalism was the keyword here. Everything, including the TV, seemed to be hidden in cabinets concealed in the walls. All that remained was the odd-looking futon with the plush indigo bedding upstairs, and comfy white sofa and triangular glass coffee table downstairs. He lived life grand, much grander than I in my small room in Newtown.

As we entered the loft he grabbed the remote control and pressed PLAY. Texas's album *The Hush* started to lullaby in the background. He began kissing my lips, neck, and then lower, until he was undoing my pants and releasing months of frustration in one mouthful. I'll admit, that was rather quick, but like an Energiser bunny I was ready for more.

Remembering that night is like looking at a dream. Almost doesn't seem real. Memories more of sensations than of actions. The heat of his body against mine, the salty taste on his lips, the vibrations of his hips with mine and that warm pocket of joy I would call his mouth.

On top of him, below him, his legs pinned back. Feeling my penis sliding against that smooth crater below his balls. He was beautiful to me then, the only person in the world, and most importantly I thought he felt the same way.

The waiter drops a plate in the café and I awaken from my flashback. I shuffle a little, feeling my erection tingle beneath the table. He always did make me hard.

I test the hot chocolate, it's cool enough, I decide. With the cup in my hands I look out at the people walking by. The sky is starting to look terrible. I wouldn't be surprised if it started to rain.

So overcast, much like that morning after. Nestled in his kitchen, wearing his bathrobe and eating his Fruit Loops while he was making an omelette. It felt divine and natural. Like that's the way it was meant to be.

When I left that afternoon, he asked for my number and kissed me. To be kissed and hugged like that was such a delight. I felt like a pre–*Who's That Girl* Madonna. It was like being touched for the first time. For the last two years the only comfort I had found was in the uncaring embrace of strangers in the dirty backrooms of Signal or the even dirtier Den.

It was nice to wake up in another's arms. My bed never felt as empty as it had that night. Maybe it was the weather but my room felt cold and the mattress seemed even colder.

The waiter drops another plate, as a gush of crisp air comes into the café. A man walks in, that familiar odour of imported soaps with a slight hint of Issey Miyake. Could it be? I look closer, but it's not him.

I became very familiar with that odour that autumn: usually for nights at a time, only not to see him for a few days. It was a repeating cycle with no obvious pattern. Those were his days, I thought. I didn't put the pieces together and on one night in May, I let him enter me as none had before. Flesh upon flesh, thrust after thrust, till he filled me with his lust. And more.

Next morning he seemed distant, taking a long time in the shower. I looked through his wall cabinets and that's when I saw it: a framed picture of Mark entwined with a guy in a Qantas flight-attendant uniform – not unlike me, but older. The jet finally landed. I slotted the two halves of his life together as I put the picture back in its hiding place. I didn't tell him what I'd found.

We were supposed to meet again that week but nothing came of it. I stopped calling him. Two weeks passed and I had heard not a word from him. I couldn't. I was having recurring nightmares of mud wrestling with his boyfriend at the Gay Games. Losing each and every time, only to be humiliated by the sneering from the crowds.

Finally, seeking some closure, I ventured to his loft, only to find him and his showroom gone: disappeared without a word. I felt worthless, and spent the rest of the autumn in my bedroom or in the toilets at university crying; having one of my Felicity moments.

Semester break came, and it rained very heavily on the day. It was a lonely time for me. I spent it in bed struck down with a mysterious ailment. Like the flu, only different. Much different, I was to learn.

My lectures resumed but I wasn't even able to get out of bed. My doctor, concerned, performed some blood tests, and the results were as he had feared. A part of Mark would always be with me and the year would prove to be very difficult. I had been diagnosed as being HIV positive.

Things went downhill very quickly from there. I denied it and rejected any form of medication for some time despite my declining health. By the end of the year I had dropped out of university, lost my weekend job and retreated into myself.

I avoided everyone. I didn't want them to see me like this. I didn't want them to pity me. There was a stranger looking back at me from the mirror, each and every morning. All spark of life was gone from my eyes. I looked wretched, like my soul was dead and I was just waiting for the body to catch up.

My doctor suggested I go to a 'young and positive' group at ACON. I was hesitant. I thought they would be all drug-fucked scene queens with monster attitudes. Eventually I did go and, though some of them *were* big scene queens, it was the best thing for me at the time.

I made some good friends who knew what I was going through and I even started to laugh and carry on the way I used to. The workshops helped me begin to live again and look at what I really wanted to do with my life.

I didn't think I could do it but I'm still here. I've survived as I always do. Working and saving these past months so that I could afford this trip and move on. So many memories here. Some good, some not so good. I keep repeating the same control dramas and getting nowhere. It's time to move, I've decided, and try life in a different city.

I pick up my backpack, and a dark-haired man not looking all that different to Mark approaches me. "Are you done here?" he asks.

I pause, thinking about it. "I think so," I reply.

I'm about to make my way to the counter, when I see the tragic waiter smirking. "What could I do to wipe that smile off his face?" I ask myself. I know it's childish, I know it's stupid, but I'm never coming back here.

I run up to the toilets where I throw rolls and rolls of toilet paper into the bowl until it is significantly blocked, not leaving till I've flushed a couple of times and made sure the water is streaming across the floor.

Back downstairs, I pay for my hot chocolate. I turn to the door and then look back. "By the way..."

"Yes."

"I think the toilet's flooded."

I give him a dashing smile and walk out.

I walk down Oxford Street pass the Saturday afternoon shopping crowd to Museum Station to catch a train to the airport. I sit in the upper deck gazing at the flashing lights of the underground.

I'm dying. I always was, only now it's a little faster. The human body decays and rots but what will remain is my spirit. If I've learnt anything, it's that everything can change in the fraction of a second. You have to seize every opportunity, every second of every day and, as clichéd as it sounds, live it to the fullest. Today a door closes, but tomorrow another opens and that's the way it's meant to be.

NISHAN RAMAINDRAN

Boy, Manson Is Gonna Fuck You

1 February
RELATIONSHIPS ARE A BORE

Bad day. Stayed in and listened to Marilyn Manson. There's actually somebody out there more fucked in the head than I am.

2 February
ANXIOLYTICS AND ANTIDEPRESSANTS

Today, while I was in bed, it occurred to me that I might be having a nervous breakdown.

Got off to a real bad start. Fell like a lame fucking alcoholic headfirst down the stairs and felt the contents of my stomach rise, burn my throat with a harsh acidity and fly out of my mouth, all over myself.

Fuck, I thought. Fuck. Took me ages to stop crying. I'm such a loser.

Antidepressants, where are they when you need them? I can never remember where I've hidden them. Not like anyone cares. He's left me. I can't believe that psychotic bastard has left me. Found the Seroxat. I am lying in bed waiting for them to work. I know they usually take a couple of weeks but these…

Been on them for ten days now and still feel like shit. Hate my GP. I'm sure he thinks I've got Munchausen's. Doctors. Hate going to see him, makes me feel stupid. Never listens, just prescribes some cheap-fuck anxiolytics like propranolol. The cunt.

5 February
LOW

Very depressed today.

12 February
LADS AND BASTARDS

I do feel a little brighter today, it's a long time since I felt this good. I think it's because the weather has improved and from my bedroom I can see people having fun. The lads from the estate are messing about near my fence again but I'm not pissed off at them today, in fact I'm almost glad to see them. Even though I feel better, I still feel kinda lost and helpless. I think it's because Ryan left me. I think he wanted to leave more than me, he is obviously fucking someone else and has been for a long time. I have just been so blind. It was great when we were together. Well, the sex was great. I tried to ignore the fact he was a total bastard and hoped that part of his personality would go away after we met, how naïve was I?

13 February
OH SWEET JESUS,
YOU STILL GONNA SAVE MY QUEER FUCKING SOUL?

Today I feel so sad.
Tried hard to cry but couldn't, I didn't know what I wanted to cry about.
Just couldn't access my emotions.
Feel like I can't cope any more. It's all too much.
I don't want a fucking education, or a stupid job.
Just want to dance all night to hard house, techno and trance.
Wanna get drunk, take drugs and fuck, fuck, fuck.

I'm going out tonight, I'm getting ready.
Ready to be fucked?
Ready to be fucked around?
I still don't know the fucking rules.
I don't even know which game I'm playing.
I'm just a fucking queer with a queer fucking soul.

I look at myself:
My reflection.
My horny eyes.
My hard cock.
My Queer Soul.
Oh sweet Jesus, you still gonna save my queer fucking soul?

16 February
PLEASE DON'T PISS ON ME

Today I let this horny eighteen-year-old lad fuck me bareback in the pub toilets. That's the last time I drink beer. I was highly strung afterwards, so I smoked some weed to calm down a bit. Got very horny. Met this Italian bloke in Kudos. Had a good hard shag with him. Quite sexy, but he kept wanting to stick his dick under my armpits. Never had my armpits fucked before. As if that wasn't weird enough, he came all over my hair. I hate it when guys come on me without asking, it's so fucking rude. It's like pissing on someone without asking first.

18 February
STUPID FUCKING QUEER

I couldn't fucking concentrate at uni today. My train was fucking late and I was really pissed off. I'm such a stupid fucking queer, I thought. A stupid fucking queer.

Had to enter the crowded lecture theatre with everyone staring, God it was so embarrassing. Sat down next to this weird fucking girl. Luminous pink dreadlocks and black Jesus boots. Gave me the creeps. Think she's a dyke, seen her hanging around sometimes with this monster-bitch. Some dumb drag king. Fucking ugly the pair of them, even for dykes. Some Indian guy with a Hitler moustache lecturing. He can't be bothered to get off his lazy fucking arse and lecture like a proper lecturer but instead reads some boring philosophical bullshit off a fucking piece of paper. Today it was Rousseau. I must admit, I love this guy Rousseau. He'd be my ideal boyfriend, he's just so damn romantic. Nowadays, romance is dead. Bring back Rousseau.

I was less interested in the lecture and far more interested in the cute guy sitting in front of me. He looked fascinated by what this Indian guy was saying. I just kept looking at this cute guy dressed all in black but he didn't look like one of those morbid Goths. He wasn't a manic depressive either, as far as I could tell, which was a shame because at least we would have something in common. Then again, what does a manic depressive look like these days? I thought he could be an artist or a thinker like Derrida. I'm really into all that post-structuralist and deconstruction bollocks, it really hits my spot every time. I looked at him closer. He was wearing these really tight Levi's, a faded French Connection T-shirt and these shiny, laddish black shoes, the ones that look like they're Patrick Cox but are from Dolcis.

Later on I ended up sitting next to him in the lunch hall. Dunno how it happened. Had a fucking hard-on and all I could think about was giving him one. He was wearing the same aftershave as me, XS by Paco Rabanne. He's gotta be gay, no straight man would wear expensive aftershave for no reason. I thought it might be something I could initiate a conversation with. Oh, what a coincidence, we're wearing the same aftershave, isn't that amazing? By the way, fancy a fuck, mate?

19 February
HARD-ONS AND PANIC ATTACKS

Fucking panic attack today. Found out it's possible to have a hard-on and a panic attack simultaneously. I'm having a bad fucking time at the moment. My anxiety's sky high, don't know why. I've been doing all that shit I was told to do by the therapist but today it's out of fucking control. He's such a total dick, my therapist, he looks like an anorexic version of Frasier but with no sense of humour. When I'm talking to him about my most personal problems – and God, do I have enough of those – he looks at me as if he's constipated or about to burst out crying. I feel I should be the one giving *him* therapy. He needs something. Can't believe I'm paying the arsehole to listen to my problems.

After lunch in the dinner hall, which was lukewarm offal and rice served in a litre of gravy, went to my tutorial. Psychological pain in a big way. Most of them are spaced out on dope or pissed on cheap beer from the Union. I love university, it really expands your intellectual horizons, and by horizons I mean the ability to catch herpes and gonorrhoea and constantly drink yourself into oblivion. On my way to this tutorial I see that total wanker Aaron. He's a sad little cunt with the intellect and charisma of a cockroach. He's also had a personality bypass. I had coffee with him once in Ku Bar. Christ, he was boring. Bored me about his innumerable lays with the world's most beautiful men, most of them heterosexuals in serious, stable relationships. I thought he was so amazing, I listened intently to all his gay-conversion stories, how he'd converted all these heterosexuals. What he meant was, he'd sucked the diseased cocks of some very confused, promiscuous hetero-bisexuals. It's just a hunch, but I think he's trying to make up for the fact he's got a tiny penis – not that it's important, of course.

20 February
HIERARCHIES AND HETEROSEXUAL INSECURITIES

Got up really late but decided to go in anyway. God, I saw Luke today. Took me right back to school. I used to really fancy that twat. Can't I get away from all these stupid, fucking tossers? He never knew. If he did he would have hated me. I used to watch him in biology, I loved his shy-sexy smile, it made my day. Made me love him more. Hate him now, hate all those wankers now. They made me feel like shit. Still do.

Walked past him in the corridor, I'm sure he knows I'm queer, felt I was gonna fucking faint with fear. I was right back in that fucking school corridor. Bastards. I saw those dreadful clouds once again and heard the vox humana weep and wail, when crowds of pubescent boys screamed with laughter at the sad freaks walking along the bastard corridors all mother-loved and humiliated as they went silently on their way.

The superficial, super-fascist, social hierarchy determined
Who you could talk to and who you could piss next to.
The rugby-lads, complete cunts.
Same fucking suits, blue-pin-striped, tight-fitting.
Same shoes, black-leather, posh-shiny-buckled.
Same haircut, short-trendy-horny-skinhead,
Same record bag, Ministry Of Sound.
Same fucking attitude,
Same disrespect,
Same shit.

These same wankers would show their knobs off
In packed changing rooms in the after-games shower,
To echoes of puerile laughter,
To prove their bonding masculinity,
To reduce their burdening heterosexual insecurity,
To undermine the sad little poofs and their perverted sexuality and
To gain ultimate popularity.

21 February

PLEASE DON'T BE MY MOTHER

Got up. Oh fuck, I'm still alive, oh well.
It's Saturday… always feel depressed on Saturdays. Feel obliged to do something.
I haven't done anything for the last five years.
I feel the whole world is doing something and
I'm not, 'cos I'm boring, useless, pathetic etcetera.
All I do these days is worry.

I spend so much fucking time worrying about what to do,
I never fucking get round to doing anything.
The phone rang today.
Please don't be my mother, I thought.
I paused for a bit before picking it up.
Thank God. It was only the weirdo giving me a crank call.

Had a fag, went to bed.

22 February
COLD SHOWER

Must have fallen asleep in front of the telly.
Woke up with a stiff neck.
Had some cornflakes. Milk's going off, must get some.
Had to have a cold shower. Went to uni.

23 February
I'M A JOKE

Went to see a psychiatrist.
He said, "Tell me everything."
I did.

24 February
PRETTY BOY

Last night I dreamt about Ryan, saw him in my neurotic visions.
I am obsessed again, he is all I can think of.
It frightens me.

I have lost him and grow more and more disturbed every minute
  I am without him.
In the night I look for him going crazy in a fucked-up world and
  I am so fucked without him.
He is my lovely whore and even the mention of his fucking name
  makes my mind so dirty.
He hates me but I still love him, that's the way it's always been.
My heart is all smashed with the blood of a pretty boy and I did it
  all for him.
I feel blood drip, drip from my bitter lips.

26 February

TOO MUCH

I'm trying so hard to be happy. My dad smoked too much and drank too much and worked too much. Sometimes I feel I'm him… I used to be a boy that had great plans, now I'm just another shitty old man. I hate where I wound up.

28 February

NOBODY GIVES A FLYING FUCK

Got up, had a shower. Started thinking. I don't think I was always this cynical, it must have crept up on me. I suppose it's an occupational hazard, even though – strictly speaking – I have no occupation. I'm a university student which means I'm usually getting drunk or getting laid and when I'm not doing those things, wanking myself into a frenzy, out of my mind on dope whilst pretending to read avant-garde bollocks like Baudrillard.

Saw the cute boy on our street (every street has a cute boy) and although this one's very straight-acting, I like to pretend he's a raving, shirt-lifting, ball-bashing arse-bandit because it makes our brief exchange of glances in the street all the more exciting. As he walks past me with a blank mesmeric stare, I can't help feeling there's some adrenaline-testosterone fuelled sexual tension in the air. I can dream. I feel dreams are all I have left. We live in this awful, alienated, phoney world full of phoney, narcissistic fuckers, the sort of fucker that wouldn't even piss on you if you were on fire. No one listens, no one cares and no one gives a flying fuck about anything. There's no place to tell our personal stories and reveal to each other the most intimate parts of our lives, to engage with each other on a deeper spiritual level and understand all those amazing things which make us human.

I guess that's why I'm so screwed up at the moment.
I mean, no one bothers to understand you.
Nobody has time to listen to you.
I wanna run…

ROBBIE ROMANO

Blood Roses

I stare at the knife in my hands. I twist and turn it in the dim light. The blade reflects the light that is coming through the window. I run my finger along the blade. It's sharp and it cuts through the skin. Blood flows from the cut and runs down my finger. It doesn't hurt as much as you think it would.

The blood drops to the floor. The impact echoes in the silence. Like a morbid storm, the drops flow from the wound, drop after drop. Their splatters look like little roses. Dark red, I can just make out their petals in my mind's eye. I can smell them. A beautiful scent, my favourite flower. The kind I want at my funeral.

I check everything again. The letter is in place, my makeshift will all in order. I look at my picture album one last time. The cover is a little worn, almost torn at one edge; I've had it forever. I open it up and lay it on my lap as I sit on my bed one last time.

My smiling face stares up from the pictures. But I know that smile is just a front. I can see through that smile, past that mask of a face, hiding behind those green eyes, to the tears that I wept that night, the tears I weep every night. My eyes fall on it, a picture from long ago.

Brian and me were just kids back then. Brian, a face I haven't seen since I was eight. He's like a symbol of my past. I didn't know I was this way back then. I was just little Corey, smiling like crazy on a summer day with a long forgotten friend. This picture was different. There weren't tears that night. There wasn't this mask that I have on in my other pictures. That smile was sincere. I was happy. I haven't felt that way in a long time.

I put the album down on my table. Time to dance. I pick up the knife once again. I look at my finger. It doesn't hurt as much as I thought it would. I can feel my hands trembling, but I know that I have to do this. It's the only way.

It's too cold. It's the middle of summer and I'm cold, cold on the inside.

Another drop of blood falls to the floor. It doesn't hurt at all.

I slide the flat of the knife on my wrist. It feels like ice. The world will have one less damned soul to contend with, one less person to shove out of the way. Everyone will be happier this way… except… He'll get over it. I'm not good enough for him anyway.

Something flutters to the floor. One of the pictures stares back up at me when I walk over to it. It must have fallen out. It's a picture of him, Matthew. He is an angel on earth if I ever saw one, with beautiful brown eyes and perfectly matching brown hair. Perhaps not exactly the most beautiful thing *you* ever set eyes on, but he's beautiful to me. He's beautiful on the inside. He'll heal. I'm not going to be missed that much. I know he's not my way… he's not gay… There now, I'll say it once before I die.

I put the picture back with the others. I don't know why I do it. It's a pointless gesture; I'll be gone soon anyway. I pick up the knife again. No games this time. This is it.

My hand grips the handle firmly.

The cold blade bites into my wrist. It doesn't hurt as much as I thought it would. The warm blood bathes my hands. It makes the blade's coldness feel even more so. I slide the blade across my other wrist. It doesn't hurt at all. Blood roses… I can see the petals as I fall to the ground. They're beautiful. That dark red colour I love. They're just like I want at my funeral… dark red. As I slip into eternity, I waver into the darkness with those roses in my mind.

It's a funny dream, yet somehow, I know it's real. It's all pretty, and I'm lying in a bed of white roses. I stare at the sky. I've never seen a sky so blue. The lightest clouds touch it. I'm in the middle of a garden. Eden, I think, apple trees and all. A waterfall rushes in the distance. I can see it from my bed. The water rushes by my feet.

There's someone by my side, I realise. He's crying. I look over, and it's an angel. He seems familiar, like a face I've seen in a different lifetime.

I stare at his wings. They flutter a little as he sobs.

One of his feathers shakes off and drifts toward me. I catch it as it begins to drift down toward my bed. I run my hands over it. They feel soft, silken, like the first few warm breezes of spring.

He sobs again. I see he's kneeling. He's naked behind those wings. His skin is white and sweet like the richest cream. His hair is a little messy, but its colour is like freshly tilled earth. It's rich and vibrant, full of life. The tears shine in the pure sunlight that pours down on us. Those eyes, red with grief, but still gorgeous, shine brown, like his hair.

The face, the hair, and the eyes, they're trying to tell me something. It's all familiar, but my mind's eye is blurred. I look down at my wrists. They're covered in something. I run my hands across them. They're bandages, I think.

"Wake up, please wake up," the angel says to me.

It is a quiet whisper, full of pleading hope. The voice is delicate and beautiful.

I feel something warm flowing on my wrists. I look back down at them. The bandages are gone. I can see the cuts in my wrist. They're ugly and pulsing. The blood flows like a lazy river from them. It flows off my wrist onto my roses, staining them dark red. They are red at a drop, red at a touch, staining the world. My once white bed is crimson soon, as the angel watches over me, crying.

"Wake up," he whispers like a chime once more, "Please wake up." He leans over me and one of his tears drips onto my bare chest. It hurts. It hurts like nothing I've ever felt before. The blood that comes from my wrists is staining everything now. It spreads to the river, soaks into the ground.

"Beautiful," I whisper, "dark red, just like I wanted at my funeral." It comes out choked and hoarse, like I haven't opened my mouth in ages. The angel leaps up. He looks excited and shocked.

"He said something!" he screams. "He said something!"

Others appear out of nowhere, dressed in white, almost as if their wings are wrapped around them like a cloak. They seem odd to me, for they don't wear the long flowing robes I imagine angels in. They seem more like nurses' uniforms – small, pert, with little hats. My vision blurs. I blink a couple of times. My eyes adjust. I stare at the angel again. He's clothed this time and his wings are gone. The face clicks in my mind. It's Matthew. I sit up, or at least *try* to sit up. My head throbs. My wrists are bandaged again.

I shut my eyes and lie back for a few seconds, groaning.

My eyes clear. The pain is an endless echo, small and constant, flaring at the slightest movement. I hear the insistent beep of the electronic equipment by the bed where I lie, like an empty hollow heart. It forces me alive.

I resent the noise, I resent the pain, and I resent the voices, because they all mean that I'm alive. I stare blankly out at the crowd of medics who come in and out.

I find myself crying. Seconds pass, minutes, hours. I can't tell anymore.

My family comes in at some time. Hugs are given, words are said. I just stare at them with red eyes, a steady stream of tears. I may not be dead to them, but I am dead to myself.

Was it really Matthew that was at my bedside? I no longer know. I find that I don't even care. He's not here anymore. He can't help me now. He wasn't crying. Wasn't crying for me. Someone is crying now though. I don't waste the energy to look at them.

Night falls and I sleep. Day comes and I wake. Soon, they blend together.

People come in. They are just blurs.

Someone tries to talk to me every once in a while.

Maybe they're a doctor trying to make me live, body and mind. Maybe they're a friend trying to find out what happened. Maybe they're a family member trying to find out why. They scream at me as well. They scream, they cry. It doesn't matter. Would they care if they knew? Would it matter? There are others out there. There are many others.

They try to make me eat. I don't. I'm on an IV. They put food in front of me sometimes. I don't look at it twice.

She kisses me sometimes. I think her name is Amanda. Kisses me on the mouth. She's a friend from school. Visits sometimes. Others from school come. I think maybe Matthew does. I can't really tell anymore. They try to talk to me. Some are trying to get a reaction; a single word, a blink, a sigh. I don't give them any satisfaction. Others just talk like I'm listening. I only notice Amanda because she kisses me. I'm not a sleeping beauty. I resent her kisses just as much as I resent the little beeps of my electronic heart.

I've started to get up to stare out the windows. They don't open far enough for me to jump through. I've already tried. I'm only on the second floor anyway. Not far enough down to kill myself. My room is on the west side. It provides me the small comfort of the view of the setting sun. But it is also a reminder that the day may end, but my life cannot.

They send flowers sometimes. I only see the roses. Too bright a red to be mine, but roses all the same. I only see the blood when I look at them. They remind me of the feeling of the blood as it left my wrists.

I shiver. If it comes from the pain or the pleasure of the memory, I don't know. It doesn't hurt as much as you think it would, to live this way.

I'm alive but dead. They can't keep me like this forever. Every day is another day closer to death.

They serve me every day, with a smile, trying to coax me. The doctors have stopped coming, the medical ones anyway. The psychiatrists come every once in a while. The attendants and orderlies are much more accommodating. They come in and go out. Don't try to talk to me. They seem to realise that it is pointless. Some come to watch me, like a caged animal in the zoo. One always seems to be writing in a notebook while he watches me. He seems vaguely familiar. He's more like a faded memory then a real person.

I find myself staring at another sunset from the top of my bed. I am bathed in the dying flames of the light, tinting me and the entire room in a blushing pink. Notebook Boy is writing, as usual. The light infuses him too. He seems more like a real person today, engulfed in that light. Noise explodes from behind me. It's an alarm of some kind. People yell and I hear the pitter-patter of their feet. The boy runs out. An emergency; I suppose they need help.

I go to close the door to the chaos outside. It shuts with a satisfying click. As I turn, I spot it on the table, next to the random vases of flowers. The notebook is on the table, neglected and lonely. The fading light tints the pages with an orange hue.

I pick a rose from a vase as I go over to the book. A sketch of me laid out on the page, in the light of the sunset. The instant is captured on the paper, sketched in graphite.

I stare at the face of the sketch. It is a profile. I realise I haven't seen my face in forever. It seems very gaunt now, rigid. I glance into the mirror and see that it is true. I look like a ghost, emaciated and lonely. The look in my eyes can only be described as one thing: *sad*.

I look back down at the page. As I tilt the book, a picture flutters to the ground. As it twirls in the air, it reflects a little of the dying light into my eyes. It hits the floor. I look down at it. It seems familiar.

I go back to the night. Memories of blood roses, blades, and tears fill my mind. With it comes a picture. It is a faded memory of happiness, of two little boys, Brian and Corey.

I see them again, staring me in the eyes. Smiling like crazy, that single drop of happiness forever caught in time in the picture in my album… and the one on the floor.

Notebook Boy had looked familiar.

I look at the sketch again. In the corner, in a messy signature that only an artist can manage, is his name, Brian.

It hurts to see the picture. It almost seems to taunt me. What happened to that smile? What happened to that face? It was before the mask, before the hiding, before the tears. It is a reminder of what I lost and what I can never regain. A tear hits the photo. I realise I'm crying.

I put the notebook on the table with the picture on top of it.

I walk over to the window. I stare out into the sun, wishing that its flames would cleanse me. The only thing it does is burn my eyes.

My tears drip onto the window, making little shining spots. When I look down at the tears, I spot them. Two young men are laughing and playing around in the courtyard. Their laughter is a pretty reminder of what I have lost. It sparkles like a shiny object just out of reach. It catches me by surprise. Then it comes, so sudden and unexpected, a kiss. In an instant it is over, burned into my memory.

They continue their laughing as they continue to hold hands. I suddenly realise that I'm still holding that rose I had pulled from the vase. I catch my reflection in my window, it's smiling. Opening the window as far as I can, I whistle. When they look up, I toss the rose to the young lovers. One smiles as he catches it, blows me a kiss, then turns and offers it to his boyfriend. His boyfriend takes it, blushing. He waves sweetly and yells his thanks to me.

They go on their way, happy; on their way to be another one of my memories. My eyes fall on my reflected smile once more, looking into my faded face. It almost seems like the picture.

The smile, it fits me. I feel good for the first time in a long time. I have caught a glimpse of happiness, surreal on one level, all too real on another. It's a happiness that doesn't seem so far away now.

Brian walks in again. I turn to him and smile sincerely. He smiles back. I can almost see that little boy from the picture, the one who was smiling his little heart out. I walk over to him, grasp him in my arms, and cry.

I don't know what I am crying for. For forgotten memories, for lost friends, for sadness, for a new-found joy, for death, for life; maybe I cry for all of them, maybe I cry for none. But these tears are different from all the others. These shine with a glimmer of hope.

ADAM ROWLAND

I'd Like You To Meet Mark

Friday afternoon. Period five. Nice one. It wasn't that Ravi liked or enjoyed PE, football was hardly a favourite of his, it ranked up there with Tit Watch, a harmless game invented by the lads at the back of maths class. The complicated rules involved a long ogle at Year 10 girls' chests before rating them out of five. A small scale, Ravi thought; therefore, when re-inventing it as Arse Watch, he had gone for a score out of twenty. The rumps in his year just weren't up to much though, with Karl Smith having the highest score of a rather sad twelve. Competition was, however, hotting up as Ravi walked into the changing rooms.

"Shift up will yer, ya fat get, you've got loadsa room."

Ravi dumped his grey Quicksilver bag in the small gap, sat down and went for his black Lacoste shoelaces. As his fingers fumbled, his eyes wandered about the room. Oh yeah, this is a good spot, Karl Smith at twelve o'clock. He watched the twelve-rated arse slide tightly around inside polyester gym shorts and his smooth body bend and twist as the bastard pulled on his T-shirt.

Karl stopped getting changed and walked over to where Ravi was sat, a cheeky smile on his face. Karl's polyester bulge came level with Ravi's face as he slowly looked up and saw the cute and cheeky smile stare back. He instantly buried his face into Karl's shorts, his hands squeezing and rubbing that prize-winning arse.

"Hey, you getting changed or what? Sat there like a muppet, you are."

Seemed like you couldn't even have a fantasy in peace, as Ravi reached for his bag and began unbuttoning his shirt. The long dark fingers tackled the buttons in a way that made Ravi feel sexy, at this moment he could be stripping off for Karl Smith, revealing his slim carob-coloured body for Karl to lick and feel. The tightly compacted and underdeveloped chest covered in smooth dark silk could be his. Dick. Doesn't even notice. Straight dick. Hm, I wonder.

A smile creased the ebony cheeks of Ravi's face above which his jet black hair stood in messed spikes shining with gel. He stopped at his trousers and started folding his clothes, something to pass the time while he thought of the muddy playing field and the rain pissing down outside. Fuck. This hard-on just wouldn't go.

He went for it and looked around to see if anyone had noticed, but they were all too busy seeing who could swing from the doorframe the longest. Straight dicks.

★

Another great game of football, Ravi had sprained his ankle and it hurt ever so much. The sidelines for him, where he'd found a girl sitting with a knackered knee. She was a bit of a tart but nice enough and they had compared FCUK and DKNY without success. It seemed to pass the time quite well as they all began piling back into the changing rooms.

"Hey if it ain't David Beckham!"

"Piss off, I thought the limp was convincing that time!" Yes, Karl Smith talking to me, just gotta get him to…

Ravi couldn't finish, the straight dicks had caught his eye. Three of them were lined up doing an unconvincing impression of 'bummin''. Most of the room laughed and cheered them on, so Ravi joined in. How little they knew, they could at least make an effort. Dicks.

Ravi went for his laces and noticed Ben, a so-called friend, staring. He knew why he was staring. Ben was the only one who knew he was gay. Ravi had only told him because he thought Ben was gay as well and always seemed up for it. Camp wasn't the word to describe him, but whatever it was it worked, popularity oozed out of him, another reason to be friends with the loser. Being the only Asian lad in his year, Ravi felt that he had no choice but to blend in as much as possible as he didn't exactly come from a background of hotpots and flat caps like the rest of them.

The staring continued. The other three were still at it, trying to perfect their technique. Ben raised his eyebrows as if to say, "I'd like some of that" and then the mobile in Ravi's pocket beeped twice.

Ravi looked down at the screen, it was from Ben.

WANNA CUM 2 DA BOGZ?

I'M HORNY DARLIN!!

BREAK – DON'T BE L8!

*

Where the fuck is he? Sat here like a lemon. Always the eager beaver, Ravi had been at the loos for five minutes already, waiting. Ravi sat on the toilet seat arranging his legs so they greeted Ben on arrival. Again the beeps of his mobile broke the embarrassing silence of the boys' loo.

SOZ HON NOT IN DA MOOD

N E MORE MAYB L8ER

MWHAHAHA – MUPPET!!

"The bastard."

Ravi flushed the toilet and walked out smiling.

Nice one Ben. Shit, I fell for it!

Ben was waiting outside.

"Ahhh, muppet!"

"Oh, suck ma dick."

"Hey I told you, maybe later."

"I've been sat in there for nearly ten minutes."

"Yeah, I know. You must be *desperate!*" Ravi smiled in agreement.

"What you got next, RE?"

"Yeah."

"Unlucky, mate. See ya around. Have a good one."

"Yeah, you too. See ya."

Usually RE was just him and Jo, the girl he sat next to, doodling pictures that took the piss out of the rest of the class. Typically, this week Mr Peters had gone for the 'Is homosexuality moral and right in the eyes of God?' debate. Technically, and legally, he wasn't allowed to, but the bigot couldn't resist an argument he thought he could win.

"It's just disgusting, innit. Unnatural and disgustin'."

One lad, Danny Holt, had taken centre stage in sharing his *valid* opinion.

"If I saw two geezers snoggin' an' stuff in the street, I'd puke. It – it just in't right, is it?"

Shelley, a peroxide blonde, piped up next.

"Aww, leave 'em alone, they can't help it, it ain't their fault. You're so narrow-minded you."

Ravi sat fiddling with his pen lid, smiling.

Fuck you, fuck you – actually in this light, Danny, I could fuck you.

Peters saw Ravi's smug smile and got stuck in.

"Something amusing you, Ravi? Maybe you've got something to hide. Would you like to share it with the rest of the class?"

"No, course I ain't."

Ravi slid down in his chair and stayed there for the rest of the lesson, admiring his drawing of a badly bleeding Mr Peters with the simple caption: TWAT.

The end of the lesson was sweet, now nothing stood between Ravi and the weekend. The Nokia tune bleeped out from his jacket pocket and when he looked down at the screen he smiled.

SEX KITTEN

CALLING :)

"Hey Ben, can't keep away today, can we?"

"Nope, and this time I have an offer you won't wanna refuse."

"Go on, is it gonna be as good as the one at break?"

"Hm, better – definitely better – oh yeah! Hehe, dya wanna come over tonight? I've gotta bottle of vodka and a hard-on and I was wondering if yer could help me empty it!"

"Empty what, the bottle or little Jimmy?"

"Ha ha, so funny – well?"

"If there's free drink, then what are friends for?"

"Nice one, sevenish. Bring a bag, you'll be sleepin' over."

"I hope there won't be much time for that!"

"Dirty bastard – see ya."

The weekend was getting better by the minute.

★

Ravi didn't know what to think as he walked up to Ben's door. In a couple of hours he could be shagging the brains out of Ben, pissed and puking his guts up, or watching some lame movie. He just wanted an idea of what was going to happen, what he could expect. He found out soon enough. Bugger, it was the lame movie, he'd fallen for it again, evil bastard: although there was a bottle of Smirnoff as promised, there was no shag – yet. Was he gay or not?

Ben lay back on the bed, his legs outstretched and wide open. Tempting. Ravi began to get tipsy and lay next to him, moving his head as close as he could to Ben's.

"Full of bullshit, you are," Ravi slurred.

Ben smiled and reached out for Ravi's hand, which he took and drew across to his grey drawstring trousers. He lifted the top of the trousers with his other hand and placed Ravi's hand onto his soft cotton boxers.

Ravi turned and stared at Ben, but he didn't stare back. He returned his arm to rest and then whispered to Ravi, "What ya waitin' for?"

All Ravi could hear was his heart in his ears. Never before had he come this close to another lad's dick. This was a first and it took a while for him to understand what exactly Ben wanted him to do. When he realised, Ravi sat up slightly and felt round Ben's boxers: the bottom of them and the start of his legs, the top of them and Ben's smooth stomach.

Ben smiled slightly and softly muttered, "Go on."

Ravi felt his way under the boxers and found the smooth, warm skin. It felt strange – not in a bad way, just different to how he'd imagined.

Wrapping his fingers round Ben's dick, Ravi found he ran out of room for his top finger and tried to slide his hand further down where he came to nothing more than the rough pubic hair. Was this it? Ravi couldn't help smiling, his nerves got the better of him and he laughed out loud.

"What?"

"Nothing."

He slowly started a rhythmic, clockwise movement, hoping that this was right, he'd never done it to anyone else, was there a difference? With his free hand, Ravi reached for the bottle and took a long swig – tipsy was slowly becoming drunk. The more Ravi thought about the lack of Ben, the more he enjoyed it.

Ravi began to giggle at the thought of it. Through his low groans Ben moaned, "What?"

"Nowt, dun't matter."

"It's you, in't it, you can't handle yer drink. You little lightweight."

"Oh yeah, whatever!"

Ravi squeezed tighter and began more fiercely.

"Hehe, it's you actually, you're the size of a flea!" He didn't mean to say it, the drink was talking.

"You what? Fuck you." Ben's tone turned serious and he grabbed the moving hand to stop it.

"Fuck you."

"I'm tryin' me best on that one!"

"You dirty fuckin' poof, finish me off, then go to sleep."

Ravi didn't take Ben too seriously – the drink wouldn't let him. He finished him off to a loud groan as Ben flinched, his eyes closed and mouth open.

Ravi took another mouthful of vodka and slurred his words, "Don't I get a good night kiss, darlin'?"

"Just go to sleep, will ya?"

⋆

Ravi went home the next morning without saying much to Ben. He had just over two hours before meeting Mark.

He had arranged to meet Mark for the second time after flirting and getting to know each other via a personal on a gayteen website, the sort of site that gay Asian lads living in Lancashire turn to in order to get laid.

The first time he'd met Mark was awkward, to say the least. After recovering from the shock that Mark was a goddamn babe, they'd sat around Manchester's Canal Street commenting on the sleazy Paddy's Goose and the S&M Rembrandt pub. They'd even taken a trip to Clone Zone, but Ravi didn't mind that, he'd loved leafing through the magazines and gawping at the toys, especially with Mark by his side. *Teenage Virgins*, a raunchy-looking video, and *Mad About The Boy* caught Ravi's attention, while a latex peek-a-boo brief caught Mark's. From thumbscrews to lilac jelly butt plugs, it had been a whole new experience for Ravi.

Ravi was expecting more of the same today (the two of them only really came alive when e-mailing), especially after Mark had said that he'd always had a 'thing' for Asian lads. This was great news for Ravi, as most people round his area had something against them.

*

The beeps from his phone were getting beyond a joke as they hit fifteen. At seventeen they stopped, his text memory was full.

U DIRTY FUCKIN POOF

Each one read the same. They'd been sent via the Internet and the sender was not proud enough to put their name to it.

Very funny Ben. Bloody hell, I was drunk. I never meant it – sad git.

Ravi began deleting the messages while trying to eye up the timetable for the next bus.

Oh great.

Ravi saw four lads from his year walking towards him in the bus station. He wouldn't have minded, but these guys were under the impression that all Pakis should go home and just mentioning the word 'gay' forced them to put their arm round the nearest girl. Lucky they only knew the half of it then. They swaggered past him, staring as they went with smug grins on their faces. Dicks.

A few minutes later, Ravi saw them coming back again while he queued to get on the bus. They brushed past him as one whispered, "Dirty fuckin' poof."

They turned and shouted back, "Dirty… fuckin'… POOF!"

Fuck, how did they know? What did they know? When did they find out? Who knew?

Ravi's stomach turned and his legs went weak. If *they* know then I'm dead.

They can't know, only one person knows.

His phone bleeped again. F-U-C-K.

Instead of abuse it was Mark.

HEY SEXY, NOT LONG NOW.

BIN MISSIN U! :)

The thought of spending a whole Saturday afternoon with Mark was a lot more exciting then worrying about something that could turn out to be nothing. Instead, Ravi turned on his mini-disc to Steve Haswell's 'Here I Come' and sat back, fantasising about him, Mark and a bubbling jacuzzi.

★

There he was, his very own Jude Law, standing there waiting for *him*, not for some camp-as-tits queen, but *him*. Ravi approached slowly, wondering how one person could be so beautiful.

Mark's wavy brown hair perfectly complemented his milky golden skin – fair enough, a sun-bed job, but Ravi couldn't imagine him any different. Levi's twisted round the long and slender legs and an old-skool T-shirt poked out from underneath a faded Gap denim jacket. As Ravi got closer, his eyes met the pure blue gaze of Mark's as he finished and stamped out a cigarette.

Hug me, please hug me.

"Hi, how are you?"

OK, I'll go along with a simple hello.

"I'm great, especially now."

Shit, that didn't work.

"So, what d'ya wanna do?"

"Dunno – go shopping?"

"Yeah, whatever, shopping's good."

Shit, this is so awkward.

But it wasn't half as bad as Ravi had thought. The narrow gaps between clothes rails were perfect for him to innocently sweep his hand across

Mark's arse and small of back. To his surprise, Mark did the same at the earliest opportunity.

The conversation eventually relaxed and edged uneasily onto ex-boyfriends. This makes me look bad. Mark's ex list could have destroyed a bedpost, never mind make it notchy.

"So what about you?" The dreaded question.

"Well, you know... um... OK, I've never had a boyfriend." Ravi blushed. "Shit, that makes me sound lame, doesn't it?"

"Nah, not really. Just means you need breakin' in, that's all."

Ravi laughed nervously.

They eventually ended back at Canal Street where the Gothic, wooden interior of Via Fossa impressed Ravi.

"What you drinkin'?"

"Erm... Bacardi Breezer."

They sat next to each other on a small Chesterfield couch in a cozy corner away from the bar. Ravi nervously sipped his drink.

It happened just like a low budget B-movie, Mark moved his lips towards Ravi, then his wet tongue was twisting about in Ravi's mouth.

Their tongues wrapped around each other's, then slipped smoothly over each other's teeth. All kinds of responses were being provoked. It felt fine.

Mark's skin felt so soft against Ravi's face. Ravi's back tingled, his stomach turned, he wanted to explore more of this gorgeous body.

Ravi's left hand slowly slid up Mark's back, his shirt creasing into ripples as he went. He finally found the back of Mark's neck and continued by softly stroking the shiny brown hair.

Mark took the cue and rubbed his left hand along the inside of Ravi's leg. Ravi pushed his weight against his hard-on to make the pleasure more intense and loosely rested his other hand on Mark's chest. He could feel the tight contours of his small pecs and the hard curves of his smooth muscular shoulders. He was kissing perfection.

Ravi lay against Mark's shoulder and casually glanced at his watch.

"Shit, I really need to go. I'm supposed to be meetin' me mum at the bus station in half an hour."

OK, that made you look a complete mummy's boy.

Ravi sat up and looked at Mark. He leaned towards Mark and their lips met for a second time.

*

He sat down on the bottom deck of the X43 as it began to turn the busy streets of Manchester before leaving the city and heading out into the suburbs. The bus made another stop and the doors opened.

Oh shit, them again.

Ravi slid down in his seat and put his arm up to obscure his face, pretending to rub his forehead. Out of the corner of his eye, he saw the gang of four go upstairs. The Rockport boots and socks pulled over Kappa tracksuit pants went well with the skinhead and thick as pig-shit look.

Fuck, that was close. The poor sods upstairs are welcome to them.

But there was obviously no room left up top and all four came looking for seats. Ravi turned to look out of the window, hoping they wouldn't be able to see his face.

It's OK, they've gone to the back. They haven't seen me, they haven't seen me.

But one of the lads *had* spotted Ravi and told the rest of his mates, one of whom moved to sit behind him.

"Oh look, it's the Paki poof."

The four of them laughed.

"Been to Queer Street, have we?"

Ravi tried to blank them by staring out of the window, hoping that people would think it was someone else they were talking about.

"Oi, I'm talking to you, ya queer cunt."

The one sat behind Ravi reached over the seat and grabbed his shoulder, the rest of the bus fell silent.

"Been to see yer *boyfriend* have yer? Had a good shag? Fuck, you lot make me sick, you come over here, take all our jobs an' shit an' then turn out to be fuckin' arse bandits an' all. Oi, don't blank me, you *bender*."

Ravi wanted to disappear down the nearest, darkest hole.

"Who the fuck are you, eh?"

The lad hit Ravi on the back, his shouts were getting louder.

"You're a dirty, fuckin', Paki poof, that's what you are. You're S-C-U-M."

The bus jolted to a stop and the driver's cab opened up. A stocky man with a shaved head approached them.

"Right you lot, either shut up or get off, I'm not havin' you causin' trouble."

"Go on *Ravi*, you heard the man, fuck off."

Ravi got up and off as quickly as he could. He heard the lads cheer as one shouted, "See ya Monday!"

Ravi sat down in the bus shelter, his face burning with humiliation and worry. How did they know? Only Ben knows. Only Ben. Ravi took out his phone.

"Hi mate, recovered from last night yet?" Ben was far too chirpy.

"Fuck off, who've you told about me, how come everyone knows?"

"What?"

"You know, ya bastard. Who've you fuckin' told? Is it 'cos of what I said last night?"

"Erm… I gotta go." Ben hung up on him.

"Bastard!" Ravi shouted down the phone, his eyes filling with tears.

*

Ravi threw himself onto his bed and punched the pillow. It didn't help.

This can't be happening.

He turned on his computer and checked his mails. Mark's name came up in his inbox:

"Hey sexy, had a great day, I can't wait till next weekend!! I've sent summat to keep you busy till then – ENJOY! :)"

Ravi opened the attachment and smiled. A picture of Mark filled the screen, a picture of Mark in just his boxers.

*

Monday morning. Shit.

Ravi hoped that he would survive the day.

Maybe I could pull a sickie and not go in... but I'd have to go eventually.

He was terrified, he couldn't tell his parents, after all, they were hoping for a huge wedding for their only child, with all the family over from India and big celebrations. They'd told him often enough how much they were looking forward to their grandchildren and spending Eid with their daughter-in-law and son. It seemed to Ravi that they'd planned his life for him and only if it were all that simple, he wouldn't be scared now. This was something he had to face alone, or so he thought.

Ravi stood in the corridor. He'd chickened out and skived the morning by wandering around the cobbled back-streets near his school, planning out his options. He'd decided to go in, to see how bad things were, how many people knew and how they'd taken it.

Fuck this, I'm gay, I'm proud and I'm out!

Now he stepped out into the yard. His heart began to thump and he could feel his cheeks burning up. If Ravi needed a reason to be scared, it came soon enough as he walked past the back of the PE building that backed out onto the yard.

A silver rail ran round the outside giving the whole of his year the perfect spot to sit, smoke and chat. This was *their* space and this was the only route to the building Ravi needed to get to.

Shit, I'm dead.

"Queer."

"Bender."

"Paki poof."

"Oi, gay boy."

Whoops and laughs came next as they cheered one lad on as he ran up in front of Ravi and stuck his arse out towards him.

"Be gentle, please be gentle!"

Ravi stopped, his path blocked.

"Fuck you. No, I don't want to give you the pleasure, you'd enjoy it too much."

"Ya what?"

"You 'eard."

There was a pause, the lad stared at Ravi, hardly believing that he'd been stood up to, and shocked that Ravi had admitted it. His ginger hair and freckled face made Ravi stare back.

Ha, Ginge! Ravi thought.

The ginger lad, called Scott, came in close to Ravi and pushed him with both hands at the shoulders.

"Come on then, ya dirty queer – wanna start sumfin'?"

Ravi just stared.

Scott pushed him again.

"Well, *Curry Boy*, you startin'?"

The whole yard had gathered in a rough circle around them, cheering and shouting. Ravi still just stood and stared. Loud shouts came from the back of the crowd behind Scott.

"Right you lot, move. I said *move!*"

A male teacher pushed his way through as the crowd drifted away.

Ravi saw his opportunity and ran.

When he cleared the school grounds he kept on running. Ravi ran until his chest choked him and he panted to a stop. He walked the rest of the way home, coming to the decision that he couldn't go back. Not only was he a Paki poof, he was also a complete dick for running off.

He stopped opposite his house, his mother was out in the front garden battling with the weeds and then his father would come home and then there'd be the three of them. The perfect family.

Ravi walked up the garden path, took a deep breath, and said, "Hi."

He went upstairs, dumped his bag and coat on the bed. Dropping to his knees he looked under the bed. He found what he wanted, got up and placed a small bottle of whisky on the bed next to his bag. Ravi unscrewed the lid and sniffed the liquid, he twitched his nose and pulled it away quickly.

The bottle was left over from when Ben had first come by about six months ago, they'd got pissed on a cheap bottle of brandy and half of that whisky, then Ravi had come out to him before puking in the loo for twenty minutes. Ravi smiled and unzipped his bag.

'Mogadon. Mrs S. Faruq: Two to be taken when required.'

He read the label of his mother's sleeping tablets carefully and stared through the amber container at the pills inside. She wouldn't miss them. After all, he was the only one, apart from her, who knew about them.

He tipped the bottle out onto the bed and counted them – forty. Taking two of the pills, he unscrewed the whisky lid and placed the tablets in his mouth.

"Cheers Ben!"

He took a large mouthful of whisky and gulped it down.

He reached out and swallowed the rest, one by one.

"Ravi?" his mother called out from the kitchen. "Hey Ravi, I'm calling you."

Ravi did not move. Feeling numb, he slowly counted down from ten. His mother pushed open his bedroom door but he sat silently, looking down at the empty bottles. He didn't see the look on his mother's face.

"What's this?"

"What does it look like?" he answered back.

"Oh, Raveed Faruq, what've you done?"

"I haven't a clue, it's all fucked up. Oh bollocks."

His mother shoved Ravi into the car while crying and muttering passages from the Koran through her tears.

"Why Ravi? *Why?*"

"I don't know."

It was all he could say. After all that was exactly it – he didn't know.

Ravi thought of Mark. He took out his phone from his grey woollen school trousers and began writing a text message:

BEEN A TWAT,

I'LL BE @

ROCHDALE INFIRMARY.

RXXX

The car arrived at the hospital. Ravi stumbled to the floor, then blacked out.

★

"Hello Raveed, I'm a nurse, can you sit up for me please?"

It wasn't like the episode of *Casualty* or *ER* Ravi had imagined, the people looked far too normal, the pain in his head far too real.

Ravi couldn't focus on the nurse as she propped him up and handed him a bottle of something.

"What is it?"

"You need to drink all of that please, as quick as you can."

Ravi brought the beaker close to his mouth, he still hadn't seen the colour of the stuff inside the bottle, he found it hard to focus. He put the nozzle of the bottle inside his mouth and took a large gulp.

He brought the bottle to where he could see it better.

"Shit, why you givin' me black sand to drink?"

"It's charcoal, it'll neutralise what's in your stomach, you need to finish all of that please."

After Ravi had finished with the bottle, he lay back with his eyes closed and groaned. When he opened them again he saw the large mass of his father standing over him. Ravi moaned again and crashed to sleep.

An hour later, he found himself in a room with three other beds that were all empty, and two chairs on his right-hand side. Mother. Father.

"Oh Ravi, my poor baby!"

His mother sprang up and grabbed Ravi's hand, but his father stayed sat down as usual, showing no emotion.

"Where am I?"

"You're in the hospital, they brought you up to the ward an hour back.

His father just sat and stared at Ravi, no hint of expression on his face.

"Do you know why I did it, why I took them?"

His mother turned slightly and looked at Ravi's father. "No."

Finally his father grunted through his heavy accent, "Ask him about the photo."

"What photo?"

"Ravi, I found a photo of…"

She paused and looked down.

"Of a… half-naked boy under your pillow this morning."

Uh-oh.

Ravi had forgotten that was where he'd put the printout of the e-mail Mark sent him at the weekend. But he was saved from having to answer by a tall brunette nurse who opened the door.

"It's good to see you're awake, Raveed. There's a lad who wants to see you, do you feel up to it?"

Ravi knew who it would be.

"Yeah."

Ravi's parents turned and looked at their son with confusion.

"Who is it?"

Ravi's father got no reply.

Mark walked into the room and paused at the sight of Ravi's parents, then carried on towards the bed. Ravi's father stood up, unsure whether to greet the lad or throw him out. Instead he stared with his mouth half-open. Ravi put out his hand into Mark's, which felt smooth and warm.

"Hi," Ravi half-whispered. Then, "Mum, Dad, I'd like you to meet Mark."

STUART SANDFORD

G-A-Y

It's Saturday night and we're in the car, heading to G-A-Y. I'm driving, as usual, which means I can't have a drink. I can't even pull and I haven't had a shag for weeks (or is that *four* weeks?). I don't even remember because it's been *so* long. I know we've got a couple of pills for later, which I may be persuaded to neck. Maybe.

Next to me is Brett, my best friend in the world, although if you asked me why right now, I don't think I'd be able to tell you. In the back are Scott, David and Matthew. Matthew's just split up with his boyfriend. Poor thing. They were together for about three years. He's tagging along because we're supposed to be cheering him up, the choice words being *supposed to be* – he'd rather be in bed at home crying, listening to Sinéad O'Connor singing 'Nothing Compares 2 U'. Scott and David aren't making it any easier for him either, going at it next to him, as they're always doing, as he tries not to look too uncomfortable. I'm wearing my brand new Versace top, just bought it today, my old 'Twisted' Levi's and my white Calvins. I look good, I know that, but I feel shitty. I know that, too.

We get there and it feels as if we're queuing for ages, listening to Kylie Minogue's 'Your Disco' blasting out from inside, and then they finally let us all in and I love it, I always do! There's always that feeling that anything, absolutely *anything* could happen, y'know? This is my church and God is a DJ. Or maybe that's Jeremy Joseph. I might meet the boy of my dreams. Yeah, that'd make a change. They're usually just nightmares. I'm not here to pull though, to be honest. Yeah, I wanna shag, boy do I wanna fucking shag, but I know there'll be no one here as usual worth a second look (or should that be fuck?) and we won't be staying long enough to find out, so, why bother? But there could be some sexy boys at this party we're heading to later in Finsbury Park. I'll just have to hope for a snog and maybe a blowjob later, I don't think I'm in line for much else. But, this guy who's twenty-five called Antoine might be there and I know he fancies the pants off me, so I might get a fuck after all.

Matthew starts straight away, "How long have we gotta be here?"

Brett tells him, "Just an a hour or so. I wanna see Luke, see what he's up to an' stuff." Luke is Brett's boyfriend, on and off, more off than on that is. "Absence makes the heart grow fonder," he tells us.

"More like it makes the dick grow harder in your case," and he slaps me on the back of the neck for that, but he knows it's right and so do I.

Scott and David (they've been together for a couple of months, they're still in that rose-coloured/semen-stained glasses stage when they can't leave each other alone for a second and they're constantly fucking and constantly telling us about it) head straight to the dancefloor and begin doing what they do with each other: snogging each other's faces off. We head to the bar.

"They're at it already..." I say to anyone who's listening.

"You're just fucking jealous," Brett tells me. And you want to know something? Yeah, I *am* just fucking jealous. I've been out for about a year and haven't met anyone yet, not anyone worthwhile. I've had plenty of shags but none that lasted more than that one night. They've been out for two months and meet each other straight away. Don't get me wrong, they're great together an' all, I just want someone too. That isn't too much to ask, is it?

Brett disappears off, looking for Luke, leaving me with Matthew. Now Matthew's a really nice guy an' that's the problem, he's too nice, he lets people just walk all over him, like his ex. We get a couple bottles of Stella from the bar, I can have a couple of bottles, I'm fine with that but I won't have any more because I'm driving, and we head up to the balcony. I spot Brett talking to Luke. No, more like shouting at Luke, actually, but decide just to leave them to it, that's just what they do, and sit down with Matthew, making sure I've got a good view of the dancefloor and who's on it as well as the entrance.

"You OK?" I ask him. I'm interested, I mean, he's my friend and I love him, but I know what he's going to say and I don't want to hear it any more, none of us do, but, you know, I ask anyway. He looks totally out of place, trying not to see the two guys next to him, rubbing up against his shoulder as they taste each other's tonsils.

"Yeah, just a bit... distracted, y'know?"

"I know what you mean."

I do, up to a point. I've never had a relationship last two days, two weeks or two months, never mind two years, not for want of trying though, believe me. His boyfriend gave him the old 'it's not you, it's me' line, something like he couldn't bear to be without Matthew because he loves him so much and Matthew's here at university whilst his boyfriend's back home in Manchester and they can't see each other so his boyfriend thought it would be best to cut him out completely, something like that anyway. Poor Matthew, he loves that twat, he really does. He's sat there drinking his drink, miserable.

And then I spot him (or should that be Him?). In he walks, all by himself it looks like, and he just has this kind of… presence, I suppose. I can't take my eyes off him. He's wearing this tight black cut-off T-shirt, revealing his pierced bellybutton that says PLAY WITH ME. He's about the same height as me, six foot(ish), short spiky black hair with dyed red tips and he is fucking stunning. I've never seen him before but I know he's the one. He's one of those that comes along maybe once, or if you're very lucky *twice* in your life. He's not like a ten, who you see every now and again walking down the street or shaking their arse on the dancefloor, but he's eleven. No, he's not even that, he's way off the fucking scale.

I know that he's the one that I want, the one I need, the one who can make me happy and the one who I can make happy and make each other come buckets. And he goes straight to the dancefloor and begins to dance and he is fantastic! I can't take my eyes off him! Oh my God, he's looking up at me and I'm looking down at him and if this were a film everything would be in slow motion just right about now…

I nearly fall off my chair and it's Matthew's turn to ask, "You all right?"

"Yeah, yeah…" I tell him. "I'm fine. I've just seen… someone that I've got to go and say… something to."

I tell Matthew to stay there on his tod and I make my way down to the dancefloor, trying to keep my eye on him as I do so but it's getting busy and I lose him in the crowd. Fuck! I stand at the side of the dancefloor but I can't see PLAY WITH ME at all. Then someone grabs me from behind.

It's Brett. "That fucking Luke! Guess what? We've just split up. He's left me, the cunt."

And although I'm scanning the dancefloor and the bar to see PLAY WITH ME, I turn to Brett and say, "Shit." I sound like I mean it. "But you've been off and on ever since the beginning." And my eyes never leave the dancefloor.

"I know," he says dejectedly.

"You'll get over it," I add.

"I know," he says again.

"Yeah, and that's the important thing, isn't it? Getting *over it*?"

"Are you trying to say I'm all about sex?"

"Brett," I tell him, "you were born with your legs apart. They'll have to bury you in a Y-shaped coffin." I'm quite pleased with that one.

"What the fuck's got up your arse? Or is that just it, nothing?" Brett gives me that fucking smile I hate, when he thinks he's just come out with the best line of his life.

I ignore him and sip my drink, still looking. Brett says something like, "Well, I'm going to find someone else, I'm copping off tonight, even if it kills me."

And he disappears off into the crowd, me thinking that if he does that, finds someone else, there won't be enough room in the car, something totally irrelevant like that, but then, remembering that Brett doesn't need a bed to fuck in, he can just use the toilets if he's that desperate, and he does, regularly. Which is what *I* need to do. To piss that is, OK? Not to fuck. Well, not yet. Maybe later.

So, I'm standing at the urinal, trying not to think about my shy bladder and being, y'know, quite successful, trying to ignore the old guy next to me with his cock out and I just know he's looking at mine with a wrinkled erection, trying not to listen to someone shagging in one of the cubicles and trying not to think that it might be Brett, when the door opens and guess who walks in? Go on, guess. That's right! PLAY WITH ME. He steps up to the urinal next to mine and I try not to look but it's genetic. Honest.

"Hi," he says, which causes me to stop midstream. I'd managed to start.

"Hi," I say back. Yeah, I know, very original, what else you gonna say when you're standing pissing, or trying to piss, at the urinal?

He smiles at me and then concentrates on his pissing. I'm so nervous that I'm beginning to sweat and I know he can see this even though he isn't looking and I can't piss any more and by the time my bladder does sort itself out, he's finished and out of there.

What a fucking idiot I am, I let him slip through my fingers. I bang my head on the tile wall, cursing, then hurry out after him. But again he's disappeared, hopefully not with a poof, and I can't see him anywhere.

That smile, that was definitely what I'd call positive. Positive eye contact. Positive body language and all that kind of positive thing.

So, I'm there, looking for him and I can't see the sod anywhere. I see Brett chatting to someone, probably some guy who looks like he fell out of the ugly tree and hit every branch on the way down. That's his usual type. Some ape. Just like Luke.

I can't see PLAY WITH ME anywhere, so I head back up to the balcony where Matthew is still sat, looking more sad/lonely/bored than ever, the two guys behind him almost shagging right then and there in front of him on the table.

"Are we going now, or what?" Matthew asks, a glimmer of hope in his voice.

"Not yet," I tell him, snuffing out that tiny glimmer. "But let's get away from them. Otherwise, they might want you to join in." Matthew follows me as we head downstairs, me having practically got to the point where I don't think I'm going to see PLAY WITH ME again, he's probably hooked up with his boyf or someone.

Past the dancefloor, where Scott and David give us a wave during a pause in their constant tonguing, groin teasing and hands down the back of each other's pants arse playing, and to the bar where I get another bottle and one for Matthew, I think he needs it, he needs a few. We pull up a seat at another table but don't sit there long because Brett appears again.

"Hey, there's this really cute guy, great arse, and he's really into me and I like him but he needs to go home." He looks to me, "Can we give him a lift?"

"No," I tell him flat. "Sorry. Car's full up."

"Oh, go on," Brett says. He looks over at where this great arse is, which I can't see because some guy's blocking my view by dancing like a twat, and then he looks back to me, giving me that smile of his. "Please?"

I mull it over for a moment and eventually I say, "OK."

"Excellent! I'll go 'n' get him."

Brett disappears again in search of his great arse and big dick.

"We're going?" Matthew asks, that glimmer of hope resurfacing again.

"Yeah."

So, we head out to the car and I start the engine, S Club 7 singing out to me and Matthew. Then I see PLAY WITH ME. And I realise he's heading in this direction. Heading in this direction with Brett. Fucking wonderful. Pulled by my best mate.

Brett opens the back door for PLAY WITH ME and he climbs in. Our eyes catch in the rear-view mirror.

Brett introduces us, "This is Tom, Tom this is Ash."

"Hi Ash," he says with that same smile from the toilets.

"Hi," I kind of croak, really gutted. "So, where we heading?"

"Notting Hill."

"Hey, nice area," Brett says.

As I pull off into traffic, PLAY WITH ME, I mean Tom, answers, "It's my parents', you know. It's OK. It's just where I live." He then reaches into his pocket, pulling out a joint and a lighter, asking me, "D'you mind?"

"No," I tell him. "Go ahead." And the smell of skunk weed fills the car, which reminds me to get the air freshener out before I give the car keys back to my mum.

They start chatting about all that getting to know you kind of shit. Which, don't get me wrong, I wanna hear because I do wanna get to know him, I'd just rather not do it with Brett in there as well. He passes the joint to me first, not Brett, me, and I just have a couple of tokes before passing it to Brett, smiling back at Tom. Matthew doesn't have any, he just sits there in the passenger seat, looking miserable.

All the while I'm trying to keep my eyes on the road, but I can't. They keep wandering to the rear-view mirror and every time they do, Tom's eyes meet mine. I can't believe that Brett doesn't notice, but he just doesn't, he obviously thinks he's got Tom eating out of the palm of his hand. But he hasn't. There's hope yet.

We finally get to Tom's house and I pull up to the kerb, turning the engine off, S Club 7 still singing at us. "This is it," he says, *still* looking at me in the rear-view.

"Nice," Brett says, then looks to Tom, straight in his eyes.

And just at the moment when they should both have their tongues in each other's mouths, if all was going as smoothly as Brett wanted it, Tom goes "I better get in," and reaches for the door handle.

But Brett bounces back with, "Can I have your number, then?"

Tom hesitates, "Er... Yeah, sure." He looks to me, then reels it off.

"Cool," Brett says. "I'll give you a call."

Tom nods and opens the door, looking to me again. "Can you walk me to the door?"

Now Brett gives *me* a look. "Yeah," I say and climb out of the car and walk him to the door just as he asked. As slowly as possible.

He whispers to me, "That's not my real number," with a conspiratorial smile. "D'you want it?"

"Y-Yeah," I tell him. "Yeah." And then he pulls his mobile out.

"What's yours?" I tell him my number and he dials it. My mobile rings in the car, once, twice, three times, then it stops. "Now you've got mine too."

I give him a smile and he looks at me for a moment before slowly moving in and, this is a moment that I love, we kiss. Not for too long but for long enough to know that it won't be the last time, and he's a great kisser! We break off and he gives me another smile. "I'll definitely call you. *Definitely*."

"And *I'll* definitely call *you*. *Definitely*." And with that, Tom opens the door and gives me another quick kiss on the lips before he goes inside. I stand there for just a moment or two, lost in his lips, his eyes, his body, his voice, his smell, the raging hard-on I could feel through his FCUK trousers and my own raging hard-on.

And then the car horn. "Come on you fucking tart!" Brett shouts at me and I head back to the car, adjusting my dick so it doesn't look super-obvious. I climb back into the car, Brett getting in the passenger seat. "I don't believe you, arsehole! He was mine." He's not genuinely hurt though, I can tell by now.

"Well, I think he was definitely more interested in me," I say, not gloating, just stating a fact. Well, yeah, of course I was gloating a bit. He wanted me.

"Well, fuck him. I don't like him any more anyway. There was another guy back there, much more attractive." Yeah, right. "I knew he was after you from the beginning, that's why I brought him back."

"You fucking liar! You wanted him to fuck you senseless and you know it. You would've been all over him," I twist that knife deeper and enjoy doing it. "If he'd let you, that is."

"Yeah, well, there's always someone else." Brett has the last word, as usual. I let him and start the engine, making our way to the party.

I'll call Tom tomorrow. I know I'll get that shag, maybe even something more.

TONY J SHAW

Thank You For Travelling On The Central Line

This is Chancery Lane. This train terminates at Woodford, via Hainault.

He was so gorgeous. He was so good looking! Such a brilliant kisser, and so much fun to be with. And he was so understanding.

This is Bank.

But he's going back to Scotland next week.

Change for Northern, District and Circle lines, Docklands Light Railway, and Network South East services.

Mum will never believe me.

This train terminates at Woodford, via Hainault.

That I have spent seven hours in Stratford, just shopping by myself? She'll never believe that. I've just got to tell her the truth.

The next station is: Liverpool Street.

But I'm so scared. "Hi Mum. Erm… I've got something to tell you."

This is Liverpool Street.

How can I say I've spent most of my afternoon in the company of a homosexual, and kissed him very publicly in Green Park?

Change for Metropolitan,

When she believes I am shopping in Stratford, for trainers. With a friend!

Circle,

How many friends have I got? Four? *Five* if I'm lucky. And they all live miles away from me… in their comfortable, contented, perfect heterosexual lifestyles, with their heterosexual posters and heterosexual thoughts and heterosexual heterosexuality.

Network South East services,

I'm not gay. It's just got to be a phase.

Woodford, via Hainault.

It's all because of the Internet! Dave is just a guy I met the other day, a name on a computer screen. My friends are names on a bloody computer screen!

The next station is Bethnal Green,

But I do like fellas. I mean Michael Owen… *mmm.*

Bethnal Green.

And how many times have I looked at that magazine in my sister's cupboard? The naughty one. *For Women.*

Woodford

Damn. Wrong train.

via Hainault.

But what will my parents say? They'll just reckon it's a phase. But why did I feel so easy today with Dave, and why didn't I care that we snogged in Green Park, surrounded by hundreds of people?

This is Stratford.

Anyway, how many people were watching us? Hardly any, I suppose.

Network South East.

Why haven't I got any mates at school? They all hate me! They all know my secret, that's even worse. "I'm proud of you for having the courage to come out to me." Yeah I bet! Another reason to treat me like an outcast in class.

This is Leyton.

So I go online. I visit gay.com. I've got my own little profile with my picture. And I'm gay to everyone in the world, apart from my mum and dad.

Woodford, via Hainault.

Mum, Dad, I kissed a man today, and really enjoyed it. I've been thinking, for a long time, that I'm gay.

This is Leytonstone.

Hey Mum, guess what? I'm gay. That's G, A, Y!

Passengers to Epping, please change at this station.

She knows. That woman over there. She's looking at me strangely. I can tell, she's looking at me weird. Yes love, I'm a homo! A queer! I like cock!

This is a Woodford train, via Hainault.

But she could be looking out of the window behind me.

This is a Woodford train, via Hainault.

What am I going to do? What am I going to say?

I think Mum would be OK, 'cos my little *test* proved that! "Mum I've just seen Ricki Lake – about kids coming out to their parents. What would you think if I did that?" She loved me then…

This is Wanstead.

Oh Christ! I've missed the station! All because of that woman. Now another half hour on this train. Hell!

Terminates at

Could read *Fluid,* I suppose. It'll pass the time. I mean, I got all that courage to buy it! Along with a Wispa and the *Daily Express.* And the A-Z, and the pencil case, and the notebook, and the CD… all that stuff just to buy a magazine!

Woodford

But everyone would look at me. "Eugh, there's a gay boy on the train," they'd say. I'd get beaten up. 'SERIOUS ASSAULT AT WANSTEAD STATION, QUEER BOY PROVOKED ATTACKERS' would be the headlines.

via Hainault.

It's all *Queer As Folk*'s fault. If I had never watched that programme, I would never have feelings for members of my sex today. Being gay is cool, it said. Yeah right.

This is Redbridge.

I'm not gay! I don't know what I like… I mean I've never been with a girl, not once. I've kissed blokes, which is lovely. But girls… well… I can still get a hard-on by looking at big tits… can't I?

Woodford

What would Alison say? Her perfect little brother: a homosexual. My mum's precious angel: a dirty poof. My grandad's prize student: a filthy queer. Ten GCSEs under my belt and a degree in shagging blokes up the arse.

via

I'm so scared.

Hainault.

I've got to tell her. It's not fair keeping it from her. She's not going to have any grandchildren.

This is Gants Hill.

But is it any of her business if I like guys instead of girls? I mean, a lot of people do nowadays. It's almost normal… they're everywhere. *We're* everywhere.

This is Newbury Park.

What am I doing? By choosing being gay, I'm taking the wrong choice. I won't ever get married, won't have children, won't be accepted into society.

This is Barkingside.

Oh no! Teenagers!

Don't look at me like that! They know. I know they know. I'm an easy target, a soft guy, and a threat to masculinity.

The next station is:

It's written across my face. They're looking at me like I'm shite. Look away… yes look at the floor. Look out of the window. Don't make eye contact. I've gotta move carriages!

This is Hainault.

Why gay? If I admitted I was a member of the BNP I would probably get more respect! … That number…

This train

Should I ring it? Maybe I should write. Enclose a stamp… then they can write back. The Lesbian and Gay Helpline. Maybe I can go to the meetings.

terminates at

"Mum, it's just a little youth group…" Maybe they can help me. I can meet some more gay people.

Woodford.

Or maybe I should just come clean… Oh, come on train. Please.

Woodford.

What will she do? How shall she react? Go crazy. Deny it. Say "Don't be stupid!"

This is

But what harm is there in kissing a bloke?

Grange

I'll never see him again.

Hill.

Now Cat Deeley. *She's* sexy.

Beep!

But so are Boyzone.

This train terminates at Woodford.

And Mr Jones. He was gorgeous when he hadn't got his shirt on, teaching me how to play cricket in front of all the other kids in my class. I loved it when he taught me how to hold the bat… his hand holding my wrist… But he was married. And had a daughter. So he wouldn't have fancied me. God. I am really gay. I fancied my PE teacher.

The next station is Chigwell.

Two people know about me. Two. Four. Eight. Sixteen. Thirty-two. Sixty-four. One hundred and twenty-eight. The whole of Year 11 in about ten minutes. Southend in one hour. Essex in a week. Britain in a fortnight. The world.

This is Chigwell.

Life isn't fair towards gays. Everyone hates them. But why? Everyone likes Elton John though, and he's kissed more guys than I will ever do. Probably!

This is Roding Valley.

I wanted Dave to kiss me.

Thank you for travelling on

I just needed some friends, not a quick snog in the park.

the Central Line.

I'm so scared.

This is Woodford, all change please.

Debden.

Boys, I think, are much nicer than girls. Sweeter. More beautiful. Gorgeous, in fact. Delicious and stunning. Fabulously attractive. And I know I love them.

This train terminates at Epping.

My life terminates here. My mum will hate me forever. I can't keep lying to her. I told her, no more lies.

This is Theydon Bois.

Nearly at the station. Dad will be there now.

Terminates

The sky is clouding up. Looks like rain.

at Epping.

Gay life could be fun. I mean, all those parties, all that clubbing, all those men… all that sex.

Epping.

Now, Damon Albarn. He's cute. He's on my wall, and Mum doesn't care. I know.

This

But how can I be sure of anything I don't know?

is

Here we are.

Epping.

End of the line. This is Epping, change for misery, prejudice, violence and the ruin of your entire life for the next eighty years. Thank you for travelling on the Central Line.

All change please.

Hi Dad. Looks like rain, doesn't it?

KAI MORGAN VENICE

Reflections

The last rays of sunshine seep in through the window and strike the bottle in Tiara's hands, turning the amber liquid within to something more resembling honey freshly harvested from a beehive. She looks at it, astonished at how beautiful alcohol can appear, before raising the bottle to her lips and taking a healthy swig.

Tiara is not used to drinking hard liquor, and her abdomen heaves slightly when the strange brew hits. The alcohol, mixed with the thirty or so muscle relaxants she has already swallowed, does not make for a pleasing combination. With a much-practised force of will, she makes her stomach settle and accept what it has been given.

Turning on a table lamp and looking at herself in the mirror of the vanity at which she is seated, Tiara sees there is a mirror behind her also, which causes her image to be replicated infinitely. She considers it ironic that her reflection has already lived forever, while in reality her time is quite finite.

The thought occurs to Tiara that maybe this is not the best solution.

There is still time to change her mind, to make herself vomit. It isn't too late, yet. She has hardly begun thinking the words before realising what a deceit they are, what a falsehood her entire life has been. How dare she ever hope that a man could fall in love with her, actually want to marry *her*? She isn't a woman, no matter how she feels, hopes and prays. No matter how many hormones she takes or operations she has, she will always have to face the unsympathetic truth: she was born a male.

Be kind, don't threaten me with love.

Midway through their courtship, Tiara confessed to Jeffrey that the name given to her at birth was Timothy Ian Rogers. Jeff was confused, at first.

Tiara didn't say a word as one and one slowly made the sum of two in Jeff's mind. It was her turn to be puzzled when his look of dawning comprehension was replaced with a beaming smile, instead of the expected hurt and disgust.

"Don't you know that I'm in love with you, and nothing is going to change that?" he asked Tiara, holding her face gently in his large hands while he looked directly into her hazel eyes.

In that moment, Tiara was lost, although it took her several months to fully realise that fact.

When Jeff took her home to meet his parents, Tiara was the epitome of grace, beauty and charm – in public, under the illumination of the sun. Late at night, with only starlight and the pale glow of the moon to guide her, she would go into the bathroom and stare at herself in the mirror, speculating as to how long she could maintain this charade in front of Jeff's parents. How long before they became fully aware and rejected her? How long before this fairy tale reached its grim ending? There was no way in hell that they would allow their only son to marry her, an imperfect woman who had been born as a man. She would cry silent, yet harsh and immeasurably painful tears, then return to bed. Before succumbing to sleep, she would convince herself once more that everything would be OK in the morning, and if she continued to play her part exceptionally well, no one would be the wiser.

Be brave, not betrayed into heroism.

Taking another mouthful of the amber liquid, Tiara is reminded of the first time one of her tricks came in her mouth. She remembers it was bitter, and tasted of smoke. When Tiara swallowed the pungent nectar, she imagined it burning as it went down her throat and oesophagus; she felt it hit the pit of her stomach like nitroglycerin. That organ had heaved in protest then as well, but the thought of the generous tip she would earn for the act made it easy to control the urge to be sick.

Let not the wind cry for my lost soul.

Throughout her teenage years, Tiara had done many things for money. She justified them all, because she believed once she had her surgery, everything would be perfect. It didn't take long after her return from Thailand for that dream to make itself known as just that – illusory, ephemeral, an infinite span of time encapsulated in a few minutes. Just a daydream, and a nightmare.

Outwardly, Tiara appeared in all aspects to be a twenty-four-year-old, caramel-coloured, soft-voiced, attractive, self-assured and full-figured woman. At one point, after a heated make-out session at Jeff's apartment, she had let him fuck her and come inside her because he told her that she had a pretty vagina.

Conversely, Tiara grew increasingly doubtful about her ability to pass.

She began to imagine that casual observers could see right through her, to the indestructible part of her that was wholly and undeniably male. When she looked in the mirror, the person who looked back was not a woman, but a tomboy: a freak who had purchased her right to be a woman by selling her womanhood. The irony of it was almost comical. Almost.

Life and circumstance had conspired to make Tiara a great natural actress. For years, she had looked up to, and modelled herself after, such film stars as Sigourney Weaver (for her strength), Michelle Pfeiffer (for her sensitivity) and Meg Ryan (for her sense of humour). But after being made into a woman, she could not stop thinking that nothing she did was real, that it was all a performance. She stopped going to the movies, because seeing such ultimate specimens of womanliness and femininity as Jennifer Lopez (seductive), Salma Hayek (sensual) and Denise Richards (sultry) made her feel like a cheap imposter.

Let not the sun die for my broken heart.

There was a meteor shower on the night that Jeff proposed to Tiara; she felt that the universe was crying for her. Quick, hot, fierce, scintillating tears – tears that she was no longer capable of producing herself. Deep inside she had known that the sky was crying because she was nearing the end.

However, caught up in the fantasy, Tiara went so far as to use the last of her SRS savings to have a wedding dress custom-made. A strapless, matte satin sheath that flared dramatically above the knee to create a natural chapel-length train, with a band of rhinestones and pearls across the bodice, which added just the right touch of flash to what was otherwise a simple dress.

Wearing the dress now, on the night before her wedding, makes Tiara feel more than ever like a stage actress. She almost made it, almost fooled herself into believing the scripted ending would be a happy one – but no more. The charade is over, the play finished, time for the final curtain call.

The angels are singing to me, lulling me to sleep.

Her left hand is full of pills, which Tiara throws into her mouth and swallows with a large mouthful of whiskey. If she had not been so tired, she would have experienced brief amazement at how easily this batch went down.

Tiara replaces the cap on the bottle with difficulty – her fingers seem to take an inordinate amount of time to respond to her brain's commands – and puts the half-empty container in the top left-hand drawer of the vanity.

She has an almost overwhelming desire to lie down and sleep, but she forces herself to stand and look at her reflection in the full-length mirror set in the door of the armoire behind her.

They keep calling me.

Only if she were wearing the item of jewellery that was her namesake could Tiara have looked more radiant. In the depths of her despair, she practically glows with emotion. The white wedding dress seems incandescent next to her skin.

Looking at herself through eyes made hazy with drugs and alcohol, Tiara accepts how gorgeous she looks, understanding that she appears this way only because she is doomed.

I don't want to go.

Before the warm, fuzzy feeling she is experiencing can intensify enough to incapacitate her, Tiara returns to the vanity and with clumsy fingers takes hold of a folded slip of notepaper lying there, then shuffles the few steps to the adjacent bed and crawls into it.

Lying on her back, Tiara feels the life draining out of her. Replacing it is a numbness that starts in her extremities and slowly extends throughout her body, taking away her senses of touch, taste, smell and hearing. The only thing left is sight, and as her breathing becomes shallower, that sense begins to fade also. Darkness closes in on her, shrouding the dim light of the lamp in fine traceries of shadow; a web that grows thicker until the room fades from view.

Tiara is startled to discover that she is still thinking. She wonders if she has become a ghost, but abandons that thought upon noticing she is still breathing. In the space between one breath and the next, she forgets exactly what it is you're supposed to do to continue breathing. A small part of her remaining consciousness tells her this is reason to panic, but she doesn't remember how to do that either.

Having no feeling or purpose, Tiara begins to believe she really *is* a ghost; obviously she is just a shade of her former self. Then her brain dies and she thinks nothing at all.

Save yourself.

Jeff is standing outside the bedroom door. Having just completed composing his vows, he is unable to resist the urge to see his beloved bride-to-be, even though tradition says that it is bad luck to do so on the night before the wedding. He knocks softly. Receiving no reply, he quietly opens the door and enters the room.

Tiptoeing to Tiara's bedside, Jeff stands over her, his gaze taking in every detail. He marvels at the awesome sight of this woman he is going to marry. Spotting the piece of paper in her hand, he averts his eyes, not wanting to spoil the surprise of hearing her wedding vows for the first time at the altar tomorrow.

Slowly, Jeff leans over to brush Tiara's lips with his own. Her mouth is cool against his, and she seems very still. Too still, as though she is not breathing at all. Straightening up, he looks more closely at the folded paper in Tiara's hand.

He stands frozen, and his heart stops beating after reading the only two visible words.

Save me.

ZIO J WALSH

No Shame In My Game

Harsh electric light gave Sean's alabaster skin a corpse-like hue. In the muggy July air he was sweaty, the tropical dampness preying on his nerves and brain.

Beyond his little pool of electric light, London was dark. In the world where Sean lived, it seemed to be forever dark, day or night. Grubby toilet cubicles in dimly lit public loos. Curtains pulled hurriedly across in cheap motels. The occasional trick in some gloomy underground car park. The shadowy back of a tradesman's van.

Dark.

Sean once told a social worker that he slept through the day, so that he could sleep his way through the night. Spoke his line totally deadpan and waited for the look of horror. It never came. But Sean suddenly saw the truth in his black humour. The hole that he was digging for himself.

It was one social worker in a succession of social workers who paraded through his life with dwindling frequency. They knew he was beyond their help. Maybe beyond *everyone's* help.

Sean was sullen and unsociable when he was eight. By ten he was truant, and a runaway by eleven. By the time of his thirteenth birthday he was laid up in hospital with his wrists open. Their insides were a pretty pink, but he hadn't had much time to look before another well-meaning social worker found him. Sean was discovered propped up against a wall in the corner of his room at the hostel, a broken toy no one wanted.

That was five years ago. He didn't want to die any more, but the trouble was he didn't really want to live. Not like this, anyway.

Sean didn't know the name of the back-street. A couple of cars had cruised past him, but none had stopped. Maybe this wasn't a pick-up spot. He preferred to meet the johns in bars, but tonight he didn't have a choice. They had kicked him out of Annie's the night before, ostensibly for letting down the tone.

Yeah, right.

The previous week, their excuse had been that he looked so young. Which he did, although he was eighteen and that should have been enough. Sometimes he felt his boyish looks and full-lipped mouth really worked against him. That, and the crossed eyes which confused many a john.

He sighed and popped some gum into his mouth. He was half-thankful for the lack of punters, but the flipside was he needed the money. Their money.

The coppers appeared magically from nowhere. Sean said, "Piss off," quite proficient in this sort of exchange. The cops smiled knowingly at each other. Laughing at him. Pitying him, perhaps. Definitely not understanding him.

Equally practised – although they knew they were on the winning side, so it didn't really matter – they intoned: "Now sir, that's not a very helpful attitude, is it?"

Sean glanced up and down the road, like he could still be there doing trade when they'd gone and left him in peace.

Yeah, right.

"How old are you?"

"Old enough."

"Got any ID on you?"

"My wallet's in my other jacket, yeah?"

"So, why don't you make our job easier and just move along."

Sean sighed. "Yeah, right."

⋆

The law wasn't about to stop him earning his living. But Sean didn't want to risk a night in jail, so the streets were off limits tonight, which left the Scrubs – and the thought of that made him sick.

A wooded hollow, the Scrubs was bounded on one side by the rear of the railway station, and sloped down towards the canal on the other side. In daylight it provided cover for schoolkids skipping class. Building companies sometimes dumped their refuse there to avoid paying the fee for commercial waste. Joyriders abandoned their stolen cars, burning them in a fiery testament to their misdemeanours.

In the dark, it was a completely different place.

The main clearing had evolved over the years, the natural flora crushed by joyriders, builders' trucks, and the secret nightlife. The usual posse of fuckers and fuckees, the mutual masturbators and the disciples of scatology. Transient lovers who might never know the taste of their partner's lips. Men who touch but don't look. A silent carnival of the fucked and the fucked up, a place where the show is all inside your head.

Sean kept his head down as he passed a couple of cruisers perched on the bonnet of an abandoned Ford. Their tapedeck was churning out hard-core techno, the minimalistic bass hardly masking the grunts and groans from the bushes.

Sean didn't want to talk to them. He wasn't cruising. He wasn't one of them.

Their eyes followed him but their heads didn't move. Sean knew they knew. This pair, whose unofficial task it was to keep this patch of wasteground safe from cops and queerbashers, they *knew* what he was.

Everyone came here for one thing only, the dirty bid for illicit sex. Strangers who didn't want to know each other, and who didn't have to pretend like they would in a bar. Men who dispensed with the lubrication of small talk. Men who wanted to cast off the trappings of civilisation for a night and be animals.

Sean hated it. It was stinking, low and dirty. The men who frequented the Scrubs were sad and desperate creatures. They embarrassed him. He embarrassed himself too, profiting from their vulgar need for degradation. But he was young, too stupid to know any better. These men were husbands, doctors and politicians. Supermarket managers and priests. What was their excuse? What made them so sick, so pitiful, so completely thick?

Keeping to the worn dirt track that wound its way through the woods, Sean fumbled in his pocket for his pack of Silk Cut and lighter. He hated smoking, but Chel suggested he try it whilst on the job, claiming it looked casual and sexy. To Sean, who was something of a romantic at heart, the terms *casual* and *sexy* sounded like the ultimate oxymoron.

Reluctantly he took a drag, trying not to retch as the foul smoke filled his lungs. The only time he enjoyed it was after he turned a trick. It went some way towards masking the taste of semen – the sickly, bitter taste of a stranger's come. He wondered idly if cigarettes should be included in the price, as an expense.

"So you think we're self-employed, do you?" Chel had said, the first time he complained. "You prick. Johnny Steele takes a cut out of everything we make. The more tricks we turn, the more he gets, the more we get, the happier everyone is. Got it?"

His cigarette burned away in the dark. From a distance, it might have looked like just one more star in a constellation of burning tips. From a distance, Sean was no different from everyone else lurking around in the bushes tonight.

*

Johnny Steele had been Sean's first pimp – a big-time gangster, notoriously vicious and quietly psychotic. Johnny Steele was rumoured, amongst other things, to be bisexual. He was renowned for his collection of pornography, gay, straight, bestial, whatever. The police, forever raiding his properties, never discovered anything more shocking than *Penthouse* and *Blueboy*.

Sean had handed over his meagre savings in four weekly instalments because he couldn't face selling himself. Couldn't face some stranger touching his body, whispering his name like he was Jesus fuckin' Christ himself.

Of course, Johnny Steele was never really a pimp, not in the strict sense of the word. He never ran a stable, only demanded a weekly payment in return for protection. Protection, not from the punters but from Steele's thugs, who might have extinguished their cigarettes in his face if he didn't pay up.

Winter had been coming and Sean had no money left. The squat he shared with several other homeless young men was due for demolition, with them still inside or not. He had to start earning. The alternative was that Steele's chums would rearrange his face in such a way that no one would ever pay him for anything again.

And then Johnny Steele was dead. Sean should have been relieved, except that Chel fixed them up with another thug right away. Another tough, another levy. Only this time Sean had no more money.

The messy set of events had led him to his present situation. But he couldn't turn the clock back. Though there were times when he would have liked to stop it.

*

The black guy was leaning against a tree. Hair growing into a neatly trimmed Afro, skin the colour of caramel.

Sean smiled at him, sensing his blood rushing from his head to another no less important organ of his body. The man smiled back, and Sean signalled that he should follow him into the trees.

"All right?" he said, touching his hand. The man pulled back, his face tense. Sean estimated that he was pushing forty, and maturing very nicely.

"So, how much to fuck you?" he asked blandly, almost as if he were asking a market trader the price of his wares. Businesslike. To the point.

Sean's face crumpled. He backed out of the bushes onto the trail again.

"Nothing, man," he muttered to himself, "that's all. It'd have cost you nothing." *If you hadn't asked me that.*

"You talking to *me*?"

Sean glanced up. Standing where the black guy had been was a white boy. Fucking perfect negative image. In his mid-thirties, maybe, kitted out in flawless skinhead drag, all leather jacket and tattoos. But the eyes gave it away. Where a real skinhead's might have been like mirrors, cold and hard, this prick had eyes like a mummy's boy. Soft. Nervous. Eyelashes batting away like an Atomic Kitten's.

Sean felt an urge to laugh, wondering if he knew how stupid he looked. A City banker, just taking a shortcut on the way back from the pub. That's what he'd say if the Old Bill caught him. Sean glanced around, looking for the rest of the 'gang', but they were alone.

Mummy's boy couldn't take his eyes off him. A sheen of sweat gleaming on his forehead spoiled his evil skinhead demeanour.

"Got a clever filtering system," Chel once told him. "Believe me, if they're in there, it's for head. Only fags get let through."

The City boy tried smiling, but it turned out as a highly strung leer. Mechanically, Sean smiled back, but inside his stomach turned over. The trick dropped his cigarette and gestured with a flick of his head towards a clump of bushes. In the moonlight, Sean could see that the grass was wet, but it hadn't rained in a fortnight. He took one last drag of his cigarette, flicked it into the damp bushes, and followed on.

They closed the distance between them, still wary, each excited in different ways by the intimacy that would follow.

Ten metres, five metres, and then two. Until they were touching and the trick had thrust his tongue down Sean's throat. His breath stank of stale coffee and Sean wondered how many skinheads had a quick cappuccino after work.

"Turn around," he slurred in Sean's ear.

Sean complied, trying not to think about what was happening. He heard a buckle opening, the rustle of the City boy's denim. Rough hands pulling down Sean's trackpants in one fluid movement.

He hugged a tree, focusing on the bird's nest up in the branches. He wondered if it had eggs in it, or a few cuddly chicks maybe. Glad he didn't have to face the trick, glad he didn't have to lie on his back with his legs in the air. This was bad enough, but at least he could crane his neck up at the bird's nest. Pretend he was taking a shit.

The trick made it easy. He didn't even use his hands as he pounded away, grunting like a pig with its snout in the trough. He didn't touch Sean. Didn't even slap his backside.

It took him ten minutes. Then he pulled out and Sean quickly turned to face him, relieved to see him peel away a condom and toss it into the bushes. Come dripped from it onto the leaves, looking like mayonnaise on lettuce.

"Great," the trick grunted, tightening his buckle. "Thanks."

He tucked in his T-shirt in and turned to go.

Sean panicked. "Wait!"

City Boy half-turned, looking like he might panic and run, himself.

"Could you spare a few quid?" Sean asked. "I'm short this week."

"You *what*?"

"I'm broke," Sean said feebly, wondering what Chel would do. The answer came back mocking him: *Get paid, that's what.*

"So what do you want me to do about it?"

"Listen, man," Sean said quietly, his voice a few octaves higher than he would have liked it to be, "Just gimme twenty quid and I'll be off. I'm not looking for trouble, right?"

A knife flashed in the trick's hand, looking like part of his anatomy as it glinted in the moonlight. This flash City boy, trying to be something he wasn't, was taking his performance to heart. His voice hushed and eyes bulging out of their sockets, he repeated, "You *what*?"

"Man, I need the money," Sean ploughed on. He wished that he'd had a knife himself. He was being used. Did this clown actually think he was the type to prowl around in the scrub looking for a fuck? He was eighteen. He could have anyone he wanted.

The trick's whole body had tensed – this was his bonus side-show, a fresh insight into the skinhead experience. His eyes were alight now, more so than when he had been fucking Sean. His lips were twitching into a snarl. His fingers grasped the knife tighter still, and he was making little stabbing gestures in anticipation of the kill.

The City boy was becoming an animal.

Sean backed off, then began to run, only to trip on a thick surface root. As the trick advanced towards him, Sean scrambled to his feet and surged through the bushes onto the path.

*

It was a sticky, humid evening and Jomo could feel his shirt sticking to his back as he waited to cross the road. He was wearing a tight white singlet and jeans by BC Ethnic, with chunky, tan-coloured construction boots. He was planning to take a stroll through the market square, shoulders dipping and the tight fabric of his jeans accentuating his physique. Jomo wasn't averse to the odd wolf-whistle or stolen glance on his way to the Flying Horse.

He was standing on the street corner, waiting for a break in the traffic, when the noise of rustling branches and snapping twigs grabbed his attention. Across the road, a boy – maybe seventeen or eighteen – was pushing his way through a gap in a chainlink fence. His face was scratched from stray branches, and leaves clung to his hair. The boy stumbled and, panting, glanced wildly about him.

"Hey yo! What happen, guy?" Jomo shouted out. The boy glanced briefly at him, confused. Then he tore off across the road, without a word, narrowly missing a passing car.

Jomo was wondering what was happening when the chainlink rattled again. A second, older man with a crop pushed his way out onto the street. Jomo gawked at him as he casually tucked away a flick-knife.

"What you staring at, darky?" the crop sneered, stomping off in the opposite direction to the one taken by the boy.

"Rass to you, an' all," Jomo yelled, flicking his middle finger at him in anger. But it wasn't worth the effort, and he had heard much worse in his time.

Crossing the road, Jomo let his mind drift back to the boy. He was oddly attractive. Not in the conventional pretty boy manner, but slightly freaky, askew. Like a comic-strip artist had dashed his angular features off in a flurry of pen strokes. Young and hard, yet vulnerable. His skin so white that Jomo wanted to touch it, to see if it was real. And those crazy eyes, sexily crossed, betraying his terror. Jomo imagined staring into them, hypnotised by the warped effect of their lack of synchronisation.

What was he doing in the Scrubs though? Tricking? Drugs? Queerbashing? Or being queerbashed himself? He didn't look your typical, furtive cruiser, but who did? Perhaps, so innocently, he was taking a shortcut home?

Jomo wondered why he should even care, and put it down to the humidity. A gap appeared in the traffic.

*

Sean was shouting at Chel, "I nearly got killed, I nearly got fuckin' killed," and he usually kept his head down and never shouted at anyone. Never ever.

Equally flustered, Chel was yelling back at him. "Look, just shut up. Just shut the fuck up, OK? I gotta think, man."

For Chel this was a major setback – he had spent months trying to convince Sean that doing rent was an easy option for them. Chel paced the floorboards of the dusty old warehouse where they squatted. His dirty copper hair matched his flushed, freckled face for tint. A rusty nail clattered at his foot and he kicked it into the corner.

"Jesus fuckin' Christ!" Sean exploded, punching one of the wooden posts in frustration. He was still breathing hard after his nightmarish dash back to safety. He had fallen twice because he was concentrating on looking over his shoulder, instead of where he was going. He looked a state.

"I said shut up!" Chel practically screamed. His mind in overdrive, he chewed on his lip. "Cooper wants paid, yeah? You gotta go back down the Scrubs or else we're both gonna be fucked."

Sean looked hard at him, his dark eyes narrowing to dangerous slits.

"No, you listen to *me* for a change," Sean said. "I'm not going back there again. Man, I'm sick of this shit, yeah?"

Chel stared hard at him for a moment, then backed off, his hands raised in a placating gesture, before sitting on the edge of an overturned crate. As Chel gnawed his fingernails, Sean watched anxiously, wondering what that devious mind would concoct next.

When Chel finally spoke, his tone was unusually accommodating.

"Right," he said. "So you won't do rent? That's your choice, man. But I can't be the only one earning. You're gonna have to do something else for that cash."

Sean wondered what else there was.

★

Jomo watched his mate Lee gulp down a pint of lager, and raise his hand for another. Jomo's fascination with Lee's state of vocational inertia bordered on obsessive. How anyone could spend their life without any goals, dreams or aspirations whatsoever – as Lee apparently did – was beyond him. Aspirations, that is, beyond the next football match, or finding a well-endowed female.

They first met three years back, when Jomo was still a fag-acting straight. As opposed to a straight-acting fag, as he now claimed to be. It was at some nameless club in the West End, and Jomo had discovered all his records had been lost somewhere between Ibiza and Heathrow.

Divine intervention, his mum would have said. She didn't like dance music, clubs or London. Or Ibiza, for that matter. She liked *Cell Block H* and Jamaican politics, which seemed to keep her happy most of the time.

Promoters were a breed apart. Jomo could hardly go running to them, "Umm, you know what, guy? I've lost all me records. Funny, innit?" Promoters, in Jomo's experience, were frequently unhinged psychos running on coke. They paid big-name DJs like Boy George and Judge Jules zillions whilst the ones with real talent – namely Jomo Lamont – barely scraped a living together. And there he was in the West End, a dancefloor full of garage-heads and him with a crate of cheap seven-inch singles left over from someone's wedding do.

OK, Lighthouse Family. 'High'. Disco mix. Twelve minutes. Sigh of relief.

Panic stations.

He recognised the Chinese lad from the gym. He was a mate of a mate whom he might have said hello to a few times. He was asking Jomo for a Jungle Brothers cut, Urban Takeover mix and nothing less, thank you very much.

"Wheel and come again man, wheel!" he grinned, and Jomo showed him his sad crate of seven inches. Lee grinned still wider and disappeared into the crowd.

Twelve minutes flew by quicker than Jomo ever imagined they could. Rummaging in the crate he found a half-decent mix of a Craig David track. He was sweating. The crowd were looking less like a crowd by the second and more like people wondering whether to cross the dancefloor to the bar or the toilets.

Two minutes were left on 'Rewind' and he peered into the box, coming up with a Whitney Houston record. Just a pity, he supposed, that it wasn't a gay club.

Then someone pushed a crate of twelve-inch vinyl into his arms. Lee, his face shiny with sweat, grinned impishly.

"Wheel DJ!"

Jomo peered into the crate. Classic garage stuff: Master Stepz, Zed Bias, London's Unique 3. He felt like crying. His ass was covered.

It later transpired that Lee had rushed around to his flat, grabbed his records and hurried back. Jomo couldn't imagine how he managed to cut a thirty-minute journey down to under twenty. He was afraid to ask.

Music was the unifying factor in their odd couple friendship, their shared passion for trendspotting and hunting out the rarest of tunes. They had come to blows only once, Lee denouncing the Ultimate Kaos remake of 'Casanova', preferring the Levert original. Jomo stood by the new version, supposedly because he liked the banging remixes. In reality he fancied the seriously underage lead singer.

Lee was one of the first people to whom Jomo outed himself. Lee had only been vexed that Jomo felt the need to make an issue out of it. After some mutual testing, along the lines of *Are you still down?*, they both got rat-arsed in the Flying Horse. It was a huge boost to Jomo's confidence, and it bonded the Chinese lad from Hackney and the black boy from the East End for life.

"Two pints, man?" Jomo exclaimed. "In two minutes? Some record, guy."

"I got issues, braa. Mum's been having a go, wants me back in school doing me leaving."

Jomo blew his cheeks out. "You're twenty-two. Bit late, innit?"

"S'what, I said, y'know?" Lee turned his attention away for a minute, clasping hands with a couple of toughs Jomo only vaguely recognised.

"Who they?" he demanded when they passed.

"The Couscous twins." Lee gestured irritably for a second round. "Old man's from Sierra Leone, mum's Malaysian. Used to hang off Jay Rogan's Yardie mates one time."

"Nice," Jomo murmured, trying to keep his eye on them through the swelling crowd at the bar. "They straight or what?"

"Yeah, guy. Fuckers used to make me go down on them though, back in the day. Heard they did some porn together one time."

Jomo wondered if his mate was just mouthing off. He wanted to press him further on the subject, but their beers had arrived and Lee was off on another tangent.

"So what about this kid, Jom? Sounds like you got the stiffs."

"He was just some kid," Jomo shrugged. "Weird-looking, man. Like he wasn't real."

"You been watching too many nasty videos, my man. Got you all twisted up here." Lee tapped his head. "Seriously Jom, you know what goes on down in the Scrubs. Fucking glue sniffers, perverts. Wouldn't catch me in there even if Jennifer Lopez was spread-eagled naked and waiting, braa."

"You're some sick puppy, Lee, you know that, man?"

"Watch this space," Lee grinned, finishing his pint.

★

Chel and Sean were standing in the stairwell of a block of flats overlooking the canal near to where they lived. They each carried an empty rucksack and Sean was looking distinctly uncomfortable. The hole in the fence from which he had earlier escaped the Scrubs gaped like an open wound. He turned to Chel.

"I don't like this," he said. "I never done none of this before."

Chel sniffed and spat a glob of phlegm down into the canal.

"Go and turn a few tricks if you don't like it. Or *you* can tell Cooper why we don't have his cut this week."

Sean followed Chel up the bleached concrete steps. "I don't know why we've gotta pay him. It ain't fair," Sean protested.

"Because, you dickbrain, it's the way it works. If we don't pay him we get fucked over – big time. By his lot or any other posse who wants an easy profit."

Sean said nothing as they continued upwards. If this was the case, then why was he almost knifed earlier on? So much for protection.

Ruthlessly, Chel said, "We do one flat each, then leg it. You savvy?"

Sean nodded reluctantly.

"We meet back at the squat. Make sure you get it right this time, OK?"

★

The night air was still sultry as Jomo crossed back over the road to his building. He hurried into the lobby, the thought of his flat and its air conditioner foremost in mind. The fire escape door banging open startled him as he waited for the lift. He turned to see a freckle-faced youth emerging from the fire escape. On his back was a bulging rucksack, and on his face a shady expression that screamed 'BURGLAR'.

"Here, what you been doing up in there?" Jomo demanded, moving between him and the entranceway.

"Fuck off, mate," the lad sneered.

Jomo pushed his hand into his chest as the boy tried to edge past him.

"What's your name?" Jomo asked, by now thoroughly suspicious.

"Chel, what's yours?"

Jomo ignored the question. "Do you live here, man?"

Chel blew his cheeks out, avoiding Jomo's suspicious eye.

"Look, my old man's just gone and turfed me out. If you want bother, go hassle him, got it?"

Jomo stared at him for a moment longer. "OK, guy, I'm sorry. You gotta be careful these days, yeah?"

"No problem, mate," Chel snorted, shoving past him and out into the night.

Jomo shrugged and returned to waiting for the lift. The indicator implied that it was still in the basement, and he kissed his teeth. The stairs beckoned.

★

Sean had dropped his torch down the fire escape. He didn't bother looking down. In the flat he was afraid to turn on any lights, and besides, Chel had told him not to. With just the faint glow from a groovy-looking lava lamp, the flat was dark.

Negotiating his way by touch, Sean filled his bag with compact discs of every cool genre: garage, drum'n'bass, hip-hop, rap, acid jazz, techno, deep house. He bagged a mini-disc player and several other worthwhile odds and ends. The DVD player, he guessed, could fit easily under his arm. And God help him if he dropped *that* on his way back down the fire escape. Whoever lived here, Sean thought, was a real music junkie. Framed posters of Roni Size, Massive Attack and a blues guitarist Sean didn't immediately recognise covered the walls.

His mind spun from the adrenaline pumping through him. Dizziness caused him to crouch down, and he heaved in a deep breath.

A Sailor In Sydney, *Caribbean Beat*, *Asian Sex Odyssey*... The DVDs stacked under the television probably weren't Lonely Planet travelogues.

The voyeur in Sean rose and stretched, as if from a long sleep, despite the danger of his situation – and was in full morning glory with it.

"Fuck," he muttered, staring transfixed at the buffed, plucked and totally unattainable sex pups gracing the covers. He licked his dry lips, feeling another dizzy spell coming on, and slipped several discs in with the rest of his loot. He decided to keep *Caribbean Beat* for himself, and slipped it into his pocket.

Flushed and panting, he stood up and glanced around for some loose cash. None was in evidence, but the fridge, like a mirage, begged his attention. He opened the door, white light cutting his eyes. He pulled a Lemon Ruski from the door, rolling its icy cold surface across his forehead. He unscrewed the top and gulped down the sweet Russian vodka, letting himself pretend, just for a moment, that this was *his* flat...

"Oh *shit!*"

Sean's heart stopped as he heard a key in the front door. His eyes stretched wide as the hinges squealed. Light flooded in from the corridor outside. A silhouette advanced on him, gigantic and athletic, all curvy thighs and broad shoulders.

Light transformed the flat as the interloper flicked a switch. It felt like an eternity for Sean before his eyes adjusted to the light. He dropped his bag, unable to tear his eyes away from the slack-jawed stranger. They stood there gaping at each other, unable to move.

Sean turned and tripped over his own bag, cursing his stupidity as the stranger sprinted towards him. Sean scrambled to his feet and sprinted for the balcony doors, ignoring the angry shouts of the black man whose flat this must be.

"Fuck!" Sean cussed, as the man seized his arm and twisted it up behind his back. Sean lashed out with his foot, extracting a yelp of pain from the man as his foot connected with his shin. Sean made a third reckless dash for the balcony door. But the man threw himself at him, driving Sean into a wall. The thud rattled the boy's teeth and knocked the breath from his body.

*

Jomo pressed his body against that of the young burglar, snatching a wrist in each hand as he struggled against him. Up close, Jomo finally managed to get a look at his face. With a shock, he recognised the youth who earlier that evening had burst out of the Scrubs.

"Wait a minute!" Jomo yelled, but his captive took advantage of his lapse and pulled his arms free, pummelling him on the back. "I'm not gonna hurt you, guy," Jomo said, grabbing again at the furiously pounding arms. Exhausted, the boy looked up at him, eyes wide with panic.

Jomo scowled at him, grinding his teeth as his anger overrode his surprise. Just who did he think he was exactly? This kid, invading his personal space. Rifling through his possessions like he had the God-given fucking right. Jomo set his jaw, fighting the urge to smack the youth one, but taking care not to release him. He wondered what the hell to do next.

Fear gripped him then. There might be another one, another housebreaker in his home. Standing right behind him with a flick-knife in hand.

"Who else is here?" he demanded, voice choked with fear and panic. "Answer me, man, is anyone else here?"

The boy shook his head dumbly, but Jomo had no reason to believe him. Then again, the boy looked more frightened than he did. Jomo had an almost uncontrollable urge to laugh hysterically, but in fact he was feeling sorry for the terrified lad. How old was he? Sixteen? Seventeen?

No, that wasn't true, he told himself, he wasn't sorry for him, he was pissed off. Who knew what damage he had done? What *might* he have done if Jomo hadn't turned up when he did? Nightmare visions of his CD collection being flogged off on some street market stall filled his head, and he had another urge to smack the boy. But really he was trying to figure out what to do.

The kid made his decision for him. Cross-eyed and flushed hot pink, he lifted his head a little and kissed Jomo on the lips, eyes fixed on Jomo's, which were wide open with sheer incredulity.

Jomo tasted cherry-flavoured bubblegum as the young burglar sucked on his lower lip. Just for a moment, Jomo let him, because the weird eroticism of the moment was getting him hard. Then anger overcame him and he pushed the kid away. *What game is he playing here?* Jomo wondered. *First he robs me blind, then he sticks his tongue down my throat. Weird, this is just too weird.*

"What up with you man?" Jomo yelled, pushing the boy back on the floor and recoiling to a defensive position.

"Shit," the thief spat, looking like he might burst into tears. Looking hungry and desperate. And angry.

Jomo wondered just who he was angry at. He turned away from the boy, suddenly unable to look at him. A half-empty Lemon Ruski sat atop an empty CD stack, and he gratefully seized it, gulping down the remainder in one thirsty gulp. He tossed the empty bottle to one side and it rolled under the sofa. Returning his attention to the boy, Jomo saw he looked scared and dangerous. Jomo wondered how he himself must look to the lad. Big, bad and black, no doubt.

He speculated again on what he should do. Call the Old Bill? Let him go, or what?

The words jumped around inside his head – *or what?* – and he wondered if the kid knew he had a hard-on. Jomo reached out to help him up, not quite sure about what he was doing. The boy was on the move anyway, scrambling to his feet and out the door.

Jomo didn't try and stop him. He waited for his breathing to slow down to normal before he crossed the room and closed the front door. His foot connected with something the young burglar had dropped in his hurry to flee.

Bending down, Jomo picked up his copy of *Caribbean Beat*, the Mendez twins gazing from the cover at him. He pondered on what the hell had just happened: why he didn't tear after the young thug and collar him; why he wasn't vexed like he should've been.

"Stay cool, guy," he muttered. "Gonna have some of that ass." Jomo smiled, and hoped. They were going to meet again sometime. And he couldn't wait.

JUSTIN WARD

Forever Geek

From our bench in James Street, the world – just for a moment – stood still. The people on the street faded away. The sound of the birds and the traffic and an intruding road drill suddenly became muted. The sun went behind the clouds. All there was to look at was your face, your beautiful eyes, and a single tear that hung on your cheek.

You said you didn't want to stay together any more.

All the air went out of my chest as it caved in on itself. For a split second, the last four years of our lives flashed through my head. A thousand shared moments hit me all at once. The time you held me in your arms when I'd had that bad day at work. The day you cried at *International Velvet*, the night you laughed at me when I pissed the bed, and the night when we shared a four hundred quid win at Bingo. How amazing it felt to share, to know someone who understood me so completely.

But then, as I watched the tear trickle down your cheek, I was suddenly seventeen years old again. Not fabulous, but freaky. All the supermodel manoeuvres I'd learnt, gone. All my confidence, evaporated. The *geek* was back. You wouldn't know him though, would you? He was the one you left alone, while you were dancing with Angel. The one you never looked at. Maybe you never saw him. He lived just below my surface. But he was there.

Geek was the one who cried when Richard Dreyfuss walked into the mothership and when Pat had that argument with Frank about Roy and when you didn't empty the ashtray. *Geek* was the boy who took lots of walks down on Bankside and shed tears on Waterloo Bridge.

I remembered all the tears of *mine* you had kept. All that power I gave away. You never really understood how my tears empowered you.

I can't believe you're leaving me just because I like Maria Callas and Depeche Mode. That boy, Angel, doesn't like Maria Callas, does he? He likes Daft Punk and techno and taking E. He likes fun and being 'fabulous'. Like life is all about having the right haircut and wearing fun fur. He thinks he can entertain you. But he's just a part of me you've never seen. There must be so many parts of me you haven't seen yet. Maybe that's why this has got to happen. Maybe we can't see those things, so close up. Maybe we'll have to get to know each other all over again, in another way. But not with Angel. He's not *me*.

You're not who you used to be. You're lost. I don't even think *you* know who you are. I know you well and it's time you were on your own for a while. You don't touch my knee any more and say "I love you", or "Who's my baby?", or "Don't worry". You've got razor blades in the palms of your hands. I get cut every time you touch me. And you've got a black tear hanging from you cheek.

If you need me, catch a bus to Waterloo Bridge. I'll be on Bankside with the *geek* and all those other parts of me you've never seen, and all the world in me. Maybe you'll see it all one day. For now, I'll just catch that tear in the palm of my hand.

As I do, I hear the sound of the birds and the traffic, and the people come back to life, and the road driller starts drilling again and the dismal sun comes from behind the clouds. I want to curse the daylight. Go now, before I start crying again.

There's a piece of me missing. Like a frozen organ, stolen from a cadaver.

You walk off with a headache. I want you to turn and say something. Anything. Just an acknowledgment, for the last four years. *Something* to say it wasn't all a waste of time. That you'll miss me. That it was important to you. That it will be something you'll never forget. That this is agony and you hate doing it and if only things were different… if only we were older, wiser… we could have worked it out… but… nothing… Just a headache.

Lunch hour over. Back to work. Deep breath, off you go. Ta-da.

I know you've just died inside. It's hurting, isn't it? Does it feel like a knife in your lungs? Like a chest infection… wheezing… you can't get your breath? That headache's like a rock! So why don't you say so? Why the *fuck* don't you say something? *Say* something!

I take a deep breath now, drawing in the Earth's energy to stand up on my own and face the world and the roaring traffic and those chirpy little bastard birds. I look at the tear in my hand. A solid glass droplet. Black and shiny like polished jet. It's hard and dense and it vibrates. I watch you walk down the street. I love you. I could even wave goodbye. But I won't do that. Why would I? I believe we were meant for this world together. Like soul mates.

Tomorrow will be different. You might not recognise me. It'll be like getting to know a new friend. But this time, don't be so sure of yourself. I might look like a *geek* but I'm taller than Angel – remember? And *know* that I have an amazing power in a tear in the palm of my hand.

DAVID WATKINS

Girl

So I'm the boy, and I'm fingering this boy but he is a girl tonight. And my middle finger gently pushes in, where the flesh parts between her legs, where it is moist and warm like olive oil and my finger is sliding in gently, slowly, and my cock – which is planted next to her left thigh – aches, and she touches me there lightly… lingering… my head tingling. Fingers of sensation slide up my thighs and around my balls, radiating like a sneeze. Jon's a girl tonight. A real girl. And he lets me push my clenched hand, fingers balled, into her damp pale skin.

In front of the mirror Jon gazes at his female reflection, his blue eyes gazing back. Shifting this way and that, irises wide open, with eyelashes in glistening, bristling curls – dark and glossy black. Marble filaments. Pouting pale lips. He puts a hand to his head, three silver bracelets slipping down his arm, and he pushes his hand, fingers splayed, through a feather-cut lawn of short, soft black hair.

★

I first meet Jen in a popular city club lit by lasers and deep gels and these fantastic lucid projections which flit across the walls like blown confetti. She leans lightly against a raised circular steel table, several metres from where I stand. She's wearing a high-collared, blue-eye coloured jacket, silver-zipped down her chest, skin-tight, defining a feminine body. Below a tan waist, a boot-black micro-dress hugs small hips. Helmut Lang–style, it covers like oil her arse and thighs. A smooth length of naked leg curves down to deep blue point-tapered Miu Miu heels. Her hair, black like space, slides past her face, falling either side of her shoulders, straight and silken.

She disappears then. Almost glides off into the crowds. But later I catch her again, on a high chair by the bar.

By chance she looks up from her hands and catches my stare. Her lips are clipped blood red and full and she winks at me, smiles at me – sending something out through the smoke. From an ice-misted glass she sips a drink, rendered luminous under the lights, and I become self-conscious and shy.

She looks at me from the distance of the bar, wrapping slender fingers around her glass and lightly flicking the straw. She steals glances from under shade-blended lids. Looking out at me and over me. Looking up and down, and away and all around – slowly scanning the scene through brilliant slashes of red and silver struck across her eyes. Sometimes she'll bring the straw to her lips, raising a finger, letting a single drop of the liquid fall into her mouth. At times I look away, safe on the verge of the dancefloor, where techno heads thrash to crisp-electro basslines. The air flickers with sheet laser beams and patches of smoke, flashed bright by spinning light machines.

The sexual attraction I feel unsettles me.

I go for effeminate guys. Girly guys. Maybe androgynous guys. Not girls.

I cannot explain why she affects me. So fuck it. Why should I care?

My friends surround me that night. Are present at my side. They tell me to 'forget her', to 'enjoy myself' and over deep beats and synth-pop vocals they shout words into my ears and their voices carry warning and urge caution because 'she's so unusual!'

But she utterly fascinates me.

She sits back on this silver high chair, her face struck by the reflected light of the chrome bar, her right leg crossed; exposing sleek lines of taut muscle, stretching down to a thin silver anklet.

Wow.

It makes me hard.

Why?

I want to know who she is. Her name? But the club excitement takes over, the music becomes more dynamic, trance-infused and, foolishly, I get drunk and dance. Get distracted seeking boys.

The evening slowly becomes a blur. In lonely minutes of desperation I rush around the club looking for her, but the green lasers blind me and the moving projections confuse me and I become lost.

*

The boy's legs. So s?he is the boy! Male. A man. He is male and he has boy's legs and a dildo. Melded to her pelvis. Arching upward through my shaking hands. But s?he smiles and closes her eyes and her hands grip the side of the bed and I notice the colour of her nails, the pearl shine that reminds me of oil on water, of oil on canvas. And I look at those nails and I look at those hands, white-knuckled, and I look at his hair where it falls over the bed like a tail but I don't look at her penis, not until the lights are dimmed and the glow of the busy neon outside flashes through the window onto our bed and our bodies and his bodice and flicks across her face like a fashion magazine.

★

A week later I am back in the club. In the corner again. She enters. Turning heads with her smiles. Emitting cool indifference, she slides across the club's ground-floor wasteland with grace and temper, pulled by something like inertia.

A black Westwood bodice and a modest décolletage give her curves and arcs. It tightens and tucks.

I've thought about her all week. The preoccupation upsets me but I cannot wait to talk to her.

She ends up sitting by my table because I've bought her a drink. I make first contact at the cigarette machine, asking for change. (I don't smoke.) So she sits there, and looks at me in the dull light of flickering UV strips. She plays with her hair, twisting it around her manicured fingers, and under the purple light it seems as silver silk in her hands. Synthetic. And femme real. But it's fake. Totally fake.

She coughs and asks me my name and then leans her elbow on the metal and rests her chin on her hand. Tells me she's called Jen. Then pauses mid-breath, her mouth caught in word formation and says no more.

Her thin fingers reach for a tiny metallic cigarette purse and tap the chrome clasp. I decline the offered upended menthol, patting my unopened pack, and she lights up.

The music is louder now. So loud I can only make out the deep boom bass and aggressive 4/4 beats and I sit there unsure of how to proceed with this boy, what to say to the girl. And when later I reach over her shoulder to set down her third drink, I try not to let my gaze slide down her neck, over strong collar-bones and down under her corset rim.

I try not to look along those lines. But my curiosity is pumping and the bpm only rises. It intrigues me and uncomfortable thoughts of desire dizzy me as I ease back into the chair.

Nothing much is said. The house sounds are tearing up the air around us and so I don't bother speaking. Wouldn't know what to say.

Jen has turned. I follow her gaze out into the club and watch her become mesmerised by the kinetic colours. The twitching bodies and punching limbs. Would she dance?

And then, finally, I place a sweating hand over hers and ask what his real name is. She can't have heard me because her face remains turned, profiling a small break in the nose, and then I feel her hand twitch beneath mine and I see her lips quiver as she brings up her cigarette to suck.

She turns back to me mid-drag and tries not to blow smoke in my eyes. But she does. And they water. So I look away, my vision becoming briefly wet and unfocused. I regain focus quickly but she just gets up and glides, drifts, then walks roughly off into the club hype.

I find her later in a tinted mirror-panelled alcove on the highest floor, slumped against her reflection, deflated. Cornered now.

She sees me and smiles and blows smoke out, way over my head, and, bewildered, I plead dazed and confused – but she just smiles, squints and tilts her head. Deciding.

Then, in one movement, she beats her left hand against her now flat chest and, smirking, thrusts forward her right hand, holding two small sculptured silicone mounds. Her breasts.

★

And I'm the boy caressing a breast – tracing the contours of his chest, running rough hands over where black corset rises in lace dunes. His breasts rise and fall to a raised respiration and the girl rolls, exposing a sleek back, slight muscles tightened to form a neat centre line which – like a rivulet – runs down to firm buttocks and her strong legs inch apart, allowing me in.

★

We arrange to meet the following week. Seven days later I stand aroused and expectant, warding off the attentions of an alpha male who attempts contact with dull eyes and dry lips.

I wait for her entrance but s?he never arrives. And so, kicking a foot against the bar and draining my drink, I prepare to leave. And then I see him.

The boy walks with bounce across the dancefloor, appearing from the smoke, and the haze and the lasers seem not to touch him. The long hair is gone, perhaps tucked under the beige suede cowboy hat that sits at an angle upon his head. I am uncertain it is Jen.

But as he crosses the space, as he comes into focus, pouting and putting out across the room, I see it *is her*. It's her in his eyes, those expressive eyes, drawn out and exposed in tribal lines of colour. They are her same blue eyes, and the same eyebrows, shaved then re-created with upward flicks of charcoal black. It's her in the same tan-coloured skin, the lips of a paler tone, lightly kissed with gloss.

But *him*... It's him in the white splash of shirt that presses against his flat chest. The fly-collared, black, slim-fit shammy jacket, which sits on and moves with broad, swaying shoulders. The loose-cut, boot-trim, faded Diesel jeans. The brown leather, silver-spurred riding boots.

Jen walks closer to me. She smiles at me again, flicks the hat backward so the lights hit her face. Coming closer. Getting warmer.

The alpha male turns to the mirror above the bar and admires himself. But I am fixed on her – her eyes remaining trained on me. She purses her lips and lowers her head and, just before she reaches me, twists round and leans back against the bar, between me and the male.

I lean forward. She looks up at me and, with low vocal tone, half-whispers, "Call me Jon."

A beat.

And I smile.

I feel honoured by her directness and I don't need an explanation and I don't care because he's here, she's here, and so what does it matter anyway?

Later, in the boys' room, Jon is laughing. We're looking at ourselves in the mirrors, aware of all the stale males around us who cannot drag themselves from their reflections. We stand in front of the basins soaping our hands and he smudges his eyes and takes off the cowboy hat, letting the hair drop.

So the men stare. But he keeps laughing: at herself, at us, at every mirror-happy gay who stands, mouth opened, confused; at those who look too serious or too similar or too pretty to be real.

⋆

We are both boys. He sucks on my tongue, each mouth swallowing mouth, clamping down with force onto wet lips, airtight seal allowing the exchange of saliva. He flicks around my mouth with warm tongue, exploring another wet hole. With strength, and control, I'm gently biting his bottom lip – gripping and sucking. I move my hand to his crotch, and with gentle palm I cup the bulge there, squeezing tighter, pressing my chest into his – pulling him to me.

⋆

I'm driving home, my car fast and low to the ground. It is Jon now who sits next to me, his hat flung to the back seat, the long unreal hair curled in his lap like a sleeping pussy. (After Jen reintroduced herself as Jon, and we both made clear our desires to meld, we fled the club.)

And we take the dancefloor with us, bottling the beats in our heads for the car ride. The car accelerates away and the CD plays crisp melodic trance – explosion loud. The car interior: a bubble of the club.

I'm driving him down the avenues now, through the city, cutting up every vehicle, the screams of their horns falling away in our slipstream. So glad she's here.

On the edge of the city district, the car starts to climb and I pull the top down. The air between us circulates with fresh energy and Jon reaches for the volume control. Again we say little. The music takes away the need. After twisted kilometres uphill, I stop the car in a lay-by, just below the crest of the peak. To our left the ground sweeps away in dust and bracken, running down towards the city limits. I get out, walk round the car, open the passenger door and hold out my hand, helping Jon out onto crunching gravel.

We stand next to each other, our hands remain connected. I cast clear eyes across the metropolis that lies stretched out before us. The brilliant landscape is expansive, and in dawn light looks impossible to cross.

Jon tells me it looks like someone has taken a butter knife and spread an inner city real thin across the desert. I nod and think of something suitable to say, but my mind is playing with crazy thoughts like kissing Jon or dating Jon. Then I think of fucking Jon and then… slowly… as I turn to his profile… I actually think of fucking Jen.

And these thoughts pump around my head, and I think of Jon creating Jen in his image. What possessed him to craft her? Why does he become her?

The unknown attracts me. This boldness excites me.

We kiss and leave soon after. I turn the car around and let gravity roll us back down to the city. Heading for bed.

★

And I am the boy and she is coming and is becoming a boy – her legs and hips jerking upwards with such force with each muscle contraction, her eyes so wild. So she is the boy again and I am the girl or she is a tomboy and I am a girly boy or she is the girl and I am also the girl or we are both girls and boys – fucking and preening and pouting and kissing.

Afterwards, I stand beside her and run a hand through her hair and in the mirror he's a girl and I notice his box of tools and – curious – I reach for the mascara, the oils and powders, the feminine gloss and in a flash, a snap of my wrist, a twist of the cap, I am painting, indulging, experimenting, unable to hold back and I am the great artiste, painting the living sculpture, I am crafting my face, redefining my look. Transforming.

And then, later, when we've washed and cleaned and our skin feels supple and smooth and we've rubbed out those painted signs… we're boys again.

Soft boys.

A wet strand of hair falls onto his damp forehead and a milky white drop of water slides smoothly down the black bang and onto his dry lips, resting there before I move in and my tongue quickly dabs it up like blotting paper.

And all this for a look.

Because she's my sexy man.

And he's my girl.

ALISTAIR WHYTE

Getting Ready

Saturday: 18:00

"It's just not natural, it's not fucking natural. It's disgusting as far as I'm concerned, it goes against everything I and most normal people believe in. I think you should get help."

I sighed, regretting ever mentioning my crush on Michael Jackson to Cevin.

"It was a long time ago," I said. "When I was a kid."

"So, if he walked in here right now you'd just tell him to piss off, would you, Richard?"

"Well," I said, wishing he'd drop it, "I'm probably too old for him now, aren't I?"

I chucked my magazine on the floor and wandered over to the window. Cevin had come round under the pretext of borrowing my Euphoria CD earlier that afternoon, but now seemed to have taken up permanent residence under my new and expensive duvet. I had told him to fuck off several times, but subtlety is always lost on the whirlpool of self-absorption that is my best mate. We were all due to go out later on anyway, so I had resigned myself to spending the rest of the afternoon in his stimulating company.

"Why does it always rain here, Cev?" I asked, gazing morosely out the window.

From my top-floor flat you could see right across the city, over the drenched rooftops, to Calton Hill, an oasis of greenery and depravity in the city centre. Calton Hill. Calton fucking Hill. Every night the place reeks of quick brutal fucks in the bushes, underage rent boys and the odd lost and panicking tourist. Not that I would know. Not that I ever went there. Uh-uh. Not me.

I turned round. 'Dooms Night' by Azzido Da Bass was thumping out of the hi-fi and Cevin was bouncing around on my bed like a monkey on speed.

Cevin. What to say about Cevin? It's hard to know where to start really. I am almost the only one who calls him Cevin, probably because I've known the prat since school. Everyone else calls him 'Witha*C*'. This is due to his habit of introducing himself as, "Hi, I'm Cevin...with a *C*."

This almost Bond-like catchphrase is usually delivered to potential shags in a low, sultry voice, which – accompanied by a quick flick of the eyebrows – results in the object of his desire either falling over laughing, or swooning. Occasionally both.

Cevin, as well as being my best mate and all round twat, is also considered by many to be a bit of all right. Not by me, I hasten to add. Apart from being camper than all the similes in the book, I've known him for so long that fancying him would almost be incest.

There's no denying the fact that, when he wants to, he can pull. Fuck, I've seen him cop off on a wet Tuesday morning in Safeways, an admirable feat – even if it did mean I was left with only my trolley for company in the fresh fruit and veg aisle.

18:30

In the next room I could faintly hear the undulating, forceful, and at times hysterical voice of my flatmate Clara. It always seems that the only people with any chance of scoring us Es are the ones we hate the most, and, as Clara is the most tactful of the three of us, she had been elected to phone round all our 'acquaintances' in the hope of sorting us out.

My mobile phone bleeped, announcing the arrival of another text message. I groaned. I knew who it would be from. I'd already had four messages that day, from a photographer called Jake who seemed to believe that if he harassed me enough, I would finally get my kit off and bare my arse in front of his camera. I'd drunkenly given him my number in the pub the other night, after he'd spent the evening following me around explaining how he regularly did shoots for *Vulcan* magazine.

HI M8. HOPE U R OK.

FONE ME 2NITE B4 10.

I'LL MAKE IT WORTH YR WHILE.

JAKE.

You can fuck off mate, I thought, as I deleted the message. Why the fuck does everyone want a piece of my body? OK, I was flashing it about last night on the podium but I was *having a laugh*. No big deal. Fuck's sake.

18:45

"So where are we going tonight?" asked Cevin from the depths of my duvet. "Yesterday was payday and I *have* to get off my tits."

"Well, let's see," I replied.

One of the joys of living in Scotland's vibrant and oh-so cosmopolitan capital is the incredible choice of gay venues. I was too skint to go to a club. This meant our evening would probably kick off in Planet Out (cute bar staff) or Café Habana (good music).

Then it would be CC Blooms. What a fucking dive. I have tried and failed to explain to people raised on a diet of Poptastic, G-A-Y, Paradise Factory and Trade, the concept behind CC Blooms. If spending your night getting felt up by ranks of coffin-dodgers – who hang around like grotesque waxworks from Madame Tussaud's – gets you going, CC's is the place for you. Or maybe you'd prefer to be crushed to within an inch of your life on the miniature dancefloor in the basement, slipping around beer, piss and fuck knows what else.

CC's is the sort of place you end up in when all other possibilities have been exhausted, when the last remaining dregs of your sanity are screaming at you to call it a night, the sort of place you are guaranteed to make a complete tit of yourself. We went there every week.

"You'd better watch yourself," I said, looking across at Cevin. "That bouncer who caught you and that Italian guy shagging in the toilets said you were on your last warning."

"We were *not* shagging," Cevin shouted, jumping off my bed. His baggy boxers flapped around his legs as he stormed into the bathroom.

19:00

"Keith, baby, hi. It's Clara." Clara grimaced at me as I wandered next door to see whether she had been successful in scoring us any gear. Fuck, I thought, she's calling Keith. This was bad news. Keith had been relegated to the bottom of our list of potential contacts after he had spiked Cevin's drink a fortnight ago. Cevin had started hallucinating really badly, and Clara had flown off the handle at Keith, slamming a door in his face and knocking one of his teeth out.

"Well I'm sure you could get them replaced… oh fuck you too, you twat." Clara put the phone down and grabbed my packet of Marlboro.

Clara is a cashier in a bank by day, and a self-confessed fag-hag by night. I glanced around her room as she groped for a lighter. A giant Lou Reed poster from his *Transformer* era hung above her bed. The floor was littered with style magazines, empty CD cases and Rizlas. Overflowing makeshift ashtrays lurked on every surface.

19:30

"Richard, you need cash don't you?" asked Cevin as he rolled a joint. Clara was still stressing out over sorting our gear, and had gone downstairs to see if that weirdo student bloke had anything decent.

"Oh, yeah," I replied. "Big time."

"Well, you should do a photo shoot for that porn photographer."

"Fuck off."

"You should."

Cevin had dabbled in the world of porn a few months back, doing a video shoot for a private collector. He's not a slut or anything – well, he is – but not in a *bad* way. He just likes shagging, and if he's getting paid for it, so much the better.

"I can't believe you've still got a copy of that video you did," I laughed.

"I wasn't going to throw it away, was I? You want to watch it again?" Cevin jumped up eagerly, but I shook my head. It had been disturbing enough the first time round. He'd suited the gimp mask. Not so sure about the latex peephole briefs though.

Clara appeared at the doorway, out of breath from running up the stairs.

"What sort of a student *is* he?" she griped, snatching the joint from Cevin and taking a long draw.

"Everyone knows students always have drugs. What a weirdo. Now, which of you two faggots is going to nip down to the chip shop and get me some nosh?"

19:45

It had finally stopped pissing down as Cevin and I sprinted out to the chip shop across the road from the flat. Well, I sprinted. Cevin minced, pausing at a convenient lamppost to do a quick Gene Kelly impression.

Back at the flat we flicked through the pitiful selection of TV programmes that pass for Saturday night entertainment. *Deep Space Nine* kept us enthralled for all of five minutes, and in the end we resorted to the neon audio and visual wallpaper of MTV. Cevin and Clara began a heated argument over whether Eminem is attractive or not. I left them to it.

I really was skint that night, and knew that if Clara *did* eventually succeed in getting us our drugs, I would be another ten quid out of pocket. Back in my room, I flicked on the radio, where Judge Jules was hammering the new Knuckleheads track.

What I hadn't told my flatmates was that I owed my brother's mate, Lee, fifty quid.

He's a bit of a headcase, Lee, but he had been persuaded to lend me enough money to go home for my brother's trial. (My brother is doing time in jail after he was busted at the airport with half a kilo of cocaine in his guitar case and one big fucker of a flick-knife down his underpants.) I'd been avoiding Lee ever since, but I knew he would be in town tonight. I was breaking out in a nervous sweat every time the phone rang.

20:00

Cevin was splashing about in the bath and Clara was hunched over the TV set, clutching her lottery ticket and praying under her breath. I wandered into the bathroom to gel my hair, a process that always takes forever.

"Richard, have you ever had sex outdoors?" asked Cevin from the depths of the bath.

"No," I muttered, glancing at him in the mirror. "Well, I had a wank with the window open once. Does that count?"

"No," replied Cevin as he lathered up the soap. "I was just wondering. It's always been one of my fantasies."

"Well, it's never been one of mine. The outdoors is risky enough. You never know what you might be rolling about on."

Cevin jumped out of the bath, shaking off the Radox bubbles, and hopped over to grab his towel. I watched him bend down to pick it up, then looked away quickly. I don't fancy my best mate, I *don't*. So fuck off.

20:55

The phone rang. I gulped nervously on my Bacardi Breezer, hoping Lee had died or something. Clara answered and it turned out to be Keith. The guy who had spiked Cevin's drink. Phoning back. With good news. It was going to cost us, but if we were desperate enough he had a few Es that he wanted to shift quickly.

I was immediately suspicious. "They'll be full of fuck knows what," I protested. Clara and Cevin told me to shut up. "He's bound to hold a grudge," I continued. "We don't know him well enough to knock his teeth out one minute and buy drugs from him the next."

"If you don't shut it, Richard, I'm going to stick this bottle where the sun doesn't shine very often," said Clara, waving her Vodka Source at me threateningly. I nervously lit a ciggie.

21:15

'Narco Tourist' by Slam vs. Unkle was my big tune that week, and hearing it grinding out of the speakers started to cheer me up. Perhaps it would turn into an OK night after all. Lee might have forgotten about the cash I owed him. I might be able to persuade Clara to buy my pill for me. Fuck, I might pull. I grabbed another Smirnoff Ice and tried to decide what to wear.

Clara came sauntering through as I was getting changed, sporting her new Agent Provocateur underwear that had arrived through the post for her that morning.

"What do you think?" she asked, dropping fag ash all over my carpet.

"Very hot, babe," I replied. I was scrabbling around in my drawer. "I've lost my fucking Hugo Boss underpants."

"No surprises there," Clara smirked.

She was right. I had recently stopped seeing this guy called Ben after I had discovered that he'd been nicking my dirty underwear and hoarding it at his place. The freak.

21:35

And then the fucking doorbell rang. Cevin leapt up to answer it. I heard two voices in the hallway. One I recognised as Keith's, our dodgy benefactor of Es. The other voice was… *Lee's?* Fuck. Then I remembered. They were mates. They came through into the living room. Keith grabbed my hand and pushed a pill into it.

"Fifteen quid please," he muttered.

"Fifteen fucking quid, what do you take me for?" I replied. "It's a tenner or you can fuck off." Then I caught Lee's eye.

"You got that cash you owe me, mate?" he asked.

Fuck, here we go, I thought. Then my phone rang. I answered. It was Jake, that porn photographer, after me body again.

*

And that's how it happened. Honest. Well I was skint, wasn't I? I was about to get my head kicked in by two of the hardest yobs I know. I *needed* the cash. You don't think I would have *chosen* to be in that filthy mag do you? I wasn't really enjoying it, that was just acting. And they didn't even let me keep the squaddie kit. Anyway, I just want to forget about the whole thing now. Would I do it again? Would I fuck. Would I fuck? Would I *fuck*? Well, you know. If the fee was right.

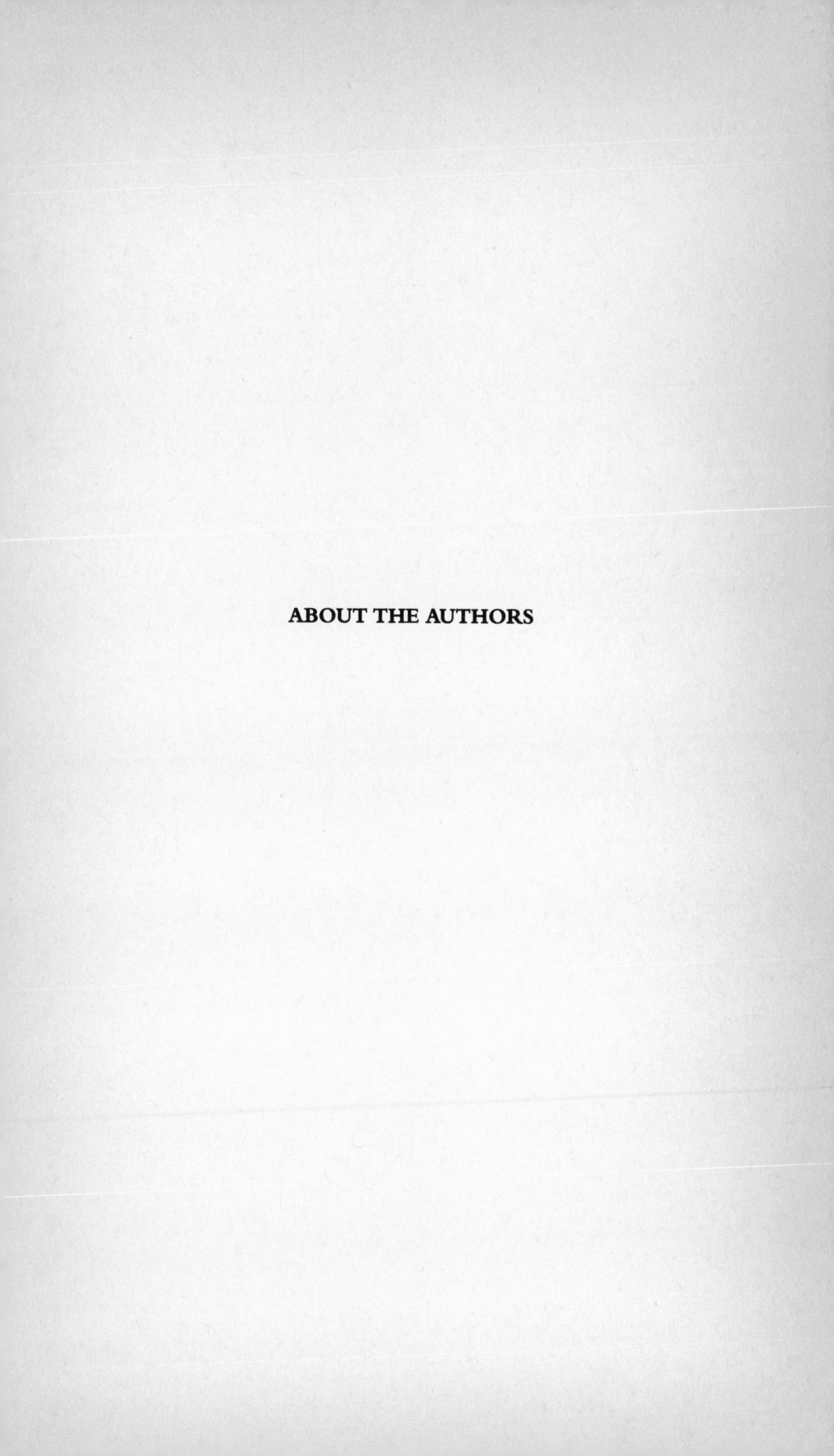

ABOUT THE AUTHORS

Anthony Baulch (DOB: 19 February, 1986) is from California's San Carlos area. He is currently a junior at San Francisco's High School of the Arts where he majors in classical voice. Anthony was recently awarded a Gold Award in Scholastic Arts and Writing at the San Francisco Youth Arts Festival. 'Telling Mother' is his first piece of fiction to be published.

Gordon Beeferman (DOB: 23 August, 1976) is a composer, pianist and writer. He was born in Boston and grew up in Cambridge, Massachusetts. He studied music composition at the University of Michigan. Gordon's music has been heard in New York's Carnegie Hall, Chicago's Orchestra Hall and in Boston, Los Angeles and Rome. Gordon lives in Brooklyn, New York, where he is busy composing and writing. To pay the bills he has been variously employed as a secretary, waiter, construction worker and pianist. 'Scar Tissue' is his first piece of fiction to be published.

Dominic Berry (DOB: 2 December, 1979) has lived in Manchester since 1999, after a move from Pembrokeshire. There, he worked with Milford Haven's Torch Theatre and as part of the National Youth Theatre of Wales. He is now a member of North West Arts' Commonword writing group, the Contact Theatre's Young Writers and Stockport's Garrick Theatre. Recently he staged his short play *Retail People* with Word Circus as part of the Campaign for the Living Wage week. Dominic participates in poetry slams and competitions in and around Manchester, including regular sets at Café Pop, the Green Room Theatre and the Frog and Bucket. 'Jerk' is his first piece of fiction to be published.

John Joseph Bibby (DOB: 1 June, 1982) was raised in Liverpool where he lived with his mother, four sisters and a brother in an old doctor's house by the docks until he was sixteen. He currently lives in Blackpool, a place he loves and hates equally. He is inspired by his boyfriend, poverty, middle-class pretences, Sheryl Crow, PJ Harvey, Madonna, Geri Halliwell, Destiny's Child, Dido, Patrick Bateman, *Sex And The City* "… and my amazing and talented friends". 'Big Exit' is his first piece of fiction to be published.

Michael Boynton (DOB: 21 March, 1978) was brought up in Richmond, Virginia. He is a recent graduate from St. Mary's College of Maryland where he earned his Bachelor of Arts in Film. As a professional actor Michael has played Romeo in a national tour of *Romeo and Juliet* and Jamie in the Virginia premiere of *Beautiful Thing*. When not on stage, Michael devotes his time to writing – mainly plays, screenplays and musicals, many of which have been produced. Michael currently attends the NYU Graduate Musical Theatre Writing Programe. 'Learning To Swim' is his first piece of fiction to be published.

David Brewin (DOB: 27 October, 1977) is a free-spirited twenty something who was born and raised in Ilkley, a rural corner of Yorkshire. David left Ilkley in 1996 to study maths and biology in Birmingham, where he feels he discovered himself. He has since returned and now lives with his family. He enjoys keeping fit and going out on the scene in Leeds and Manchester, plus bell-ringing. He drew inspiration for his story from his experience as a member of the Gay Christian Movement. 'Double Life' is his first piece of fiction to be published.

Nathan Buck (DOB: 24 December, 1976) grew up in small towns in the mid-western United States after he was born in Chicago. He has worked as a volunteer for several queer advocacy groups in Madison, Wisconsin, where he currently resides, now working with teenagers who are cognitively delayed. He admits to having slightly unhealthy obsessions with author Francesca Lia Block and singer/songwriter Tori Amos, as well as an in-the-closet love of young adult novelist Christopher Pike. '8' is his first piece of fiction to be published.

Miles Donohoe (DOB: 24 May, 1979) was born in Enfield, Middlesex, but grew up in Welwyn Garden City, Hertfordshire. He studied an art and design foundation course at Hertfordshire University before moving to London in 1998. Miles has just completed his English literature degree at Middlesex University in North London. He has been working for a gay web magazine (gay.uk.net) since September 2000, writing various feature articles and stage reviews. 'RU FREE 2MORO NITE?' is his first piece of fiction to be published.

Dean M Drinkel (DOB: 11 December, 1976) tries to lead a more settled existence nowadays in Surrey, following a somewhat turbulent childhood – most of which was spent on various American air bases around the world. The outbreak of the first Gulf War was the final straw and the family relocated to Black Head, near Lizard. He recently completed an honours degree in transatlantic Gothic writers and is currently researching a biography on German footballer Robert Enke. 'The Child Fucker' is his first piece of fiction to be published.

Mat Dunne (DOB: 30 August, 1979) lives in a small town named Shepshed, just outside Leicester. Mat had the chance to pitch story ideas to the producers of *Star Trek* when he was seventeen, after they were impressed by a script he had sent them. He is currently working on several projects, all in various stages of completion. 'When A Smile Is All It Takes' is his first piece of fiction to be published.

Alex Fínean-Liáng (DOB: 14 April, 1976) is a political conference promoter in London. He writes for a number of gay publications, including the *Pink Paper* and *QX*. Having lived in six countries on three continents, Alex describes himself as being "from all over". Right now, Alex is happily living in Kensington with his boyfriend, Robert. A recent graduate from University College London and l'Université de Paris-IV Sorbonne, Alex spends his free time doing charity work with a variety of London gay, youth and HIV charities. He also enjoys gymnastics, theatre and having a boogie at G-A-Y with friends on a Saturday night. 'Blue Eyes In Green Park' is his first piece of fiction to be published.

Geezer (DOB: 25 December, 1982) lives in Redditch, Worcestershire. FTM (female-to-male) issues are very close to Geezer's heart. 'Bloke' is his first piece of fiction to be published.

Lewis Gill (DOB: 8 July, 1981) was born in Chesterfield. At sixteen he left school and went to work with the civil service in Sheffield. He soon decided that he was not going to stay and at eighteen he moved to Blackpool. Lewis is currently in the process of developing a first novel. 'A Picture Of James' is his first piece of fiction to be published.

David Gue (DOB: 4 August, 1977) was born in Baltimore, Maryland. After briefly studying literature at the University of Newcastle Upon Tyne, he graduated with a degree in English and Writing from Loyola College in 1999. David did a short stint recruiting for the college and moved to Ireland shortly thereafter, where he has been living for the past two years. David teaches at the secondary level, mentors roughly one hundred young men at the university level and is pursuing a graduate degree in psychology/counselling. He lives on Dublin's south side. 'Men At Work' is his first piece of fiction to be published.

Robin Ibbeson (DOB: 30 April, 1977) was born and raised in Sheffield until his late teens when he finally packed in his job at the local steelworks to move to Manchester. Since then, he has worked in a variety of occupations, ranging from tarot phone-line operator to medical testing volunteer, in an attempt to fund his writing habit. Robin recently returned from several months on a beach in Thailand, tanned and relaxed, having splashed out the advance he received for an erotic novel (published by Idol) about footballers, created by one of his alter egos.

Morgan Melhuish (DOB: 4 April, 1982) has had his poetry published in *Manifold* and has been one of the winners of the National Young Playwrights Competition for three years in a row since 1998. He has also written articles for his local newspaper in Surrey and *Seren*, Bangor's student newspaper. Morgan is currently studying at Bangor University for a degree in English literature and creative writing. 'Like When You Swallow Ice Cream' is his first piece of fiction to be published.

Keith Munro (DOB: 14 December, 1976) grew up in Bathgate, in Scotland's West Lothian area, and is a graduate of the Manchester Metropolitan University. His CV includes stints in stockrooms, classrooms, chemists and toy shops, but he regards himself principally as an actor, writer and musical director. As a musician and composer, Keith has produced scores for everything from Shakespeare to pantomime. As an actor, he has appeared in a wide variety of roles in Britain and abroad, as well as creating his own one-man show entitled *Prone*. He currently lives in Crewe, Cheshire, and is working on his first novel. 'Pornography' is his first piece of fiction to be published.

Arden Pryor (DOB: 24 December, 1978) is a freelance comic writer by trade. Romanian-born, he writes features focusing on lifestyle and relationship issues for the gay press in the UK and Australia. Primarily based in Sydney and London (where he has been known to do an occasional spot of stand-up comedy), Arden is an active member of the Gay London Writers Group. He is currently developing his first novel, 'Boy London'. 'The Golden Mile' is his first piece of fiction to be published.

Nishan Ramaindran (DOB: 10 November, 1978) was born in Jaffna, Sri Lanka, a country torn apart by civil war. His father, a doctor, came to London hoping to return, but following the civil unrest and riots against the Tamils in 1978, his mother also left and emigrated to England. Nishan is a poet and writes about contemporary art. He is mainly interested in conceptual, feminist and performance art. Based in Petts Wood, Kent, he is currently studying for a degree in sociology and cultural studies in London. 'Boy, Manson Is Gonna Fuck You' is his first piece of fiction to be published.

Robbie Romano (DOB: 25 August, 1983) admits to having suffered from severe depression throughout his adolescent and teen years in North Charleston, South Carolina. He cites his major literary influences as Paul Monette and the Japanese writer Banana Yoshimoto. 'Blood Roses' is his first piece of fiction to be published.

Adam Rowland (DOB: 19 February, 1984) was born and raised in Bacup, East Lancashire. Now, at the age of seventeen, Adam is studying for his A-level courses in Oldham, Greater Manchester, before going on to university in 2002 to study ancient history and archaeology. Adam's main interests include dance, pop and indie, with his favourite bands ranging from Steps to Stereophonics. He enjoys shopping and going out with friends on Manchester's ever-growing scene "... which provides a refreshing change from where I live". Adam is currently working on his first novel and hopes to make a career out of writing. 'I'd Like You To Meet Mark' is his first piece of fiction to be published.

Stuart Sandford (DOB: 16 April, 1978) was, until recently, studying Politics at the Manchester Metropolitan University – until realising that he had made a terrible mistake by surrounding himself with politicians instead of artists. Having studied acting at college, he then moved behind the scenes and discovered his love for film and writing. At the age of nineteen he co-founded, co-edited and contributed to a national GLBTQ youth magazine entitled *One In Ten* that now rests online. He is currently in the process of developing a feature screenplay, 'G-A-Y', on which this piece is based, whilst preparing for his MA in screenwriting at the Northern Film School in Leeds. 'G-A-Y' is his first piece of fiction to be published.

Tony J Shaw (13 October, 1982) hails from Bobbingsworth, Essex. He describes himself as 'str8 acting' whilst also being Shirley Bassey's number one fan. Currently working in a year out, Tony will be going to a uni somewhere in the South East in 2002 to study English. 'Thank You For Travelling On The Central Line' is his first piece of fiction to be published.

Kai Morgan Venice (DOB: 21 August, 1977) was born and raised in Philadelphia, Pennsylvania, but escaped to San Francisco, California, as soon as he was legal, to pursue his dream of being a writer in more liberal surroundings. He is an HIV tester/counsellor by day, a writer in Duboce Avenue by night, and has published under a previous moniker. Kai is currently working on a book of short horror stories.

Zio J Walsh (DOB: 23 January, 1979) was born in Belfast, Northern Ireland, migrated with his family to Western Australia in 1989 and has endeavoured to leave ever since. As he was never in the closet, he never had to come out "… though I corrected the common misconception that I was straight when I was seventeen". Since then he has lived in New York and London. He has recently completed his first novel, 'Coffee, Blood and Beatz', and whilst seeking a publisher is working on a second, 'Boys' Home'. 'No Shame In My Game' is his first piece of fiction to be published.

Justin Ward (DOB: 2 March, 1977) grew up in the industrial wonderland of Wolverhampton "… where I was considered to be a perverted weirdo". He studied art and design in Northampton, Birmingham and Staffordshire, where he began his career as a teacher of art and English. He now lives in London where he teaches on a part-time basis, whilst also working as an assistant to the writer and film-maker Philip Ridley and doing the occasional feature for the *Pink Paper* and *Fluid*. 'Forever Geek' is his first piece of fiction to be published.

David Watkins (DOB: 10 January 1979) was born in Bridgend, Wales, and brought up in Southampton, England. Recovering from a three-year drama and theatre arts degree at Goldsmith's College in London, he decided to go west and spent last year on the minimum wage in California. He's back now, working on a novella about a bulimic bisexual in a future San Francisco. He is a regular contributor to *G-News* and a member of Gay London Writers. 'Girl' is his first piece of fiction to be published.

Alistair Whyte (DOB: 14 September, 1977) is a student living in Edinburgh, studying for a masters degree in tourism. He grew up in the North-East of Scotland, moving to Edinburgh back in 1995 to study environmental biology. After graduating, he worked for an environmental organisation in the Highlands and then in Yorkshire, before returning to Scotland's capital city. He enjoys clubbing, DJ-ing, playing guitar and drinking. He is also a keen traveller and is currently planning a trip to Nepal. 'Getting Ready' is his first piece of fiction to be published.

Have you checked out this book's big brother?

The Gay Times Book of Short Stories:
New Century, New Writing
edited by P-P Hartnett

This exciting collection from the same editor as *The Next Wave* contains an innovative mix of stories by established writers and adventurous new voices, from across England, Ireland, Scotland and Wales.

Includes stories by Michael Arditti, Nicholas Blincoe, Toni Davidson and Christopher Whyte.

"A new wave of voices, a landmark collection" Justin Webb, *Pink Paper*
"Simply the best Homothology out there ****" *The List*

ISBN 1-902852-19-2 UK £9.95 US $14.95
(when ordering direct, quote GAY192)